SEVENTH INNING HEAT

THE VEGAS ACES

LYSSA KAY ADAMS

LKA PUBLISHING

1

Eric Weaver rarely missed a pitch, but this was one curve ball he didn't see coming. And just like a line drive to the balls, it left him with a burning need to bend over and heave.

"You can't be serious."

His eyes darted back and forth between the two men before him. Las Vegas Aces owner Devin Dane sat behind his desk, feet up and arms crossed over his pansy-assed tie as if he hadn't just dropped a potentially career-ending bomb in Eric's lap. Team manager Hunter Kinsley stood on his right flank, looking like a slightly remorseful lieutenant who tried to talk his superiors out of shock-and-awe but followed orders anyway. Behind them both, the sinking St. Augustine sun streamed through the window and illuminated the Aces' spring training field in the distance.

This had to be a joke. Some kind of twisted, preseason

prank, right? Eric waited for a signal, a flicker of a smart-assed grin or something that would indicate Hunter and Devin were just dicking him around.

Instead, they met his gaze head-on.

"Sonuvabitch." Disbelief sent the air from his lungs and the strength from his spine. He sank against the leather cushion of his chair.

They were talking about moving him to the bullpen. The *bullpen.* After seven years as a starting pitcher, being busted down to the ranks of reliever would not only be a major demotion but also one cocksucker of a humiliation. He could see the blog posts already. *Eric Weaver, son of retired Texas Rangers pitcher Chet Weaver, could never live up to the legacy of his storied father.*

He shot to his feet. "You can't do this to me."

Devin tented his fingers beneath his chin. "It's not about you. It's about what's best for the team."

"Keeping me on the mound is what's best for this team." Even as Eric said it, though, self-doubt churned in his gut. For two years, he had felt the magic slipping away. It didn't matter how hard he worked, how much he trained and drilled. His curves fell flat. His fastballs lost their heat. And when it had mattered most, he failed in brutally spectacular fashion. Four months ago in the last game of the World Series, he gave up five home runs. His teammates would have championship rings if not for him.

But dammit, Devin and Hunter couldn't do this.

"Who—" Eric had to stop and clear his throat. "Who would take my place?"

"We're looking at Zach Nelson," Hunter said.

For fuck's sake. Talk about rubbing salt to a wound. Zach Nelson was an untested rookie known more for his lumberjack beard and his surfer-boy lifestyle than his prowess on the mound.

Eric couldn't let it happen. He wouldn't. "What do I have to do?"

"You need to work your ass off these next six weeks and do everything your coaches tell you." He tossed a plain manila folder onto the desk. "Especially that one."

"Who is that?"

Hunter straightened and crossed his arms across his chest. "We're bringing on a new pitching coach, Eric. One with a reputation for kicking asses and whipping people back into shape. We think she'll be good for you."

Eric blinked as one key word sank in. "*She?*"

2

THERE WAS ONLY one *she* anywhere in the United States Eric could think of who met Hunter's description and was even remotely qualified to be a pitching coach for a Major League Baseball team.

There was no way his luck was that bad.

Eric stared at the folder a moment before swiping it off the desk. He opened it and felt the world tilt beneath his feet.

Correction: His luck was that bad.

He actually felt dizzy as he met Devin's gaze. "You have to be kidding me."

"It's just a new coach," Devin said, smirking. "What's the big deal?"

A new coach he could handle. Hell, he'd sign himself up for Little League again if it meant ending the two-year shit spiral that had stolen the velocity from his fastball and turned his curve into a flat-line meatball.

But Devin and Hunter weren't bringing on just any coach.

They were bringing on *Nicki Bates*.

Sweet jeezus.

Devin dropped his feet to the floor. "You seem bothered by this. I'm surprised. Didn't you and her brother play together at Vanderbilt? I thought you were friends."

Eric snorted. *Friends*. He dropped the folder back on the desk. "This is a disaster waiting to happen."

"Because she's a woman?" Hunter said. "She's more qualified than ninety percent of the coaches in the bigs right now."

"It's not because she's a woman!"

Devin raised his eyebrows. "Then what's the problem?"

Eric jerked his fingers through his hair and swallowed against a cocktail of surging anger and simmering lust. The first one was a feeling he was well acquainted with these days. But the second was an emotion he thought he'd doused long ago. His mind called up the image of her. Long limbs. Seductive eyes. Lips that could make a man's imagination head straight for the foul line.

That was the problem. He couldn't be within fifty feet of her without wanting to *conference on the mound*. It was a distraction he couldn't afford, not if he wanted to save his spot in the rotation.

He couldn't explain any of that to Devin or Hunter, though. The one and only promise he'd ever managed to keep to her was never to tell a soul about them, and he wasn't about to break it now. He was already having a hard time looking at himself in the mirror these days.

Devin and Hunter stared at him with matching smirks, waiting for his response.

He searched for something that sounded at least plausible. "We can't take this kind of attention right now, Devin. The guys were barely talking to each other at the end of last season, and this is going to only make things worse."

"I realize the media coverage will be intense. The first woman ever to coach for a Major League ball club is going to bring a lot of scrutiny."

"It'll be a fucking circus."

"That's where you come in. The players respect you and will follow your lead. You're still the team captain."

For now. The unspoken threat hung in the air. No relief pitcher would ever be chosen by his peers as team captain.

Devin suddenly stood. "The deal is done, Eric. We're announcing her tomorrow morning. She's already here."

Shit. He'd spent the better part of seven years doing everything in his power to stay as far away as possible from her. And now here she was.

Same state.

Same city.

Same fucking team.

"Where is she staying?" He barely got the words out.

Hunter cocked an eyebrow. "Going to welcome her to the team?"

"Something like that."

Devin rounded his desk. "We put her up in the four-thirty-two house."

Eric stalked across the office and threw open the door. It crashed against the opposite wall as he stormed into the hallway. Nicki's talent was unmistakable, but her presence on the team would only bring trouble. If he was going to save his career, he needed absolute focus on one thing and one thing only: the game.

That would be impossible with Nicki anywhere near him.

Which left him with only one certainty.

Nicki Bates had to go.

ERIC WHIPPED his Escalade into the only available spot on the street and groaned. Five other cars were parked in front of the house where Nicki was staying.

That could only mean one thing.

Her family was there.

Shit.

But why wouldn't they be there? This was the culmination of her life's work, the realization of a dream she'd had since she'd first put on a ball glove as a kid. Eric should have expected them to be there to celebrate with her. But their presence wasn't going to make this any easier. Eric couldn't wait, though. Not if Devin was determined to announce her to the world in the morning. He had to make her see reason before then.

He crossed the street and walked up the brick pathway toward the door. The house was a smallish ranch with palm trees out front and a lawn full of that spiky green shit that passed for grass in Florida. In Eric's seven years with the Aces, the house had been home to everyone from marketing temps to college prospects. And now Nicki.

Sweet jeezus.

The closer he got, the louder the noise grew. The Bates family had no concept of inside voice. They yelled. They fought. They ran with scissors. Nicki was the youngest of four and the only girl. As an only child, Eric had always felt like he'd walked into a sitcom whenever Robby invited him home from school.

It felt more like walking into The Godfather this time.

Seven years had passed since he'd been welcomed into the family. Though Robby played for the Red Sox and they saw each other on the field several times a year, they barely spoke. Some betrayals couldn't be overcome.

Eric rang the doorbell and waited, hands in the pockets of his jeans.

A few seconds passed before the door swung open.

Ah, shit. "Robby-"

Nicki's brother let out a growl and threw a punch. It connected with Eric's mouth before he had time to duck. Eric stumbled back, his hand covering his now-throbbing jaw. He pulled his fingers away and swore at the blood. "What the hell, man?"

Robby stormed out the door. "I warned you."

"The fuck you did."

"I told you if you ever came near her again, I would beat your ass."

Eric dabbed at the blood again. "Well, in case you haven't heard, she's apparently now my coach. It's going to be a little difficult to stay away from her."

He should've known Robby would be there. The first few days of spring training were only for pitchers and catchers. As a first baseman, Robby wouldn't have to head to the Red Sox training facility in Fort Myers for at least a week. Just fucking great.

"Robby? What is all the commotion?"

Nicki's mom appeared in the doorway. "Oh my goodness. Eric, dear." Her Italian accent was as strong as ever. "Robby, why didn't you tell us he was here? Eric, dear, come inside. Are you staying for dinner? Are you bleeding? What happened?"

Robby glared one more time before moving aside to let his mother grab Eric's hand and pull him in. "Oh, Eric, I'm so glad you are here. Isn't this wonderful? You and Nicki on the same team."

Yeah. Wonderful.

She pulled him into a living room with furniture that had seen its fair share of shenanigans. There was a rumor that a college prospect had even lost his virginity on the couch. *Note to self: Don't sit down.*

Sliding glass doors on the far end of the room opened onto a patio and a fenced-off pool. Through the glass, Eric spotted Nicki's two other brothers, two women he didn't recognize, and some children that hadn't existed the last time he'd been around. Her father stood over a flaming grill poking meat with a giant fork.

"How many steaks do you want, dear?"

Eric found his voice. "Thank you, Mrs. Bates, but—"

"Isabella. How many times do you I have to tell you to call me Isabella?" She pinched his cheek. The throbbing one. "All these years, and you're still so polite."

"*Isabella.* Thank you. But I just came by to talk to Nicki. I can't stay for dinner."

"No. You will eat."

Robby grunted. Or growled. It was hard to tell the difference.

Eric ignored him. "Is Nicki here?"

"Of course, dear. She'll be out in a minute. She's in the shower."

Great. Just the image he needed—Nicki, wet and soapy.

The sliding glass doors suddenly opened and her father walked in. He stopped short, and Eric waited for another blow to the face. Instead, Andrew Bates smiled and held out his arms.

"Eric. It's good to see you, boy."

Eric let the man pull him in for hearty back-pounding hug. Robby let out another indecipherable noise.

Isabella smacked his arm. "What is wrong with you, Robby? Is that any way to treat an old friend?"

That answered one question he'd always had. Did her parents ever know about them? No, apparently.

Isabella brushed past him toward a hallway that led to the bedrooms. "I will go see what's taking our Nicki so long."

Just when she disappeared around the corner, the sliding glass doors opened again. Andrew walked back out to the grill as Nicki's other brothers—Vincent and Anthony— walked in. They joined Robby in an offensive line of crossed arms and glowering stares that would've made any NFL team proud.

That answered the other question. Her other brothers *did* know. Great.

They glared for a long moment while Eric glanced around the room. This was ridiculous. They were all adults here. Couldn't they behave like it?

He looked at Robby. "When you going to Fort Myers?"

"Don't talk to me."

"Gotcha."

Eric shoved his hands back in his pockets and looked at his feet. Somewhere down the hallway, a door opened and closed. Isabella appeared and smiled. "She's almost ready."

A minute later, Nicki walked out.

And Eric went dumb.

She was even more gorgeous now than she had been at twenty-two. Her skin glowed like a damn skin care commercial, and her long, dark hair hung wet across her shoulders. She wore a white Aces t-shirt that left little to the imagination about the curves and well-honed muscles underneath. Her long legs were encased in beat-up jeans that hugged her in all the right places and made him want to drop to his knees and thank God for creating the thing called woman. *This* woman, in particular.

His tongue was thick in his mouth. "Hey."

She tossed him a smile, but it was meaningless—the kind reserved for players you only saw a couple times every season.

"Eric, hey. I'm glad you're here. I was going to call you tonight to go over a few things before tomorrow, because we really need to get started as soon as possible. What the hell happened to your face?"

Eric blinked. She was staring at him like he was supposed say something. "What?"

"Your face—" She groaned and glared at her brothers over his shoulder. "What did you do?"

"I warned him," Robby said.

She shook her head and refocused on Eric. "Do you want some ice?"

"Do I need ice?"

"You're starting to swell."

He touched his jaw and winced. "Can we talk in private, please?"

"No." That was from Anthony, who had moved to stand next to Nicki as if she needed protection.

The door to the back yard slid open again, and her father leaned his head in. "Eric, medium for your steaks? Or you like 'em a little more done?"

Nicki pulled a phone from her pocket and swiped the screen a couple of times. "Give me your email address. I need to send you a schedule of the new workouts."

He blinked again. "New workouts?"

"Eric, medium or well-done?"

Nicki looked at her dad. "He likes them pink in the middle."

"I'm not staying for dinner."

Nicki returned her attention to Eric. "Your email address?"

Isabella yelled from the kitchen. "Eric, what kind of dressing do you like on your salad, dear?"

"Um—"

"Just oil and vinegar for him, Mom. He needs to take some weight off."

What?!

"Butter and sour cream on your potato, dear?"

"Mom, I'm putting him on a diet. No sour cream."

Eric looked down at his stomach. He didn't need to lose weight. Sure, he'd been eating like shit lately and maybe he had gotten a little softer than his usual playing shape, but.... dammit. "Nicki, I need to talk to you. *Now.*"

"Great." She turned the phone so he could see the screen. "This is a schedule of—"

"You have to quit."

The words were out of his mouth before he could even think about pulling them back in.

Another fist met his face.

There were some gasps, a few yells, and one loud curse —which probably came from him—as he toppled and landed with a thud on his back.

Anthony leaned over him with a steely glare, his fist ready for another throw. He'd played football at Ohio State and majored in meathead. He was now apparently making a career out of it.

Nicki pushed him away. "Oh my God. Will you guys please stop trying to break the merchandise?"

"Did you just call me *merchandise?*"

Nicki crouched next to him on the floor. "You arm is worth eighty million dollars. You're merchandise."

He grabbed her hand. "Nicki, I really, really, really need to talk to you alone."

Nicki swallowed and sighed. "Fine."

She stood, offered her hand, and helped him to his feet. Just holding her fingers in his was like a hundred Red Bulls to his system. If she felt the same jolt, she hid it well.

She headed back down the hallway, holding up a hand to stop her brothers from following. "Give us a few minutes, guys."

They grunted in unison.

He followed Nicki into a room at the end of the hallway that looked like some kind of home office. She swung the door shut behind him and then crossed her arms. "Well?"

Seven years. That's how long it had been since he'd been alone in a room with her. The realization brought his brain to a halt.

She cocked her head and raised her eyebrows. The move brought his attention to a small scar above her left eye that hadn't been there the last time he saw her.

"I believe you were saying something about me quitting," she deadpanned.

Right. That. "We both know this is a bad idea, Nicki."

"I think it's a great idea, actually. I'm living the dream."

"I'm talking about us!"

"There is no us."

"Nicki—"

"But I'm glad you brought it up, because there is something I want to discuss with you." She uncrossed her arms and settled her hands on her hips. "Your promise still stands, I hope."

"Don't worry, sweetheart. Except for your brothers out there, I'm still your dirty little secret."

"Good. Because I'm sure you can see how uncomfortable it would make things for me if people knew about our little fling."

"*Little fling?*"

"Should I call it something else?"

"It was a helluva lot more than that, and you know it."

She snorted. "Which one of us are you trying to convince?"

"You of the selective memory."

"My memory is perfectly clear. I especially remember the part when you disappeared."

Bam! Nicki could throw a verbal fastball as powerful as the real thing, and this one hit its target. He had to fight the urge to rub his chest even as he admired her aim. She was the only woman he'd ever known who wasn't afraid to knock him off his pedestal. In a different situation, he might even enjoy the sparring. But there was too much at stake now, and Eric was an all-star competitor.

He closed the distance between them and lowered his voice. "I get it now. This is revenge. I dumped you, so now you're getting back at me."

To his surprise, Nicki tipped her head back and let out a booming laugh. "Yeah," she gasped in between guffaws. "I orchestrated this entire thing just to get back at you." She smirked. "I hate to burst your bubble, Eric, but it really wasn't that good."

Bam! Fastball number two. This one whipped past his bat and landed with a humiliating thud in the catcher's mitt. He shook it off and stepped back up to the plate. "You know what? You're a rotten liar. Because I seem to recall you calling my name over and over again."

"And I seem to recall faking it a lot."

Bam! Fastball number three. This one nailed him in the head. Which meant it was time to charge the mound. "I don't think so, darlin'."

He moved toward her. She backed up until she collided with the wall. He planted his hands on either side of her head.

His eyes dropped to her lips, and that was all it took. Blood rushed to his groin as memories came back in carnal clarity. Her body beneath his. Her eyes closed. Her voice calling his name.

Shit. Whatever he thought he was starting, it was something else now. Because when he tore his gaze from her mouth back to her eyes, he could barely remember what they'd been fighting about. He didn't know what the fuck came over him —the casual dismissal in her eyes, the smell of her skin, the memories suddenly slamming him from every direction.

She cocked an eyebrow. "What are you doing?"

"Jogging your memory."

Eric claimed her lips.

And felt an explosion of pain as her knee met his nuts.

He doubled over with an oomph just as her hands shoved at his shoulders and sent him reeling. He stumbled backwards and then fell to his knees. He couldn't breathe. Couldn't talk but for a single, guttural groan. His hands covered his junk and he fell forward. If he ever hoped to have children, he was pretty sure that dream had just died.

Her feet appeared in front of his face. "Don't ever do that again."

He tugged one hand free from under his body and managed a thumbs up.

"Are you all right?"

He mumbled into the carpet. "I think you broke it."

"Do you want some ice now?"

He thought about asking her to kiss it for him, but he liked his life, thank you very much.

"Look at me, Eric."

He moaned and rolled onto his back. She glared down at him. He immediately pictured her naked, and his dick twitched in response. Thank God it still worked.

"You think I don't know what you're doing?"

Shit. Was it that obvious?

"You think you can kiss me and touch me and I'll just come running after you?" She didn't give him time to respond. "You nearly derailed me from my dreams once. I won't let you do it again."

He pushed himself off the floor and stood, swallowing away a wave of nausea as his balls dropped from his throat. "What are you talking about? I always supported you."

"I almost gave it all up for you. Remember that?" Her voice took on a mocking tone. "*I don't know if I can do this without you, Nicki. I almost left school for you!* And then you dumped me, thank God."

She jabbed him in the chest. "I'm not the stupid girl I used to be, Eric. You might have hurt me back then, but you leaving me was the best thing that ever happened to me. And do you know why? Because you taught me a lesson I've never forgotten, a lesson that has gotten me here."

"What lesson is that?"

"The game is all that matters."

She wasn't even bothering with fastballs anymore. She was full-on cheating. Throwing in the dirt. Wiping pine tar on the ball.

And it worked. He was out. For now. "Are we done here, *coach*?"

"We're done."

She stepped around him and jerked open the door. He wanted to stomp behind her, but he had to settle for limping to the living room. Isabella, oblivious to the tension radiating between them, passed him a plate covered with tin foil.

"Robby told me you're not staying, so I put your food here. You can take it with you."

"Thank you, but I—"

She shoved it at him. "You eat."

Nicki smirked as he accepted the plate. He tried to smile at Isabella, but that only further cracked open the corner of his mouth. He winced and dabbed at the bleeding with his tongue. How the hell was he going to explain his face to the guys on the team?

Nicki marched to the front door and swung it open wide.

He walked outside and turned around. "Nicki—"

"Batter up, babe."

She slammed the door in his face.

3

Sometimes Fate was hell bent on kicking a man when he was down. Eric felt the blow of Her steel-toed snake skins as soon as he pulled into his driveway and saw the Ford truck with Texas plates blocking his garage. He had just enough fight left in him to consider ramming it with his Escalade, but he also had just enough throb left in his groin to subdue the urge.

Eric found him in the kitchen, stirring something on the stove. In the two years since they'd last spoken, his hair had faded into the color of a stormy sky and the small paunch he'd developed early in retirement was once again flat with athletic tautness.

Eric glanced around the room. The tower of pizza boxes was gone. The sink was empty of the dirty dishes that had been piling up for a week. The stench of laziness had been replaced by a lemony clean aroma. The place was goddamned spotless.

Eric dropped the plate from Isabella on the counter. Chet Weaver turned around as if that were the first he'd noticed Eric's arrival.

"Hello, son."

"How'd you get in here?"

"You gave us a key."

"I gave *Mom* a key."

Chet nodded toward the pot. "I kept it warm for you."

Eric snorted. "You don't expect me to believe you cooked, do you?"

His father faked a chuckle. "I got pretty good at it when your mother was sick."

Eric clenched his jaw and stormed to the fridge. He threw open the door and stared inside, searching for a beer that wasn't there. It took him a second to realize that he was looking at fresh produce and full gallons of milk. Things that hadn't been there this morning.

Eric slammed the door and whipped around. "What is this? What are you doing here?"

"Your mother used to help you get ready for the season. I thought I would, too."

"Mom was invited. You're not."

"Just the same."

Chet was refusing to take the bait. His tone suggested a practiced patience, like an umpire standing stone-faced in front of an unhinged manager. It made Eric want to throw things. He didn't need this. Not now. Not today. Hell, not *ever*.

"I want you gone tomorrow."

"Fair enough. But why don't you at least sit down for a few minutes and tell me what happened to your face."

"I ran into some fists."

"Wanna talk about it?"

"With you? Fuck no."

Chet showed the first signs of life. He rolled his lips in and out as if he were literally biting his tongue.

Eric tried to summon some satisfaction but couldn't find it. He shook his head and headed toward the hallway on the other side of the kitchen. "I'm going to my room. Be gone in the morning."

"It's time to end this, Eric. It's been long enough."

"Maybe for you."

"Eric—"

His father's voice faded away as Eric rounded the corner and trudged upstairs. The world had a sick sense of humor. In the span of one hour, the two people he most needed to stay in his past had parked themselves front and center in his life.

Eric emptied his pockets onto his dresser, avoiding the mirror on the wall. If he looked up and studied his reflection, he would barely recognize the face staring back at him. He'd see his mother's green eyes, his father's square jaw, and a dark complexion that hinted at a Sioux ancestry. But they were all just pieces. Parts thrown together in a puzzle that used to fit, back when he still knew who he was and what he wanted. Back when the ball felt right in his hand and he could control his entire world from a mound of dirt.

Long enough? Not even close.

Not with Nicki.

Not with his father.

Not by a long shot.

CHET LET out the breath he'd been holding as his one and only child walked away. Again.

He turned off the stove and reminded himself that he'd never believed this would be easy. He'd also known it was risky—surprising him like this—but desperate times called for desperate measures. What was it his counselor in rehab used to say? *It won't be easy, but it will be worth it.*

There was a special kind of torture in knowing your child was hurting. It was even worse knowing it was your fault.

But, hey, Chet had managed to wrangle one night out of it. Score one for Dad.

In the morning, he'd figure out how to convince Eric to let him stay the week. Then all of spring training. Then he'd find a way to let Eric know he'd rented an apartment in Vegas and had purchased season tickets.

Chet covered the pot and carried it to the fridge. Chicken noodle soup always tasted better the next day, anyway. He hoped it was still Eric's favorite. A good father would know for sure, but Chet had never been that.

He heard the sound of running water upstairs, as if Eric had turned on the shower. It was barely seven o'clock. Eric had made it clear he was going to stay in his room all night, which certainly wasn't the worst outcome Chet could have imagined. Eric could have tossed him out on his ass. He could have called the cops. Or he could have repeated the last words he'd spoken to Chet two years ago after the funeral.

"She was the only good part of this family, and now she's gone. And there is absolutely no point in you and I pretending to be anything other than strangers."

"I'm your father."

"Took you a little too long to figure that out."

Eric was right. It had taken Chet too long. Too many years wasted—figuratively and literally. Too many years when he thought the game was the most important thing in his life; that the people he loved most would simply be there when it was all gone. Too many years assuming they understood why he did the things he did; that the pressure of being Chet Weaver justified the women, the booze, the yelling. Too many years thinking the best way to show his love for his son was to push him hard to succeed.

He always believed he would have time later to make up for the shit storm he rained down on his wife and son.

He was wrong.

Chet let out a breath and wiped the counter one last time with a wet cloth, scrubbing away the miniscule remnants of the disturbing mess he'd found when he arrived. His son had never been a slob. Eric was meticulous, disciplined.

But crumb by crumb, stain by stain, Chet would scrub until the slate was clean.

Whatever Eric threw at him, he was ready to catch. He was prepared to go all nine innings and then some if necessary.

Because a man will do just about anything to get his son back.

4

THEY WERE FOLLOWING HER. Nicki could hear their footsteps, their voices. But the faster she ran, the closer they got.
The alley ahead was a shortcut. It was dark, but if she could
outrun them, she could get away.

"You're that bitch on the baseball team."

Nicki gasped and shot up in bed. Her arms swung out
but connected with nothing but air. Sweat drenched her
back, and her heart galloped in her chest. Her eyes darted
around the room. Where was she? Whose curtains were
those? This bed. It wasn't her bed. What was going on?

Then reality returned as the remnants of panic faded.
This was the Aces house. This was her bed, at least for the
next six weeks. And the dream had been just that, a dream.

She swung her legs over the bed and grabbed her phone
from the beat-up nightstand. The time display read *4:15
a.m.* Fifteen minutes before her alarm was due to go off.

There was no point in returning to bed, so she got up and pulled on her yoga gear.

Her parents, Anthony, and Vincent were all staying in a hotel. Robby was sleeping in the bedroom next to hers, and she did her best to be quiet as she shoved the couch out of the way in the living room for her morning yoga routine. Robby was a bear in the morning even in the best circumstances, and she really didn't need one of his lectures right now on whether she got enough sleep. Someday, he was going to be a helicopter parent of the worst kind.

She put up with him, though, because he was also her biggest champion. When she was old enough to start playing Little League, he'd endured more than his fair share of teasing from their teammates. When she was named starting pitcher on the boys' varsity team as a sophomore, he'd thrown punches defending her right to be there. When she made national news as the first woman to land a college pitching scholarship for a men's team, he stood beside her at the press conference with tears of pride in his eyes.

And he was the only other person besides her parents who knew how far some men were willing to go to keep her from succeeding.

She almost made it through her entire hour-long yoga practice when he emerged from his cave.

"Shit, Nicki. What time is it?"

She looked up from her downward dog position. "If you're awake, then it's time for a morning run."

He groaned. "I should've stayed in the hotel."

She stood with a stretch. "Please? I need to burn off some energy, and it's too dark for me to go alone."

He mumbled some creative curse words and shuffled back to his room. Nicki quickly changed into running clothes, dug out a hat and some gloves—even in Florida, February was cold—and then waited for him at the door. He was still scowling when he joined her.

He followed her outside. "How far?"

"Five or six."

"I hope that means minutes."

She laughed and took off down the sidewalk. They ran in silence for the first few miles until Robby slowed and stopped. She turned and jogged in place with a teasing grin. "You're weak."

He bent and placed his hands on his knees, his breath creating white puffs around his face. "Do you have any idea how fast you're going?"

She checked her fitness watch. She was running under a six-minute pace. Not her fastest, but definitely faster than Robby was used to going for any length of time. Baseball players were sprinters, not marathoners. "Sorry. I'm distracted."

He stood and put his hands on his head. He studied her face for a second.

"What's wrong?"

She toyed with the idea of telling him about the dream but opted against it. "Just nervous about today, I guess."

"The press conference?"

"And meeting the team and everything else." That part was at least true. She'd been walking onto men's teams her entire life, but this was literally a whole other ballgame. Things had changed in the past decade, to be sure, and she wouldn't be the first woman to coach a professional men's team. There was already a woman serving as an assistant coach for an NBA team, and an NFL team had temporarily hired a woman as a coach during training camp.

But Nicki wasn't naïve. For every fist-pump of support she received there would be a middle finger flipped in her face. Some even from within the Aces organization itself. She had perfected the face of bravado over the years, but it still burned whenever she was faced with the realization that some people would simply never accept her or see her talent simply because she was a woman.

Even knowing how deep that sentiment ran in some men—how much hatred they could carry and heap upon her —it still smacked when she was forced to deal with it. And the question she faced with every new achievement was how many supporters she would find.

Knowing Eric Weaver likely wasn't one of them stung more than it should.

Nicki had imagined a thousand different ways he might react to the news that she would be his coach, and she had braced herself for the chance that he wouldn't exactly be overjoyed. After all, it had been seven years since the breakup—seven years since she'd climbed out of his car, slammed the door, and vowed to never look back.

But of all the possible greetings she had conjured up in her mind, demanding that she quit before kissing her was not one of them.

She was proud of how she handled herself last night, but hearing him tell her to quit had hurt.

Still, she hadn't been lying when she told him he actually did her a favor by dumping her. She never would have made it this far if she'd been distracted by him and his career. The only thing that mattered now was proving herself. With or without his support.

As usual, Robby read her mind. He started jogging again. "This is about him, isn't it?"

"A little."

"I should have broken his arms last night."

"My job depends on his arms *not* being broken, thank you very much."

"I don't trust him."

"You blame him. There's a difference."

"You're goddamned right I blame him. I always will. You wouldn't have gone out that night if Eric hadn't dumped you."

She had blamed Eric at one point, too, but time and therapy had helped her focus the blame squarely where it belonged—on the men who had hurt her. The only crime Eric had committed was to reveal himself as a lying jerk who turned her into a sniffling, weak mess when he left.

Never again.

"It was a long time ago, Robby."

"Is that why you had another nightmare this morning?"

She glanced over at him and stumbled in her stride. "How did you—"

"I heard you yell, and then you got up. What else would it have been?"

"It was just a dream."

"It's never just a dream."

"I'm just nervous. Everything is fine, Robby."

His pinched expression told her he wanted to say more, but she didn't give him the chance. "Race you."

She punched up the pace to a sprint and beat him home. She heard him call her name from the corner of her street as she skidded into the house, but she ignored him and headed for the shower.

She braced her hands against the tiled wall and let the hot water cascade down her quivering muscles, carving tiny rivers through the ridges of sinew she had earned through hard work and total dedication.

Few things felt as good as exertion, of pushing herself harder and farther, and achieving what others insisted was impossible. Proving the doubters wrong made everything worth it—all the sacrifices, the punishing workouts, the isolation, the hostility from men who never would accept her.

All her life, people had told her it couldn't be done. All her life, she had proved them wrong.

Nicki tipped her face into the water and traced the scar above her eye with her fingers. Her doctor told her they could fix it with plastic surgery, but she refused. She needed it. Every day when she looked in the mirror, she stared at the visible reminder of how weak she'd once been, and she made a vow to herself. To the girl she had been *before*.

She was going to succeed, no matter the cost.

She was going to beat them.

And then the nightmares would end.

5

LIGHT BLINDED Eric as his eyelids flew open. He bolted upright and regretted it immediately. He was as hard as a Louisville Slugger. He tried to get his brain to focus, but the only organ that seemed to be working was the one waiting to bat in his boxers.

After a long hazy moment, the details began to fall into place. He was on top of the covers in his bed, wearing the same clothes he'd had on last night. The melted ice pack taped loosely to his elbow explained the cold, wet spot beneath him, and snippets of a dream involving a very naked Nicki explained the boner. He'd been one imagined thrust away from a grand-slam orgasm until something woke him up.

Then he heard it again. The noise that had pulled him from the dream. Someone was knocking on his door. What the hell?

Oh, yeah. His father. Sonuvabitch.

With a groan, he pulled himself off the bed, dropped the ice pack onto the dresser, and stormed to the door. He yanked it open.

His father stood on the other side, wearing a rise-and-shine smile and holding a heaping plate of scrambled egg whites and cut-up fruit.

Eric turned away. "You're supposed to be gone."

"No reason I can't make breakfast first."

"I'd rather eat dog shit than whatever you cooked up."

"Sort of childish, don't you think?"

"You know your way home if you don't like it."

"I think I can gut it out."

"Yeah, well. I can't. Pack your bags and get out of my house."

Eric heard his father set the plate on the dresser.

"Eat, Eric. I know how shitty the food is in the clubhouse."

Eric scrubbed his hands over his face. It did smell good, and his stomach grumbled in response. Fuck it. No use wasting a home-cooked meal. His father was right. The food in the clubhouse sucked.

Eric spun around and grabbed the plate. If his father showed one sign of satisfaction, though, Eric would throw him *and* the food out the door.

Eric sat down on the edge of the mattress and started shoveling eggs into his mouth.

"Big news about Nicki, huh?"

Eric looked up. "How do you know about that?"

"It's on CNN."

Fuck. How the hell did CNN know? The team hadn't even been told yet.

Eric grabbed the remote from the bedside table and turned on the TV. He punched in the number of the news network. CNN came to life on the screen with a banner along the bottom.

BREAKING: *Vegas Aces to announce woman as pitching coach today*

Shit. The team could not find out this way.

The CNN anchor ran through the basics as she knew them from "an unnamed source" in the Aces organization. *Minor League pitching Coach Nicki Bates, who had spent the past four years with the Boulder Peaks double-A team, would work with the Aces at least through spring training. Owner Devin Dane would decide before opening day whether to keep her on full time.*

Wait. What? Her job was only secure through spring training?

The screen split in half as the anchor introduced their "team of experts." Ray Fox's smug face appeared, and Eric swore.

Ray fucking Fox? Why the hell would they ask for his opinion? The man had literally made a career out of being a sexist asshole.

Breakfast forgotten, Eric set the plate on the table and stood.

"She will ruin the game of baseball," Ray declared. "I mean, let's face it, I might enjoy watching her wind up in a pair of tight pants, but that doesn't mean I want her anywhere near a Major League ballpark."

Eric growled.

Chet turned up the TV as the show's moderator turned to another commentator, Avery Giordano, a baseball writer for The New York Times.

"I have been covering Nicki Bates for years," the woman said. "She was an exceptional finesse pitcher in college who became one of the best pitching coaches in the minor leagues. Two of last year's Cy Young contenders came from her instruction. And let's not forget her Ph.D."

Chet looked at Eric. "Nicki has a Ph.D.?"

Eric shrugged, just as confused as his father. How much else did he not know about the woman he once swore he would spend forever with?

Avery Giordano continued. "Nicki Bates knows more about how an athlete's body works than every other team manager combined. The Aces were smart to hire her, not because she's a woman, but because she knows what she's doing."

Ray snorted. "That is nothing but VS."

The anchor's eyebrows drew together. "VS?"

"Vaginal solidarity."

Chet snorted. "That's a new one."

Eric growled again. "I don't share your amusement."

"Mark my words," Ray continued. "This is nothing more than a publicity stunt from an owner who needs a distraction from the way his team imploded during the World Series. And does anyone really think it's a coincidence that of all the teams to hire her, it was the team Eric Weaver plays for?"

The anchor interrupted. "What are you suggesting, Ray?"

Ray smirked again. "What do you think?"

Eric went cold. Shit. This was exactly what Nicki was afraid of. She was going to go apeshit. Five minutes into her first official day on the job, and someone had already suggested they were *chasing the long ball* together. He was going to kill whoever leaked this.

His phone rang. He didn't recognize the number, but he suspected who it was. He answered and turned away from the TV.

Nicki's voice was hard and cold. "You asshole."

Wait. What? "Excuse me?"

"I wouldn't quit last night, so you're trying to ruin me in the media?"

"You think *I* leaked this?"

"I can count on one hand the number of people who know about the Aces hiring me, and you're the only one who has a motive to hurt me. Do the math, Eric."

"I didn't fucking leak this!"

The fact that she suspected him made him want to hurl, which made no sense. She was right. What better way to make sure Nicki left the team than to play up the very romantic rumors she was terrified would get out? He should be celebrating that Ray Fox had done it for him. He should be capitalizing on it. But the thought of that made his stomach clench. He wouldn't do that to her.

Just because he couldn't afford the distraction of her as his coach didn't mean he wanted her ruined publicly.

"Christ, Nicki. Is that what you really think of me?"

"Give me one reason why I should think anything else."

He heard another voice in the background. "Give me the phone."

Robby. Great.

There was the sound of some shuffling, as if her brother was wrenching the phone from Nicki's hand.

"You sonuvabitch," Robby hissed.

Eric ignored the accusation. "Why don't you do something to protect her instead of trying to blame me?"

"You've got some fucking nerve," Robby said, his voice dangerously low. "First you tell her to quit, and now you're ordering me to stand up for her?"

"I happen to care."

There was some more shuffling, as if they were once again fighting over the phone.

Robby won. "You gave up your right to care when you broke her heart."

His voice broke off, replaced quickly by Nicki's. "Excuse my brother. He doesn't like you."

"Someone needs to defend you. We need to put out a statement or something."

"We? *We* aren't doing anything. In case you've forgotten, last night you were begging me to quit. Why the hell do you care now?"

"Excuse me for giving a shit."

She snorted into the phone. "When you asked me to quit last night, was that your version of giving a shit?"

He ignored the jibe. "So, you're just going to ignore it?"

"No. I'm just telling you to stay the hell out of it."

"Nicki—"

"I've been taking care of myself for a long time. I don't suddenly need you to do it for me."

Eric sank back onto the mattress and scrubbed his free hand over his hair. "Put your brother back on."

"Good-bye, Eric."

"Dammit, Nicki!"

She hung up.

Eric clenched the phone in his hand and thought seriously about throwing it against the wall. If he needed any more proof that Nicki was going to be nothing but a distraction, he had it now. The start of spring training usually left him feeling like a kid on summer vacation. The entire season was before him. A clean slate. A new chance to chase the dream. He should have woken up this morning with a jolt of competitive adrenaline and old-fashioned boyhood enthusiasm.

Instead, his stomach churned. Guilt mixed with anger. Nicki was right. He didn't have a right to be pissed on her behalf, but he was. He wanted to throw Ray Fox into a dark room and practice fastballs on his face.

Chet cleared his throat. "Is Nicki OK?"

Dammit. What the hell was he still doing there? Eric held up a finger to silence him. "Don't. You don't get to say her name."

Chet's face twisted in something that looked like real regret. "I'm sorry, Eric. I made a mistake back then, and it's probably too much to hope that you or Nicki can ever forgive me for it. But I also know—"

Eric shot to his feet. "You know what exactly? You don't know shit. You don't know anything about Nicki *or* me."

"I know you're in a bad place, and I'm to blame for that."

"For fuck's sake. Leave me alone." Eric stormed to the bathroom and slammed the door, hoping it would snap the strings in his chest that had tightened at his father's apology. They had never talked about it before. Ever. Eric would rather break his own arm than discuss it now.

He listened for the sounds of his father leaving the bedroom. There was the clink of the fork against the plate, the soft shuffle of his father's footsteps on the carpet, the quiet click of the door.

Eric let out the breath he'd been holding and braced his hands on the bathroom counter.

Why the hell do you care now? Jeezus, he fucking hated karma. All his lies, all his mistakes. They were coming back to bite him in the ass, and there was nothing he could do about it.

Nicki believed he didn't give a shit about her, because that's exactly what he had wanted her to believe all those years ago.

The truth was exactly the opposite.

He cared too much.

A different voice filled his memory. This one slurred and angry.

She'll be nothing but a distraction, son. Don't be an idiot. No man goes to the Majors saddled with a wife.

Eric spun away from the counter, from his reflection in the mirror, from the taunting voice he could never silence.

His father was right about one thing, at least.

He *was* to blame.

And Eric would never forgive him for it.

6

THE PRESS CONFERENCE was as painful as Nicki knew it would be. A hundred reporters, cameramen, and God-knows-who-else had packed into the Aces media room with their tiny weapons of mass exposure. Microphones. iPhones. Video cameras. All pointed straight at her.

It was twenty minutes of pure hell.

She hated dealing with the media. She respected them and the job they had to do, but she despised the lack of control. On the field, she was the one in charge. In front of reporters, it was their game.

When the press conference was over, she sought safety in the quiet of a conference room across from the clubhouse —baseball's term for locker room. Hunter was supposed to meet her there and escort her across the hall to introduce her to the team.

She turned on the TV mounted on the wall and settled

on ESPN. Ugh. Ray Fox once again filled the screen. Of all the people in the world for the media to interview, the networks had to choose him?

If men were pigs, then Ray Fox gave them the mud to roll in.

She'd been relieved to scan the press room and not see his face in the crowd. Apparently, he instead was spending his morning making the rounds from cable network to cable network suggesting she was either a politically correct stunt or Eric Weaver's personal ball bunny.

Nicki rubbed her eyes and tried to drown out Ray's voice. All it did was let her brain remember another voice. *I didn't fucking leak this!*

She still wasn't sure if she believed him. Who else would have anything to gain from it? He had actually sounded convincing, but he also had been convincing seven years ago when he told her he loved her.

Nicki had learned the hard way that Eric was one helluva good actor, and the timing this time was too perfect. One day after telling him to make sure no one found out about their history, Ray Fox suddenly goes on TV and starts hinting she and Eric were playing a secret game of catch?

Her face burned. She could already hear the late-night TV monologues. *Are Nicki Bates and Eric Weaver hitting homers off the field?*

She hadn't even met the team yet. Now she would have

to walk in there and wonder what was going through their minds. They were probably high-fiving Eric.

The TV suddenly zapped off.

Nicki jerked around. Standing in the open doorway, the remote control in her hand like a weapon, was one of the smallest but most intimidating women Nicki had ever seen. A tall man stood behind her, and next to him was her agent, Gary.

"From now on," the woman said, "you stop watching this junk."

"I'm sorry. Who are you?"

Gary stepped further into the room. "This is Abby Taylor, your new press agent."

"I have a press agent?"

"You do now," the woman said.

"We bring her on for particularly high-profile circumstances," Gary explained. "We tried to get her here in time for the press conference, but her plane was delayed."

Abby crossed the room, hand extended. From the looks of her tiny physique, Nicki feared she'd crumble in anything harder than a polite squeeze of the fingers. But her grip was as strong and fierce as the hard set of her eyes.

"It's a pleasure, Nicki," Abby said. She motioned to the man behind her. "This is my colleague, David Ross."

The man nodded, and suddenly the names clicked in Nicki's mind. "Ross, Taylor and Associates?"

"That's right."

"Don't you guys specialize in image repair following a scandal?"

"Yes."

"My image doesn't need repairing."

"It will now that Ray Fox has you in his radar. Surely, you must know that."

Nicki cocked an eyebrow at the woman. A straight shooter. She liked that. She didn't have time for someone who would tip-toe around kissing her butt. If she could get Ray Fox and his innuendos under control, even better.

The woman motioned to David. He swiped the screen on his iPad a couple of times. "Social media chatter from someone who lives one block over from you says Eric Weaver was seen leaving your house last night. Care to comment?"

"Are you kidding me?"

"I give it a half-hour before it's trending on Twitter," David said. "Ray Fox will be sure of that."

"But nothing happened! My family was there!"

"Still," Abby said. "I think we need to be prepared with a statement."

"The only statement I have is unfit for the airwaves."

"Just give it to us straight," Abby said. "Do you now, or have you ever had, a romantic relationship with Eric Weaver?"

"No," Nicki lied, stomach in a knot. How had it come to this already?

"We'll deal with it," Abby said. "Are you ready to continue?"

"Continue what?"

"Prepping for interviews." Abby glanced at her watch and pursed her lips. "Everyone is asking for first dibs, but we can't afford to start out pissing off anyone at the national level by favoring one of their competitors. So my recommendation is that we piss them all off equally and give the local guys the first crack at you."

She nodded at David again, and he produced the iPad once more. "We've blocked out two hours," he said, swiping the screen. "TV will go first since they have to make their evening newscasts. After that, we'll let in the print guys and blogs."

Nicki shook her head. "No."

Abby raised her eyebrows. "We know what we're doing, Nicki."

"I meant no media. Period."

"This is a joke, right?"

"I'm not doing interviews. That's what the press conference was for."

Abby whipped around and glared at Gary. "What the hell is this? Is she serious?"

Gary's eyes grew big and round. "Um, Nicki, I don't think that's going to cut it."

"I'm not doing this for media attention."

"I don't care if you're doing this to raise money for

Tibetan monks with cancer," Abby snapped. "I did not drop
everything in my life so I could come out here and issue
press releases."

Nicki crossed her arms. "How much is Gary
paying you?"

Abby matched her pose. "More than you make."

"Then it's certainly enough for you to speak to the
media on my behalf."

"You can't be serious."

"I am. I have no doubt that you and David know what
you're doing. But so do I. I've been walking onto men's
teams since I was in training bras, and the absolute worst
thing I could do at this point is to steal their spotlight any
more than I already have. They will never accept me if I go
prancing around like some kind of media whore. I can't start
out that way. And I won't."

Abby's eye twitched as they stared each other down.
The woman barely came to Nicki's chin, but she had an iron
will that belied her slight stature. Suddenly, Nicki recognized something in Abby's eyes. A woman in a man's world
had to develop a special kind of determination, and Abby
Taylor had it. Her eyes never wavered, never blinked—a skill
she no doubt had to learn the hard way as she faced down
men much bigger than she.

Just like Nicki.

An unfamiliar sense of kinship began to grow. Nicki
could count on one hand the number of friends she'd had

her in life. Most women—*girls*—considered her either a freak or a threat. In high school, the other girls assumed she played baseball to steal their boyfriends. In college, the girls assumed she was a lesbian. Either way, it was always about sex and never about baseball.

Abby sighed, and the hint of a smile tugged at her lips. "I don't like taking orders. Most of my clients trust my advice."

"I'm sure they do, but on this one, *you're* going to have to trust *me*. The best thing you can do for me is to act as my spokesperson and keep the reporters away from me."

Abby considered Nicki's words one moment more. Then she nodded. "Deal." She turned to David. "Make it happen."

David spun on his heel and walked out.

Abby eyed Gary. "Leave us alone for a minute."

Nicki almost laughed out loud at the way Gary snapped to attention and hustled from the room, shutting the door behind him. Abby was a bona fide ballbuster.

And she now was aiming her steely stare at Nicki. "I agreed to your terms. Now you need to agree to mine."

"I'll do my best."

"Do not ever lie to me."

A chill went through Nicki. It was a promise she'd already broken.

"I can't do my job properly if I don't know everything, so when I ask you questions before speaking to the media, I need the absolute truth. Is that clear?"

"Crystal."

"Good. Now, if you'll excuse me, I have some asses to kick over this morning's leak."

Nicki watched Abby march from the room and immediately felt sorry for whomever was next on her list. Her amusement faded quickly, though, only to be replaced by guilt.

She *had* lied to Abby, and not just about Eric. She'd left something out about her reluctance to do interviews. Every time she thought about sitting down with a reporter and opening herself up to them, she remembered the last time she had done so. And what had happened afterward.

"You're that bitch on the baseball team."

Nicki gripped her purse tighter against her side. "No, I'm not."

"Yeah, you are. I recognize you. You're on the cover of Sports Illustrated.*"*

Nicki shook off the memory. No, media exposure had never done Nicki any good. Abby would just have to live with it.

7

Devin Dane sipped his coffee—an organic, Tanzanian bean that was nearly impossible to get—and stared out the window of his office.

The hush of the empty stands below was broken only by the hurried pace of the grounds crew as they prepared the diamond for the start of training camp.

He turned away and shook his head to clear it of the doubts that had kept him awake most of the night.

Wouldn't that shock the world? Yes, even Devin Dane, the arrogant playboy of the Dane family dynasty, feared failure.

And right now, failure was very much an option. The bases were officially loaded against him.

The team was losing money. Fans were turning on him. They said he was too young. Too inexperienced. He'd been hearing the whispers for five years, ever since his uncle died and he took over the team.

But the whispers became screams after the Aces lost the World Series.

He and Hunter had been taking a beating for their decision to let Weaver start that last game. Even the local Vegas press—who had been mostly kind in their coverage of Devin—had started wondering if his critics were right all along.

His older brother, Bennett, loved to rub it in his face every chance he got, including last night when he called to complain, yet again, about money. The conversation had robbed him of sleep.

"You paid two hundred thousand dollars for a painting?" Bennett's voice was deceptively muted.

"It's an original Faragamo. They don't become available very often."

"Where the hell did you get the money?"

"My trust fund."

Bennett snorted. "Right. You mean you put it on a credit card that I'm going to have to pay."

"Actually, I had to wire the money."

Bennett made a choking sound. "From what fucking account?"

"It's my money, Bennett. Dad left me the same amount as you."

"Your trust fund is almost gone, Devin. Don't think for

one second I'm going to let you start dipping into family money."

"The team is going to start turning a profit. You have to trust me."

"That's the thing, little brother. I don't trust you. And neither does Mom. We only agreed to let you run that damn team because we had to give you something productive to do before you bled us dry. But I swear to God, this is your last warning."

Devin fought to keep his voice calm. "What exactly does that mean?"

"If you can't dig yourself and that team out of debt, we're taking the Aces public and cutting you off. Period."

Bennett had more than enough money and influence to make it happen, but Devin knew the real reason for the threat. Bennett always felt the need to remind Devin he was older, wiser, and richer. It was one more salvo in a twenty-year sibling rivalry. And Bennett had finally found a way to stick it to his *little brother* in a way that really mattered.

What he wouldn't give to see Bennett's face right now.

One leak on his way to the ballpark this morning, and the entire sports world was talking about exactly one thing: The Vegas Aces. There wasn't a press outlet or sports blog in the nation that wasn't scrambling to report on the rumor that the Aces were hiring a woman as their pitching coach.

He sat down at his desk and grabbed the remote to flip from CNN to ESPN.

"You can't go in there!"

Devin dropped the remote at the sound of his secretary's shriek. A moment later, a woman threw open the door and stalked inside. He barely had time to notice toned legs and a tight skirt before she stormed to the front of his desk and crossed her arms. Long red nails tapped her elbow. Luscious red lips pursed in displeasure.

Shit. He knew those lips.

He *dreamed* of those lips.

Even when they were snarling in his direction.

He stood, sloshing coffee onto his tie in the process. "*Abby?*"

"Do you make a habit of screwing your staff," she said, "or is Nicki Bates a special case?"

His secretary ran in then, breathing hard. "I'm sorry, Mr. Dane. I tried to stop her."

Abby shrugged. "If you're not going to play by the rules, neither am I."

Next through the door was Todd Marshall, the team's public relations director. He, too, was panting. "Devin, I'm sorry. Meet Abby Taylor."

"Don't worry, Todd. Devin and I are well-acquainted with each other."

That was one way to put it. Devin stood and hoped his face didn't betray the emotions rioting in his mind. He swallowed and wiped at the wet spot on his tie. "I didn't realize Nicki had retained an independent publicist."

"Yes, well, it's a good thing she did, isn't it? Because if she can't even trust the team owner to protect her, I'd say she needs all the independent help she can get."

"I'm afraid I don't know what you're talking about."

"Bullshit."

Devin's eyebrows shot north as his lips broke into a grin. Few people ever dared to speak to him like that. Or get in his face. Or barge in uninvited.

Except for Abby. She was the only woman who had never treated him like *Devin Dane*.

"Let me be clear," she said, bending forward to grab the remote from his desk. He got a tantalizing glimpse of silky white skin as her blouse pulled away from her chest. She straightened and pointed the remote at the TV. "I won't put up with any more stunts like the one you pulled this morning."

Todd puffed up with indignation. "Now wait a minute, Abby. You can't run in here and—"

She glanced over her shoulder. "Shut up, Todd."

To Devin's amazement, Todd actually obeyed. Devin's smile grew. "Abby, I don't know what you think I've done, but I assure you, you're mistaken."

She zapped off the TV. "You left her high and dry this morning. You let Ray freaking Fox get nearly four hours of major network time with absolutely no statement from the team or Nicki. You let him set the narrative, and now I have to un-do it. You don't just leak information to the first person in your contacts list, Devin. Leaks take a lot of strategy."

"You think I'm the source?" Ok, so he *was* the source. But she didn't need to know that.

She rolled her eyes. "God save me from the tyranny of amateurs."

A laugh burst from his chest.

Which was the clearly the wrong thing to do. She rounded his desk and jabbed a finger in his chest. "You think this is funny? It's going to take me hours to clean up the mess you created. The next time you get the urge to manipulate the media, leave it to the professionals."

For one of the only times in his life, Devin was truly speechless. Of course, the only other time had also been in the face of her rage. The irony was not lost on him.

Abby tossed the remote onto the desk and leaned in. Devin caught a whiff of something spicy and feminine. His body reacted predictably, and he shifted his stance to hide it.

"Let me make something very clear," she said. "You may have hired Nicki Bates as a publicity stunt, but I won't let you ruin her reputation or her career for your own agenda."

His amusement disappeared, along with his smile and his boner. "The only agenda I have is to see my team succeed. I resent any implications otherwise."

She leaned back. "Good. Let's keep it that way, or you're going to have to deal with me."

Then she spun on one dangerously high heel and

stormed out. And the only thing he could think as he watched her disappear through the door was that he'd spent the better part of twelve years wishing he could deal with her again.

Except, in his fantasies, she didn't still hate the very sight of him.

8

THE SCENE outside the ballpark was unlike anything Eric had ever seen for the start of spring training. Press vans from every recognizable network lined the road to the players' parking garage. News crews scrambled to raise satellite dishes and erect shade tents, a sign that they had no intention of leaving anytime soon.

Eric slowed his Escalade and blared the horn to ease through the throngs of reporters, cameras, and gawkers blocking his path. Today was just a team meeting and a light warm-up, for Christ's sake, but the leak and the press conference had clearly turned a normally quiet day into a circus.

No doubt about it. This was going to be one rat-fuck of a day.

A pair of security guards shouted at the crowd to back up as they swung open the gate to the parking garage. Eric parked quickly, hoisted his duffel bag over his shoulder, and then dodged nervous grounds crew and anxious team staff as he jogged the hallway to the players' lounge.

He slipped in the back. The entire pitching and coaching staff stood with their backs to him, their shoulders tight and stances wide. The room seethed like a collective clenched fist.

The row of muted flat-screens against the opposite wall were all tuned to different stations, all covering the same story. Nicki.

Standing before the team, Hunter glared. He was already in his uniform—the long, loose pants he favored covering his prosthetic leg. In between baseball stints, Hunter had served in Afghanistan and, according to press reports, lost his leg in some kind of ambush. He was only a few years older than most of the guys on the team, making him the youngest manager in the MLB. Even with his threat to move Eric to the bullpen still fresh in his mind, Eric's respect for the man was bone-deep.

"We did not make this decision lightly," Hunter said. "And I'm as pissed off as you are that you had to find out from the goddamned press. But what's done is done, and I'm not going to stand here and debate that with you. We have more important shit on our plates right now."

"Like getting rid of the bitch," someone mumbled. It sounded like Al Kasinski, long relief pitcher and all-around asshole.

Eric's teeth ground against each other. It was bad

enough hearing Ray Fox bash Nicki on TV. Hearing a team-mate do it sent rage through his veins.

Yet one more reason why this had all the makings of a disaster. Competitive anger was a good thing. Jealous, protective fury was not.

"Like doing our jobs," Hunter said, his gaze pinned on Kasinski. "And some of you have a helluva lot more work to do than others."

Hunter's cell rang, and he paused to look at it. He muttered a cuss word. "I gotta take this."

Hunter left the room, and the guys began to shift and grumble. Eric snuck around the back to his open stall and dropped his duffel bag inside. Cal Mahoney, a fellow starter and his best friend on the team, appeared by his side.

Eric looked over and braced himself for the inevitable.

Cal delivered. "Jeezus, dude. What happened to your face?"

"I ran into some fists."

"How many?"

"They were big fists."

Cal raised his eyebrows like he wanted to know more, but Eric cut him off. "How's Sara?"

Cal's face fell, and he sank onto the bench in front of the stalls. Eric sat next to him, cringing with guilt that he'd been so caught up in his own drama that he hadn't asked about Cal's twin sister earlier. Sara had been diagnosed with ovarian cancer at the start of last season, and the entire team was devastated. Sara and her three daughters were regulars at Aces games.

Eric dropped his voice. "The chemo isn't working?"

"She has one more round, and then they'll do another scan. But it's not—" Cal stopped and cleared his throat. "It's not looking good."

Eric lightly pounded his fist on Cal's back. "I'm sorry, man."

Cal nodded and stared into the emptiness of his stall.

Fellow starter Harper Brody suddenly shouted Eric's name and made a beeline for him.

"Dude. Is it true you know her? She's fucking hot."

Eric felt his eyes narrow as he looked up. Brody was a good guy, but Eric was feeling less than friendly right then.

Brody peered closer. "What happened to your face?"

"He ran into some fists," Cal offered.

"Shit. How many?"

"They were big fists," Eric said.

Brody shrugged. "Whatever. Dude, Nicki Bates. Do you think she'd go out with a player? She's fucking hot."

A sound emerged from Eric's chest—some kind of cross between Grizzly bear and drunken Tommy Lasorda.

Brody raised his hands and backed up. "Whoa, dude. Sorry. I assumed all that Ray Fox stuff was just bullshit."

"It *is* bullshit."

Their conversation drew the attention of their teammates, and the floodgates burst open. Guys crowded around him, all talking at once.

A rookie, some cocky little prick from Arizona whose name Eric couldn't remember, pounded his fist into his other hand. "I didn't wait four years in the minors so I could get called up and ordered around by a chick. No freakin' way."

Kas shook his head. "I give her two days. She won't last. Not if I have my way."

Eric's chest tightened until it was hard to breathe.

"I tell you what, though," the rookie said. "I wouldn't mind pitching to her after the game."

Eric shot to his feet. "Shut the fuck up!"

The room went silent. Eyes widened. Feet shuffled.

Kas was the first to pounce. "Shit, Weaver. Something we need to know about you and little miss hot pants?"

Eric's hands clenched at his sides, and he took a step closer to Kas. "The only thing you need to know about *Coach Bates* is that you will treat her with respect."

Kas inched forward, a menacing hue to his face. "Is that right? And what if I don't?"

Eric reacted out of pure rage and adrenaline. He grabbed the front of Kas's jersey and shoved. Kas toppled back but quickly righted himself and surged forward.

"Hey!" Cal got between them, a hand on each man's chest to hold them apart. "Knock it off. Now."

Kas pointed over Cal's shoulder. "You'd better watch

yourself, Weaver. Lotta guys in this room still aren't happy with you right now."

Cal got in his face. "Shut up, Kas."

"You standing up for that asshole?"

"You're goddamned right, I am. Now back the fuck up."

Kas straightened his shirt with an angry tug. The team held its breath to see if he'd push it, push *Cal*. No one messed with Cal these days, but Kas was a special kind of dumb fuck.

He must have finally gotten a fraction of sense, though, because after a moment he turned away. The guys broke into smaller groups again, and Eric sank back to the bench.

Cal joined him. "I have no patience for that prick. Not this year."

"Don't get into it with the guys on my account, Cal. He was right."

"No, he wasn't. No one blames you for that loss."

"They should."

"Kas was the closer that night. He gave up a homer, too."

"It wouldn't have mattered if they'd started you in the first place."

"It's over, Eric. A new season starts now. You have to forget what happened and focus on getting us back there for another shot at the championship."

Focus. Right. As if that were possible.

Another round of raucous laughter drew their attention to the other side of the room. Eric could tell from their faces they were still talking shit about Nicki. The tightness in his chest grew.

"Did you see she has her own damn press agent already?" Kas said. "Who does she think she is? Queen fucking Elizabeth?"

"Actually, my name is Veronica Marie Bates."

9

THE CLUBHOUSE WAS INSTANTLY SILENT. Every head swiveled toward Nicki as the swinging door flapped, flapped behind her. She steeled her spine and let her eyes do the talking.

That's right, boys. I heard every word.

This wasn't how she planned or hoped to meet the guys, but now was as good a time as any. She'd gone to the lounge to look for Hunter in his office, because he hadn't come to the conference room for her. But when she overheard the guys talking, she knew she needed to make her presence known. They needed to know she wasn't intimidated by them.

Eric included. Apparently, he thought she'd been kidding on the phone that morning. The last thing she needed was for him to add fuel to the Ray Fox fire.

She let her gaze stop on the source of the last remark, Al

Kasinski. She closed the small space between them and stuck out her hand. "But you can call me Nicki. Or Coach, if you prefer."

Someone snickered. Kasinski stared at her hand and then, with deliberate slowness, turned his back on her. Which was a victory, as far as Nicki was concerned. When they stopped throwing punches, you knew you won.

The rookie, Alex Palmer, was next. Nicki thrust her hand in his direction. "Nicki Bates."

He leaned over, opened his mouth and hacked. A blob of oozing, brown chew landed with a squishy thud on the toe of her shoe.

Charming. She'd been spit on before, but chew was a first.

Nicki kicked her toe against the cement floor until the offensive mass slid off, leaving a brown smear in its place. "That stuff causes cancer, you know."

"I'll take my chances," Palmer smirked.

"Not if you want to make this team. The next time I see you with that stuff in your mouth, you're headed back to Arizona."

The rookie's face went red. "You can't do that."

"I can, and I will." She turned away from him, but stopped at the last minute.

"By the way, the reason you spent four years in the minors is because you're inconsistent after about fifty pitches. You also have a tendency to drop your shoulder on your fastball, and it floats across the center of the plate like an open invitation to the sweet spot."

"You bitch."

"That's Coach Bitch to you." She pointed to the glob on the floor. "And clean that up. The clubhouse isn't your toilet."

She turned around and found the rest of the crew staring, wide-mouthed. She planted her hands on her hips. "Anyone else want to measure dicks?"

Harper Brody stepped forward and dropped to his knee. "Will you marry me?"

Eric whacked him in the head. "Shut up, Brody."

Nicki ignored the short exchange and faced Eric square. "Weaver, may I have a word with you in the trainer's office, please?"

The request sent a murmur of smart-ass snickers through the staff. Eric stood and extended his hand to flip off his teammates before stalking across the room.

He opened the door to the attached office that would soon be her makeshift locker room. Nicki followed and ignored the laughter behind them as she closed the door.

Eric leaned back against a row of cabinets by the door and crossed his arms over his chest. Nicki tried not to notice how his black t-shirt pulled taut across his defined chest and biceps. She thought she would be immune to him after all this time. Couldn't fate have thrown in a little male-patterned balding or a missing tooth over the years? Or a rash. A rash seemed fair.

She'd have to settle for the temporary satisfaction of his split lip and purple jaw.

She matched his cross-armed pose. "Are you trying to ruin me?"

Eric blinked. "Excuse me?"

"I don't need you to fight my battles. I thought I made that perfectly clear this morning."

"What are you talking about?"

"I'm talking about your little jealous boyfriend routine in there! What were you thinking, taking on Kas like that?"

Eric straightened. "I was standing up for you!"

"Well, don't. You just make it worse."

"I swear to God, Nicki, I have no idea why you're so pissed at me right now."

"Use your brain, Eric! How long before someone leaks it to the press that there was nearly a fight in the clubhouse this morning? I give it twenty minutes, tops."

"Ballplayers fight all the time. It's hardly newsworthy."

"But this time I'm involved. And you know what that means? They're going to want to know what would make the Vegas Aces turn on each other. And you know who they're going to blame? Me!"

"May I point out one small thing?"

"No."

"We were, in fact, fighting about *you*."

She rolled her eyes. "I provoke people just by being here. Is that what you're saying? You think I haven't heard that before?"

"You provoke *me!*" His outburst echoed off the painted cement walls. He jerked his fingers through his hair and stared at the floor. After a moment, he looked up at her again. "You can't ask me to stand by and do nothing. If you had heard what they were saying—"

"I heard every word. I was standing just outside the door."

"Why the hell didn't you do something?"

"Because it wouldn't matter. If I took on every guy who made a crude remark about me, I'd be a heavyweight champion by now. I learned a long time ago that if you ignore their punches, they eventually stop hitting you."

"Bullshit. If you ignore their punches, you end up bloody and broken. Guys like Kas and Ray Fox speak one language—brute force. They would respect you more if you gave it right back to them."

She scoffed. "I'll never win against guys like that with brute force, Eric. They're bullies, nothing more. They want you to hit back. That's why they do it. The best way to beat them is to win. Period."

"At some point you have to come out swinging."

"Spoken like someone who's never really been hit."

Shit. The instant the words left her mouth, she regretted them.

His eyes narrowed. "What are you talking about?"

"Nothing."

He closed the distance between them in three long strides. Nicki backed up against the trainer's table in the middle of the room. Eric stared at the scar above her eyebrow and then dipped back down to meet her gaze. His eyes darkened with an unreadable expression, and a vein popped along his forehead as he clenched his jaw.

"What happened?"

"Nothing."

She tried to sidestep him. His arm snaked out and blocked her escape. From any other man, it would have seemed aggressive. From him, it felt protective.

"Tell me."

They stared each other down. His eyes shifted to her lips, and her breath stuck in her lungs. Was he seriously going to kiss her again? And why the hell did that possibility fill her with heat?

The door suddenly swung open and Abby stalked inside.

Nicki jumped back as if scalded.

Abby's eyes narrowed at the scene before her and then zeroed in on Eric. "You idiot."

Eric looked down at her and then back at Nicki. "Who is that?"

"Abby Taylor. My new press agent."

"Yeah. Your press agent. Who thought you might like to

know that someone already leaked it to the press that there was an altercation in the clubhouse."

Great. Nicki glared at Eric. "Less than ten minutes. That has to be a record."

"Nicki—"

She held up her hand. "Get yourself under control, Eric."

Abby held open the door. "We have work to do. Let's go. Both of you."

Eric gripped her wrist. "Nicki, wait."

She yanked free of him. "*Coach.*"

"Excuse me?"

"It would be best if you call me Coach."

ERIC TAILED Nicki and her press rep whose name he couldn't remember down the dim, cinderblock tunnel that ran from the clubhouse to the dugout. The tunnel buzzed with activity as team staff ran around finishing last-minute tasks.

Coach. Nicki wanted him to call her coach. What the fuck?

"Where are we going?"

"Conference room," was the woman's muffled response.

She shot him a dirty look that would make Black Widow wither as she held open the door for him. He followed Nicki inside and practically jumped when the door slammed behind them.

Jeezus. Who was this woman?

"Can someone please tell me what the hell is going on?" he asked.

Black Widow circled around him from behind. "I should be asking you that."

Eric looked at Nicki, who stood with hands planted on her hips and a peevish tightness to her lips.

Black Widow narrowed her gaze at Nicki. "Not thirty minutes ago, I asked you point blank if there was anything I needed to know about you and Captain Dipshit over here."

Captain Dipshit?

"And I told you no," Nicki said.

Black Widow pursed her lips and mm-hmm'd like she didn't believe it. She turned around, and Eric noticed for the first time a man sitting at the end of the long conference table. His computer was hooked up to the TV on the wall with his Twitter account projected on the screen.

"How's it looking, David," Black Widow asked him.

"I'm monitoring hashtags and all references to Nicki and Eric."

"And?"

"Ray Fox is having a field day."

Great. Eric spared a glance a Nicki, who gritted her teeth and crossed her arms.

"What do we do?" Nicki asked.

"You can start by being honest," Black Widow snapped.

"I already told you. We're just friends."

"Bullshit. What I just walked in on was *not* just friends."

Eric glanced at David, who was suddenly engrossed in his keyboard. Black Widow followed his gaze and sighed. "David, give us a minute, please."

The man shot to his feet and raced from the room like Alex Rodriguez dodging a subpoena. As soon as he was gone, Abby—yes, Abby, that was her name—faced Nicki again.

"I can only help you as much you'll let me."

Nicki's face was pure ice. "We were friends, Abby. That's it."

Abby looked at Eric. "You sticking with that story, too?"

"It's not a story," Nicki jumped in.

Eric sucked his lips in and rolled them back out. Was she being purposely naïve? He faced Abby. "What happens if the truth comes out?"

Nicki clenched her jaw. "The truth about what?"

"Us, Nicki."

Abby piled on. "He's right. If there was a relationship in the past, it's best to get it out there now."

"No."

"People tend to get much more bent out of shape over cover-ups than the scandals themselves."

"There's no scandal. No cover-up. There's nothing to tell."

What the hell was wrong with her? "Don't be crazy, Nicki. You are the single most famous woman in American sports right now. Abby's right. Ray Fox will dig up anything he can get on you."

"This is not your decision," she ground out.

Eric let out a frustrated sound and jerked his hands through his hair.

Nicki's lips thinned, her posture ramrod straight as she faced Abby again. "Are we done?"

Abby let out a long sigh. "We're done, for now."

Nicki spun on her heel and beat it out of the room. Eric clenched his hands into fists to fight off the urge to follow her.

If he had any sense, he'd leave it alone—leave *her* alone —and walk away. He had enough to worry about with his own career. But there had been a moment back there, a fleeting one, when her face lost some of its bravado and she looked almost scared. There was no way he could let it go.

Nicki shot him a dirty look when he followed her into the multi-media room where players and coaches analyzed game footage. He shut the door behind them.

She dropped into one of the desk chairs in front of the video equipment with a side-eye in his direction. "Can I help you with something?

"You can lie to everyone else, but do not lie to your press agent, Nicki."

She swiveled in her chair to face the line of computer screens. "I don't have time for this."

He planted his hands on the desk beside her. "Abby is right. You really think there isn't at least one person out there who's going to remember seeing us together?"

"We were always careful. No one can prove we were ever anything more than friends."

"Dammit, Nicki!" He straightened and ran his hands down his face. "You need to be prepared for this thing to come out. Tell Abby the truth and let her do her job."

"No."

"Why? Why is it so bad if people know?"

She shot to her feet and got in his face. "You have no idea what it's like! You put on a uniform and people accept you! You belong here. They never question it. But people look at me and either assume that I'm *batting for the other side* or that I slept my way to the top. Can you imagine what would happen if word got out that I had actually slept with one of my players?"

"*Slept with?*" That was how she defined their relationship?

She shook her head. "I can't risk it. Not after everything I've been through to get here."

He almost missed the significance of that last sentence,

but then her fingers fluttered to the scar above her eyebrow. He doubted she was even aware she'd done it.

His stomach clenched. He knew she'd been too evasive before when he asked her about it. "What happened to you," he asked again.

"I worked my ass off. That's what happened to me."

"Bullshit." He pointed to her scar. "What happened?"

"It was nothing."

"Then why not tell me about it?"

"Because it's none of your business."

He gripped her elbows. "*You* are my business."

She yanked away from him. "Since when?"

"Since the day I met you."

Her mouth closed. He watched the muscles of her throat work as she swallowed against whatever protest she had planned next.

Dammit! He couldn't do this. Not now.

He let out a long breath and set his hands on his hips. "This is why I asked you to quit, Nicki. My career is on the line. I can't afford any distractions. I can't worry about you *and* save my career."

She stiffened. "So it's all about you, isn't it? Your needs. Your career. Why doesn't that surprise me?"

"That's not what I meant."

He reached out to touch her, but she backed away and transformed in front of him. Her eyes slid closed, and she sucked in a deep breath. Her posture straightened, her spine grew rigid. And when her eyes opened, he was looking at a stranger.

"This is the last time I'm going to say this, Eric, so I need you to listen. I won't quit. Not for Al Kasinski. Not for Ray Fox. But especially not for you."

"Nicki—"

"My *name*," she ground out, "is Coach Bates. The Nicki you keep referring to is gone. She quit the game a long time ago, and this is what you get in return. Is that clear?"

"We're clear," he said, voice rough.

She sat back down but spoke over her shoulder. "Good. You have ten minutes to get on the field. Go get changed."

Eric yanked open the door and stormed into the tunnel.

It was time he got his head out of his ass and put his focus squarely where it mattered most—the game.

Because at least *Coach Bates* was right about one thing. The game was all that mattered.

10

Mac's Bar was about as lively as the clubhouse after a rout
when Eric tipped back his bottle and sucked down the last
foamy remnants of a Budweiser. He'd been nursing the
same beer for an hour, and it had long since gone piss-warm
and skunky.

Sort of like the atmosphere.

Bonding over a cold one at the greasy dive on the
outskirts of St. Augustine was an Aces' spring training tradition, but there wasn't much backslapping or story-swapping
going on tonight. The few guys who had chosen to come out
following the day's warm-ups were now silently hunched
over half-empty beers, their squinted eyes glued to a
hockey game.

It was well past nine o'clock. Eric should have
headed home long ago to ice his arm and hit the
sheets, but the thought of falling asleep and dreaming

of Nicki kept his ass rooted to the cracked vinyl barstool.

Nicki—who had tortured him with her mere presence on the field. He had vowed to ignore her but couldn't. No matter how hard he had tried to focus on his own throws that afternoon, his eyes kept straying to her on the far end of the practice field where she warmed up with Cal and Brody.

Christ on crutches, he had been jealous. *Jealous.*

Distracted and pissed off, he had thrown like shit.

The baseball writers jumped all over it.

A lackluster start for Eric Weaver, one blogger wrote.

Still struggling, was the headline of another.

He hadn't even made it one fucking day without giving the vultures a reason to circle. And now here he was, bent over a beer like a moody teenager. He didn't know what was worse—his forlorn sulkiness, his shitty performance, or the sinking realization that no matter what he did, he was good and truly screwed around Nicki.

That wasn't the only thing bothering him, though. *The Nicki you keep referring to is gone.* The words alone had sent a chill down his spine, but the look in her eyes had turned his veins to pure ice.

He could take her fire, her anger. Hell, he could even take her knee to his nuts. But the *nothingness* in her expression, the empty determination ...

It was unnerving.

It was frightening.

It was like staring into a mirror.

Eric planted his elbows on the bar and scrubbed his hands over his hair. He had long ago accepted the facts of his life. He was nothing but the game. He was nothing *without* the game. But not Nicki. She was purpose and passion, a streaming comet who sucked everything and everyone into her orbit. She was the one person in his life, other than his mother, who had seen beyond the uniform for the man he wished he could be.

That was the woman he'd fallen in love with.

He didn't know this woman.

A fresh beer suddenly appeared on the bar in front of him. Eric looked up at Mac, whose crusty, crease-lined face wore an expression of something resembling sympathy.

"Bitches," he grunted.

Eric choked on his own spit. "What?"

"Women. They mess with your head."

"What makes you think I'm having woman trouble?"

Mac's old-man eyebrows shot north.

Jeezus. You were officially a pathetic loser when Mac started feeling sorry for you. Time to call it a night.

Eric stood and dropped some bills on the counter. With a nod of thanks to Mac, he dragged himself out to the parking lot and to his car. Twenty minutes later, he turned onto his street and rounded the cul-de-sac.

And slammed on his brakes.

Un-fucking-believable.

His father's truck was still in the driveway.

Teeth clenched, Eric pulled into the garage and let himself in through the back door. It opened into a mud room —that's what his mother always called it—before leading to the kitchen.

His father was loading stuff into the dishwasher when Eric walked in. The aroma of something awesome lingered in the air. Which only pissed him off more.

"What the hell are you still doing here?"

Chet looked up. "I'm not done cleaning yet."

"I say you are."

"There's a lasagna in the fridge. Want me to warm up a plate for you?"

Lasagna. Sonuvabitch. Eric loved lasagna. His mouth watered and his blood pressure skyrocketed. Chet was manipulating him with food.

"Just give me a sec," Chet said, adding a few more forks to the dishwasher.

"I'm not hungry," Eric lied, because he was actually starving.

Chet shut the dishwasher. "Your mom used to get pissed at me for putting the cups on the bottom. Remember that?"

"Mom had a lot of reasons to be pissed at you."

"True. But that one seemed to really set her off."

"That's because if she ever confronted you about the other shit, you'd threaten to leave us."

Chet opened the fridge. "True again. I never deserved her or her forgiveness."

"Finally something we agree on."

Eric watched as Chet cut a large piece of cheesy pasta and set it on a plate. He popped it in the microwave and turned around to lean against the counter. "How'd it go today?"

Eric hesitated, not liking where this was going. Chet was too calm, too nonchalant. "Fine," he ground out.

"Glad to hear it. I brought my glove. Let me know if you want to throw it around."

"How about I just throw you out?"

Chet chuckled and turned at the sound of the microwave beeping.

Somewhere between watching the steaming food being pulled out of the microwave and Chet setting it in front of him, Eric's stomach made the decision to eat. He sat down and dug in.

"Good?"

Eric shrugged.

"Your mom was so patient teaching me how to make all of your favorites. I used to roll her wheelchair into the kitchen, and she'd walk me through each step."

Eric's fingers tightened around his fork, the food suddenly heavy in his stomach. "Don't."

Chet chuckled. "It took me a while to get the lasagna right."

"I said stop. I'm not doing this with you. I'm not talking about Mom."

Chet barely missed a beat. "You want something to drink?"

"No."

"I got a call today from Joe Wheeler."

The sudden change in topic brought Eric's head up with a snap. Wheeler was a baseball columnist for USA Today and an old friend of his father's. Chet was always good with the press. A media darling, they called him.

Eric used to dream about secretly recording one of his father's drunken outbursts and leaking it so everyone could hear what he was really like. But the thought of his mother's humiliation always stopped him from actually doing it.

"And?" Eric asked, not really wanting to hear the answer.

"He said there's a rumor that you're being eyed for the bullpen."

The world went still.

The fork fell from his hand.

The food in his stomach threatened a violent return.

"Is it true, Eric?"

"What if it is? You still gonna stick around and cook for me, or will you be too ashamed to have such a loser for a son?"

"I could never be ashamed of you."

"Right. You're just afraid I might ruin your precious, bullshit legacy."

"That's not true."

Eric shot to his feet. "What the hell are you doing here, really? Did you come here just to rub it in a little more? Make sure I remember who the potential hall of famer is in this family?"

"If you think that, then I have more work to do here than I thought."

Eric pointed at his father, but then let his hand fall when he realized it was shaking. "I want you out of my house."

"Do you know what your mother said to me after she was diagnosed?"

Eric's throat tightened, like a noose had been slipped around his neck. "I told you to get out."

"She told me to fix things with you."

Fuck. His chest. Something in his fucking chest was trying to claw its way out.

"She said she could be OK with dying if she just knew that you and I could repair our relationship."

A dam broke inside. All the confusion. All the anger. All the history and its goddamned chains snapped and broke. With a sudden roar, Eric swung his arm across the counter and knocked everything off. The plate and fork and uneaten lasagna crashed to the tiled floor in a violent cacophony. Then he raised his fists and slammed them onto the counter.

"There is no relationship! I don't need your apologies or your fancy new cooking skills. All I need is for you to pack your shit, go back to Texas, and practice your twelve steps on someone who gives a shit. Just leave me alone so I can save my fucking career."

Eric spun on his heel. He was out the door and in his car again before he even knew where he was going.

11

Abby peeled one white-knuckled hand off the steering wheel and punched the power button to the radio. She didn't need to hear one more radio host replay the events of the day. Nicki had enjoyed one good hour of positive coverage following the morning press conference, and then Captain Dipshit had to go and hit his teammate.

Abby had spent the next twelve hours dealing with the fallout. The idea of two players fighting over the first woman to coach baseball—especially one who looked like a super-model—was too sexy to pass up.

Abby's body cried out for a hot bath and her bed, but her day wasn't over yet. She fished around on the passenger seat for her cellphone and voice-dialed David. He answered almost immediately.

"How's it looking?" she asked.

"Nicki is still leading ESPN and the sports sections of

every daily newspaper with circulations over a hundred thousand. We're still working on the smaller circs, but it looks like most of them at least grabbed the AP story."

"How prominently are they running our statement about the fight?"

"You're either quoted directly in the headlines or within at least three paragraphs of every article."

Abby shifted the phone to her other ear. "Anything new from Ray Fox?"

"The AP quoted him, so he's everywhere."

"Great."

"He knows too much. He definitely has an inside source."

Yeah. And Abby had a pretty good idea who it was.

David promised to keep her posted, and Abby hung up. Her GPS told her the destination was a quarter-mile on the right. She was getting close. If she opened the windows, she could probably sniff her way there, following the mingling scents of arrogance and bullshit that always seemed to be the unique cologne of men like Devin Dane.

Correction: *Especially* Devin Dane.

She spied a dark entrance ahead. This was it. The long, paved driveway wound her up a small hill and brought her to a soaring wrought-iron gate. Her headlights illuminated gold scrolled numbers, and she automatically double-checked the address on her phone.

Yep. This was the place.

OK, she knew Devin was a trust fund baby, but this was ridiculous. This was just his spring training home? The gate itself probably cost more than her parents' entire house in Milwaukee.

Disgusted, Abby lowered the driver's side window. She reached out and pressed the call button on the intercom.

A moment passed, and then a crackly, upper-crust voice answered. "Yes?"

Abby burrowed her eyebrows in confusion. "Devin?"

"Mr. Dane doesn't answer his own gate."

Abby rolled her eyes. "Right. Of course. That would just be so middle class."

Silence.

"Can you please tell *Mr. Dane* that Abby Taylor is here to see him?"

"I have no record of any appointments with an Abby Taylor this evening."

"I don't have an appointment."

"Then I can't let you in."

"I'm not leaving until he sees me."

"Miss, I have no idea who you are—"

"Tell Devin that I know he's the piece of shit who alerted the press this morning, and I'm going to make him regret it if he doesn't let me in."

Silence again. Then, "One moment please."

Several minutes went by. Just when she was about to blare the horn, the gate swung open. Abby shoved the car into gear and roared up the long, paved driveway. Her mouth dropped open as she squealed to a stop. Built in the Spanish Mission style, the stucco home was only a single-level ranch but boasted a soaring, arched courtyard entrance that screamed opulence. The curved driveway was shadowed by mature Banyan trees and a thick lawn that was far too lush for the climate. As if on cue, sprinklers sprouted from the ground and began to drench the grass.

Abby smirked and threw open the door. *Rich people.*

She slammed the door shut and stomped up the brick stairs that led to the front door. It swung open before she could even knock. An older man with graying temples and a major attitude stood just inside the threshold.

He literally looked down his nose at her. "Ms. Taylor?"

"How'd you guess?"

"I'm Mr. Dane's butler. Please follow me."

Butler? Good Lord. Devin really did take himself seriously.

Her footsteps echoed inside the cavernous foyer. She hated herself for being impressed, but she couldn't stop herself from marveling at the home. A marble floor gleamed in the dim light of an antique, iron chandelier. A round table sat in the middle of the entrance and boasted a massive, fragrant bouquet of orchids and exotic lilies that had to have easily cost a thousand bucks.

Abby was no stranger to wealthy people and their cribs. Her clients were all multi-millionaire athletes who draped themselves in lavish displays of disposable income. But Devin's place was different. Its beauty was understated. Subtle.

Old money. The worst kind.

The butler cleared his throat. "Ms. Taylor?"

Abby blinked. "Right. Lead the way."

She followed him down a long hallway. Her eyes took in the artwork decorating the walls. All originals, no doubt. She thought about the Van Gogh reprints in her apartment back in New York. The hallway dead-ended at a 'T.' The butler turned left, but Abby screeched to a halt. Her breath hitched in her chest when she spotted the painting on the wall.

The butler sighed. "Ms. Taylor."

"That's a Faragamo."

"Yes."

"Is-is it *real*?"

She was greeted by silence. She looked at the older man. His deadpan gaze was all the answer she needed.

Abby swallowed and nodded. "Of course."

"This way, please."

She practically shook with rage and jealousy. Devin wouldn't even know about Faragamo if not for her. She was the one who had introduced him to the obscure artist in college. He'd laughed at it back then. *Looks like something my brother used to paint in pre-school,* he'd mocked. And now he had an original?

The butler showed her into a spacious home office lined with book-filled built-ins and a desk that rivaled something from the Oval Office.

"Wait here," he intoned.

Abby rolled her eyes again and went to one of the bookshelves. She trailed her fingers down spines that had never been cracked, as if the books were there merely for show.

"If you see something you like, feel free to take it."

Abby sucked in a gasp and spun. She hadn't heard Devin come into the room, but now he stood behind her looking way too arrogant, way too relaxed, and way too sexy.

He pointed to a wet bar along one side of the room. "Can I get you something to drink?"

"This isn't a social call, Devin."

"Wine?"

"No."

He strolled to the bar and pulled out a bottle of a dark red and two glasses. She watched as he masterfully uncorked the merlot and filled them both. She wasn't surprised when he lifted one, twirled it, and admired the lines that clung to the glass. *Rich people.*

"It's a private label," he explained, as if she cared. "I bought a case of it during a trip through Napa a couple of years ago. I save it for special occasions."

"Then you just wasted a bottle."

He looked up with his eyes alone. "I disagree."

Her stomach gave a little jolt.

"Try it. It has a smoky undertaste and just the faintest hint of spice."

"I'm afraid it's going to be lost on me."

He chuckled. "I remember. You're a beer girl."

"And proud of it."

"I assure you, no offense was intended."

"Good. Because none was taken."

He held out a glass. She stared at it for one split second before crossing the room and accepting his offer. In the exchange, his fingers touched hers, and she felt a zing all the way up her arm.

"What should we drink to?" he asked.

"Faragamo."

He smiled. "You saw the painting."

"What I saw is that you're still stealing other people's ideas."

His lips tightened at the corners, an unexpected show of discomfort. He seemed to quickly shake it off as he raised his glass.

"To Faragamo."

She took a sip and looked away. He was right. The wine was good. But she'd chew off her own tongue before giving him the satisfaction of admitting it.

"So," he said. "To what do I owe the honor?"

"Someone leaked the news of the fight to the press."

He cocked an eyebrow. "And you think it was me, I assume."

She mirrored his expression.

"What possible motive would I have for leaking a negative story about my own team?"

"Your motives have always been a mystery to me."

"Not true. You've just never *understood* my motives."

"Is there a difference?"

He grew silent. He stared at her as if he could see everything, and she squirmed under the scrutiny. Then his eyes suddenly widened with some kind of understanding. "This is personal to you."

"I take all of my clients personally."

"I think it's more than that."

He stepped closer. Her breath caught in her throat as his eyes seared a path deeper into her soul. She wanted to look away, knew that she should. But she couldn't stop from drinking him in like the fine wine in her hand. She already knew he tasted as good as he looked, but she also knew he would come with a painful hangover.

Devin's eyes narrowed. "Why did you really come here tonight?"

"I think we already covered that."

"You haven't asked me anything that couldn't have been discussed over the phone. You came to see me in person for a reason."

"I—"

"You know what I think?" he said. His voice dropped to a seductive hush.

"No."

"I think you were curious."

"About what?"

His eyes darkened with hunger. "If the spark between us is still there."

Somehow, without her even noticing, he had closed the last few inches of distance between them. The warmth of his body reached out to her, wrapping around her like a seductive blanket. A masculine scent scrambled her senses, a tantalizing mix of aftershave and merlot. Her hand trembled, sloshing wine over the rim of the glass.

Without a word, he took the glass from her and discarded it on the bar behind him, along with his own.

"Abby ..." Her name on his lips was barely a whisper, a caress of sound and sigh. And then, before she had time to react or to think or to object, his mouth claimed hers.

Shock waves wracked her body and then instantly gave way to intense pleasure, the kind that made her knees go limp. Her hands sought something to hang onto and found safety on his shoulders. But the fire that erupted beneath her fingertips was anything but safe. There was nothing safe in the way his mouth molded more deeply against hers or the way his tongue plundered in and out with an erotic rhythm.

There was only danger in the way she gave to him freely, moaning in acceptance as his hands found the hem of her blouse and inched it upwards, baring her skin to cool air and hot caresses.

There was only danger in the way one hand snaked up her back and cupped her head.

Only danger.

Danger!

Abby pushed him away and whipped around. Panting, she wiped her mouth, desperate to erase the taste of him and the humiliation of being such an easy conquest. How could she have let him get to her like that again? Had she learned nothing?

Behind her, Devin's raspy voice was the only sound in the room. She felt his hand on her back. She had to keep it together. She couldn't let him see how he had affected her. She focused on her breathing. In and out. In and out.

She pulled away from his touch and turned around. "Wow," she smirked. "You're good."

His chest rose and fell with every labored breath. As if he'd really been affected by her. *Right*. She knew better than that.

He swallowed hard. "Good?"

"You've clearly had a lot of practice at the whole seduction thing."

"It's easy when the attraction is mutual."

"I'm not attracted to you, Devin."

He answered silently, arching one perfectly groomed eyebrow over hooded lids. God, he was sexy. A little voice whispered things she didn't want to hear. That maybe this time it could be different. Maybe *he* was different.

No. Those were dangerous thoughts. He was a dangerous man.

She had to escape. Now.

She backed away, pissed at the betrayal of her body—the racing heart and dizzy breathlessness. This couldn't be happening. Not again. She couldn't possibly be this stupid again.

"I have to go." She turned toward the door and was halfway across the carpet when he spoke.

"Abby, wait."

She faced him again.

"I've apologized a thousand times for what I did back then," he said. "What is it going to take to convince you I've changed?"

"You could find out who the leak is and punish him."

"Already working on it."

"I'll believe it when I see it."

His jaw tightened. Abby watched a line of muscle twitch along his jaw. "Fine. I assume you know your way out."

Mustering as much dignity as she could, Abby smoothed her disheveled blouse and spun on her heel. The door seemed a mile away.

"And Abby?"

This time she didn't turn around. "What?"

"Make an appointment next time."

The only thing that kept her from breaking into a full-fledged sprint was her pride.

She climbed into the front seat of her car. She drove with one hand and held her phone in the other. She scrolled through her contacts until she found the number she and her firm only called in emergencies.

The man answered on the second ring. "Sanchez."

"We have a job for you."

"Give me the details."

"Someone is leaking stuff to the press. I need you to find out who it is."

"On it."

He hung up, and Abby tossed her phone onto the passenger seat.

Devin had been right about one thing, at least. She could've handled this meeting over the phone. But a small part of her—the naïve part that could never stop hoping for the impossible—had wondered. *Who was Devin Dane today?*

Now she had her answer.

Devin Dane hadn't changed.

Thank God she had.

12

"AND IT's time for one last round!" Ray Fox raised an empty beer glass. The live audience inside the Los Angeles soundstage burst to its feet, whistling and cheering, so pumped up on testosterone and booze that the theater shook.

A siren shrieked, strobe lights flashed, and from the back came a sashaying line of barely-dressed women who fought like cats for the chance to serve as one of his waitresses.

In string bikinis that barely passed decency rules, the girls hoisted enormous trays that were designed to tip and douse them with just enough brew to keep the men in the audience happy.

Ray allowed one named Rita to pour him another glass. She bent forward, giving him a face full of luscious flesh. He waggled his eyebrows at the camera. It was no secret in the cable television world that Ray liked his

Foxies with big hair and bigger tits, earning him a permanent place on the Most Wanted List of most feminazi groups.

But, hey, the way he saw it, if his show was so degrading to women they wouldn't line up in droves and offer him blow jobs for a chance to pour his beer.

Ray clapped Rita on one smooth butt cheek as she walked away, earning a roar of catcalls and applause from the crowd. He smirked. This is why they came, why they camped out all day for a ticket. His show, "The World According to Ray Fox," was the last place anymore that a man could be a man. Where it was OK to ogle women and drink beer. Just like God intended.

He took a quick drink and then raised his hands. "Let's hear it again for the Foxies."

The noise rose to almost painful levels. He hadn't seen an audience so riled up since he got that beach volleyball player to demonstrate a few moves on his show in a string bikini. But it wasn't lust that had these men going nuts. It was *blood* lust. Hatred for Nicki Bates surged through every man in the room. She was going to be ratings gold.

He supposed he should feel guilty, but he didn't. He didn't actually give a flying fuck if the Vegas Aces filled their entire coaching roster with chicks. But there obviously were a shit-ton of men who did. So what if he capitalized on it?

Thirty seconds left in the show, Ray nodded at his producer off-stage, and the back screen was suddenly filled with her picture. Empty beer cups showered the stage, and the boos drowned out every other sound.

He jumped up and pumped his fist in the air. "This is Ray Fox. Out."

The red lights on the cameras went black, and they were officially off the air.

His assistant ran onto the stage, a cellphone in one hand. "It's him."

Ray grabbed the phone and stormed off the stage. "It's about fucking time."

"If you're going to insult me, you can forget about this whole thing."

"Don't be a douchebag. I told you I would pay you."

"I already tipped you off about the fight this morning."

"Right. And what have you done for me tonight?"

There was a pause. Then, "What do you need me to do?"

"Get me anything you can. Video. Pictures. Unsubstantiated rumors. Anything."

"I'll do my best."

"Do better than that."

Ray ended the call as he reached the parking lot. He slid into the front seat of his red Porsche, his dick hard in anticipation.

An inside source was the best kind of source.

13

NICKI LEANED BACK in the rickety desk chair in the video room and stifled a yawn. It was only seven in the morning, and she already felt weary.

She'd had the dream again. It woke her up at three, and she couldn't get back to sleep, so she finally gave up and drove to the ballpark to work out before the guys arrived.

A punishing hour later, she showered, changed into her uniform, and went to the video room. She had intended to simply drag a couple of clips onto a flash drive to show Zach Nelson later that day. Instead, her curiosity got the best of her, and she called up the last game of the World Series.

She spent the next hour hitting play and replay, zooming in and out, studying every angle, until she couldn't ignore facts that should have been evident all along.

Eric had been flawless on the mound that night.

Mechanically perfect.

Every throw was technically correct, yet the ball wouldn't cooperate. It was as if someone else had been inside Eric's body. Someone else's soul.

Whatever had been wrong with him during that game— whatever continued to be wrong—it wasn't something she could fix with a tweak of technique or a shift in his hold on the seams.

Pitching was only fifty percent throwing the ball. The other half was entirely mental. No one but the pitcher himself could fix that.

"Enjoying my humiliation?"

Nicki jumped in the chair and swiveled around. Eric leaned against the doorframe, arms folded across his chest. He wore the team's spring training sweatshirt over his jersey. It was loose and big but did absolutely nothing to hide the bulges of muscle that defined his upper body. His baseball cap was pulled low over his forehead, hiding his features.

"Just watching game film," she said.

"And what have you learned so far, *Coach*?"

"That you did everything right that night."

"Yet I tanked miserably."

"Any idea why?"

He pulled away from the doorframe and shrugged. If he did have an idea, he didn't seem keen on sharing it with her.

"I can't fix it if I don't know what's wrong," she said, rising from the chair.

"I thought it was part of your job to find out, *Coach*."

"Can you please stop saying *Coach* like that?"

"Yesterday you ordered me to call you that. Make up your mind."

"You say it like it's an insult."

He pulled off his hat with a frustrated sound and scrubbed his hand over his face. When he looked up, the overhead light illuminated things that had been shadowed before under the brim of his cap.

His eyes were bloodshot and rimmed with dark circles. The creases in his forehead seemed deeper, and it looked like he had forgotten to shave. He had a gaunt, couldn't-sleep look she knew too well.

She felt her annoyance soften just a touch. "You OK?"

"Don't worry, *Coach*. My head's in the game."

"You look tired."

His lips tightened into a smirk. "Yeah, well, I never sleep well in someone else's bed."

Knife. To. Chest.

He'd been with a woman last night.

And he was throwing it in her face.

There was probably no hiding her reaction. She blinked quickly and straightened. She didn't care. *Wouldn't* care. Even if she had to repeat it a thousand times to make it true, she would not care.

"You can sleep in a different bed every night if you

want, Eric, but do not ever come to training camp strung out like this again."

She hated herself the instant the words left her mouth. She sounded bitter and hurt, and his smirk told her he'd noticed. He looked like a bat-flipping runner who takes his time rounding the bases after sending the ball over the wall.

She spun around and sat back down. "I'm busy."

She didn't realize he had snuck up behind her until she felt his breath tickle her ear. "You let me know if you want to offer up your bed instead."

Nicki leaned forward and away from his touch. "Are you looking for another knee to the balls?"

He laughed.

Her teeth practically cracked as she clenched her jaw. "I'm glad you find all of this so funny, Eric. But after your performance in that last game, you might want to take things a little more seriously."

His voice lost all signs of teasing. "Wow. That's quite a mouthful."

"Just speaking the truth."

"Sure you're not just pissed off that I didn't sleep at home last night?"

She spun in the chair and shot to her feet again. "Let's get one thing straight, Weaver. I am here for one reason, and that is to win. Don't delude yourself into believing that I care about *anything* other than how well you throw the ball."

Eric winced. It was such a tiny, fleeting emotion that she almost didn't see it. But then his face hardened, and his angry footsteps carried him toward the door.

He stopped at the last second to look back. "You know what? You were right yesterday, *Coach*. The girl I knew is long gone."

He slammed the door in his wake.

Nicki stared at it for a long moment, and then sank back into her chair. She let out the breath she'd been holding. As the air escaped, her spine lost its steel, and she turned to press her forehead to the desk.

The girl I knew is long gone.

He had only been parroting back her own words to her, but it stung. She'd been nasty, vicious, and for no good reason other than what he had rightly pointed out. She *was* mad that he'd been with someone else last night. She was furious that the instant he mentioned someone else's bed, her mind concocted an image of him naked, sweaty, and rolling around with a lingerie model.

She needed to be honest with herself. She cared about a lot more than how Eric performed on the mound, and that was a problem she hadn't been prepared for.

She'd had seven years to get over him. Seven. That should have been more than enough time for her to be around him now and not feel anything.

Apparently, it wasn't.

The question was, what was she going to do about it?

She had to start by getting her own head in the game. Fast.

Nicki sat up and closed her eyes. She practiced her breathing, deep and slow. She pictured herself on the mound. Felt the glove slide over her fingers. Saw the batter take his stance. Listened to the air in her lungs.

No emotion. No emotion. It was the mantra she used to chant to get herself ready to pitch, to get in the zone where nothing existed but the ball in her hand and the plate sixty feet away. No stress. No fear. No intimidation. *No emotion.*

Now, it was how she centered herself when she needed to beat back the tiny traces of the girl she used to be whenever they threatened to rise to the surface. That girl—the one who used to laugh, used to revel in the flutters of awareness in her stomach at the touch of a man, used to have a life outside the ballpark—was gone.

She had to be, because that girl was weak and broken.

Nicki would never be broken again.

She opened her eyes.

Traced her finger along her scar.

It was time to take the field.

The tunnel outside the video room was packed with players, staff, grounds crew, and dozens of other people hustling to get where they were supposed to be.

Cleats clicked on the cement floor. The whir of a leaf blower outside added a low hum. Male laughter bounced off the walls as a huddle of eager and hopeful college prospects walked by. Energy coursed through the cinderblock hallway like a vein delivering blood and oxygen to a beating heart.

This was why she was here. Baseball *was* her beating heart. It had been from the moment she had first tagged along with Robby to a neighborhood game of catch and threw the ball like she'd been born to do it. She'd had no idea back then how hard her chosen path would be, and she had endured far too much over the years to let Eric throw her off course now.

The door to the clubhouse swung open at the end of the tunnel, and Hunter Brody and Cal Mahoney walked out together. She pulled away from the wall to meet them halfway.

They slowed at her approach and eased into smiles—Cal's warm, Brody's goofy.

She stuck out her hand at him first. "We didn't officially meet yesterday."

Brody took her hand and held it. "I'm still waiting for an answer to my proposal."

"Sorry. I'm going to have to decline."

He let go of her fingers and covered his heart with a mock stumble.

Cal elbowed him and rolled his eyes. One of their starting pitchers, the press often referred to Cal by the nickname "Thunder" because his fastball had the velocity of a sudden storm—the kind that came out of nowhere and left you stunned. He was also a fan favorite, not just because he brought in the wins but because he'd hit some kind of genetic home run at birth. He had the looks of a Greek god —tall, dark and drool-worthy. Nicki avoided men in the romantic way at all costs, but she wasn't blind.

He extended his hand. "Cal Mahoney."

"Nicki Bates. I'm looking forward to working with you."

"Likewise. I saw you pitch once in college. A friend of mine played for NC State. I went to one of his games and you were pitching that day."

"Did we win?"

"You struck out seven."

She smiled. "I remember that game."

"You still throw?"

"Every day."

"Maybe you should be on our roster, not coaching."

Brody snorted. "Kiss ass."

"You coming to Devin's tonight?" Cal asked.

Shoot. She had actually forgotten about that. Devin was throwing a party at his house for the pitching staff. It was apparently an annual thing. She had a ton of work to do— more game film to analyze, the play book to work on, a drill schedule for the prospects. But the party would be a good chance to get to know some of the guys and start cementing her place on the team.

Thanks to Eric, she had gotten a rough start. He'd

shaken her with his demands that she quit and his confusing ambivalence.

It was time to get back in the game.

From this point forward, Eric Weaver was just another player.

14
___

DEVIN LIVED outside St. Augustine in a luxury subdivision where the mansions were hidden by long driveways, gentle hills, and lazy Banyan trees. Nicki slowed and squinted at a house number on a stone archway that soared over an open wrought-iron gate.

She drove through it and followed the winding, paved driveway until the house came into view. Her mouth dropped open. Wow. Was Jay Gatsby going to come strolling out?

She stopped in the center of the large circular drive and glanced down at her outfit. She felt underdressed just sitting in the driveway. She had on jeans, tall brown boots and a white tunic. This place screamed black tie.

Then again, this *was* a baseball party. There was a good chance at least one of the guys would have on rubber sports sandals with socks.

A valet appeared next to the driver's window. He opened Nicki's door and extended his hand to help her from the car.

"Good evening, miss."

She laughed out loud. Couldn't help it. So this was how the other one-half of one percent lived. The valet took the keys and handed her a ticket with instructions on how to retrieve her car when she left.

Nicki followed a torch-lit path and the mingling sounds of laughter and Latin music until she reached the back of the house. Her mouth fell open again. The backyard was just as magical as the front. String lights hung over a massive, immaculately landscaped yard, where linen-topped cocktail tables had been set up around a twinkling pool, interspersed with tall portable heaters to take the edge off the night air.

By the looks of it, she was one of the last to arrive. Small groups of players and staff with their significant others clustered around food tables and a bar. On the opposite side of the pool, a giant inflatable movie screen displayed a video game in action. Three guys sat in a line in front of it, locked in an epic, meaningless battle.

Nicki felt conspicuously alone as her arrival began to draw attention. She watched as more than one woman leaned to her man and whispered, their eyes cast in her direction.

Walking onto men's teams was hard.

Meeting the wives and girlfriends could be excruciating.

Which raised another thought. Had Eric brought Miss Shitty Mattress?

Scratch that. She didn't care.

Her eyes scanned the crowd until she spotted a friendly face. Hunter Kinsley stood alone at a cocktail table at the far corner of the pool. A half-full glass of something clear sat in front of him. He acknowledged her approach with a tilt of his head.

She hoped it didn't show on her face that she was more than a little star struck by him. Hunter was a bona fide American hero whose story had been told and retold a hundred times in every imaginable media outlet. He'd been a top draft pick when he signed with the Aces in 2000, but after his childhood best friend was killed in the Sept. 11 terrorist attacks on the World Trade Center, he gave it all up to join the Army Rangers. When he came home after losing his leg on a mission, Devin hired him to run one of the Aces' minor league teams, and he'd worked his way up from there.

He had a reputation for being secretive and standoffish, but she knew the guys had a reverent, protective respect for him.

She leaned against the table. "Is this place for real?"

Hunter chuckled. "I had the same reaction the first time. Devin is actually pretty laid back when you get to know him, though."

"Where is he?" She hadn't seen him when she walked in.

"He'll come out for a few minutes to say hi, but then he usually spends the rest of the night inside."

"He doesn't attend his own parties?"

"He doesn't want to get to know the prospects at this point."

"Why—oh. In case he has to send someone packing."

He looked at his water. Awkward. Nicki was just as much a prospect as the college boys.

"You settling in OK?" Hunter asked.

"Great. I'm almost done with the initial play book, and I'm planning to get some new plans finished tonight for Zach Nelson. I think if we really focus his attention on—"

Hunter was laughing.

She stopped short. "What?"

"You really are all business, aren't you?"

She blinked, cheeks warming. "It's who I am."

Hunter suddenly tipped his chin up to acknowledge someone behind them. Nicki followed his gaze.

And screamed a little inside.

Eric approached their table in a group that included Cal, Harper Brody, and catcher Riley Quinn. Each man carried a beer and walked with the cocksure swagger that only professional athletes seemed to master. They were the kings of the universe and knew it.

Except that Brody was wearing rubber sports sandals with socks.

The guys circled the table and set down their drinks. Nicki avoided Eric's gaze, but she felt the heat of it searing her skin.

"Want a drink, Coach?" Brody parked himself next to her and flashed her the goofy smile she was quickly finding endearing.

"No, thanks. I'm good for now."

"They don't make Cherry Bombs?" Eric's voice dripped with sarcasm.

"What are Cherry Bombs?" Brody asked. "I want one."

"Nicki's favorite drink," Eric said.

"I'll go get you one," Brody said. "Want anything else? Shrimp? Cheese cube? Diamond ring?"

Eric growled. "Shut up, Brody."

Nicki tried not to clench her jaw. "It was a drink they made at this dive bar in Daytona that we went to during spring break one year," she explained to Brody.

If she weren't afraid it would tip off the rest of the guys, she would've glared at Eric for bringing it up. Only the two of them knew what he was really doing—reminding her of what else happened during that spring break trip.

As if he read her mind, his lips curled up in a mocking smile. "That was a good trip."

"I've always sort of regretted it, actually."

His smile vanished.

"You gonna hide out at my house again tonight?" Cal asked, oblivious to the silent argument going on between her and Eric.

"Don't know," Eric answered, looking directly at her. "Haven't decided yet."

Wait. What...?

Two things happened at once.

Eric smiled.

And she realized she'd been duped.

Her nostrils flared with an angry intake of air. "You spent the night at Cal's last night?"

"He has the new Madden game."

"Thought you didn't sleep well in strange beds."

Cal looked back and forth between them. "Why do I feel like I've just walked into the middle of a conversation with you two?"

"What about strange beds?" Brody asked.

The topic quickly shifted to trade deals on other teams, but Nicki's mind was still stuck on Eric's lie. She wanted to bolt right then and there, but she knew it would only raise suspicions. So she stayed for five agonizing minutes before finally pushing away from the table.

"If you'll all excuse me, I think I'm going to call it a night."

"You just got here," Brody whined.

She pretended to yawn. "Tired."

Shaking from the inside out, Nicki forced her long legs to carry her back through the crowd to the pathway along the side of the house.

"Nicki, wait." Eric's voice behind her was quiet but insistent.

She ignored him and kept walking.

"Nicki, come on."

She finally stopped and whipped around. "Go ahead. Gloat. Get it over with."

"That's not—"

"Why did you lie to me?"

"I didn't lie."

"You let me believe you spent the night with a woman." She let out an argh. "You know what? It doesn't matter. I don't care."

She spun around to search for the valet, but Eric's voice once again stopped her.

"I spent the night at Cal's to avoid my father."

Just like that, he threw a curve and changed the game.

Her feet slowed, and when she turned around to look at him, she forgot for a moment why she'd been mad. The cocky smirk that had taunted her about Cherry Bombs was gone. His hands were in his pockets, his shoulders slumped. He looked *small*. In all the time she had known Eric, the one and only person who had ever had that effect on him was his father.

Chet Weaver was a dying sun, swollen and hot, burning everything and everyone around him. Eric especially. Most baseball fans had no idea that behind the amiable public image of the future Hall of Famer, Chet Weaver was little more than a mean drunk who serially cheated on his wife and once made his son practice pitches in the dark until Eric's hands blistered and bled.

The Adam's apple in Eric's throat struggled against a swallow. "He showed up uninvited two days ago. I can't get him to leave, and I couldn't deal with him last night, so Cal let me crash at his house instead."

The naked vulnerability on his face made her heart catch. "Why didn't you just tell me that this morning?"

"I might have told Nicki, but I wasn't sure how much I trusted *Coach Bates*."

"Coach Bates cares about anything that affects your performance, Eric."

He did it again. He winced. "Do you really regret that spring break trip?"

She groaned and looked away. They were getting nowhere. Was this how they were going to act with each other for the rest of spring training? She was going to be exhausted within days, not to mention suffering from a bad case of whiplash from trying to keep up with his mood swings.

"We have to stop doing this, Eric. We have to stop fighting and, and—" She waved her hands around. "Doing whatever this is. If we can't find a way to work together, we're both going to go down in flames."

"Then maybe we should spend some time getting to know each other again."

She snorted. Right. Except his expression was stone-cold serious.

"Are you crazy? You and I can't spend time together. Ray Fox has practically offered a reward for incriminating pictures of us."

He let out a frustrated sound as if she were being unreasonable.

"Can you at least give me a ride back to the ballpark?"

Her brows pulled together. "Why do you need a ride?"

"I came here with Cal. My car is still at the yard. No one can raise any eyebrows about you and me being together at the ballpark."

"What about the party?"

"I'd rather hang out with you."

Her mouth fell open. "Fine. But you have to stop that."

"Stop what?"

"Looking at me like that."

"How am I looking at you?"

She waved her hands. "Like that."

"Sorry, Nicki. This is just my face."

She bit back a groan and spun on her heel. "Fine. Come on."

The valet emerged from whatever darkened corner he'd

been paid to sit in. He took her ticket, spoke quietly into some kind of walkie-talkie, and then told them her car would be around in a moment.

It was the longest moment of her life. Neither of them spoke. She had no idea what Eric was thinking about, but her brain was on a hamster wheel of racing thoughts. The faster she ran, the more they chased her.

Her car pulled up in the circular drive. She didn't even wait for the valet to get out before rounding the hood to get in. Eric followed silently, sliding into the passenger seat while she willed herself not to look at him.

This suddenly seemed like a bad idea.

"You're quiet," he said as she headed down the long driveway.

"I'm fine," she lied.

She was *not* OK. She was itchy and antsy sitting next to him in the car, where the scent of his soap overpowered her, and his impossibly broad shoulders filled up the passenger seat. And she was pissed off that she noticed any of it. She did not want to notice the veiny strength of his forearm as it rested lazily on the console between them. She didn't want to notice the deep timbre of his voice. And she especially didn't want to notice the tuft of dark hair that poked above the neckline of his faded Dallas Cowboys t-shirt.

Because if she noticed that, her mind would immediately remember how that dark hair spread deliciously over the hills and valleys of his entire chest. She would be forced to remember tangling her fingers in it, rubbing her cheek against it, and turning her lips to press kisses against the taut skin beneath it.

Nicki hit the button to lower the window. She suddenly needed air.

15

GOD, she was beautiful. Eric did his best not to stare, but that was like asking a starving man to ignore a buffet.

Her hair fluttered softly in the breeze from the open window, and the glow of the digital display illuminated the fullness of her lips. Eric had nearly collapsed when she walked into the party. She wore jeans again—tight ones that showed off every minute of hard work—and those tall brown boots women always wore, probably because they knew it made men dream of peeling them off. If she'd been wearing a string bikini, she couldn't have been sexier.

Of course, he had also seen her in a string bikini before, and that was pretty fucking sexy, too. Especially when she wore it to sneak into his hotel room late one night during spring break and stand before him with a shy invitation on her face.

"I'll go if you want me to," she said.

He shook his head, barely able to speak. "Come here."

She approached the bed slowly. He drank her in with every step, his eyes hot and greedy. When her knees hit the edge of the mattress, he pushed the covers aside and her eyes dropped to the inescapable evidence of how much he wanted her.

He let out a growl and reached for her, gripping her hips to tug her closer. Then he leaned forward and pressed his lips to a spot just above her belly button. She threaded her fingers in his hair and let out a moan.

He raised his eyes to hers. "Do you know how long I've dreamed about you coming to me in the night?"

"Do you know how long I've wanted to?"

Nicki might want to avoid those kinds of memories, but he relived them often enough to be embarrassing.

He had only been partially honest with her before about why he let her think he had spent the night with another woman. It was true that he hadn't been entirely comfortable admitting to her that he was hiding from his father. But the bigger truth was that when he walked into that video room and found her hitting the replay button on the most humiliating failure of his career ... Well, what could he say? Fear and embarrassment rarely brought out his mature side.

And if he really wanted to be honest, at least with himself, he had wanted to see how she would react to the idea of him being with someone else.

So, yeah. Real fucking mature.

"You're doing it again," she said quietly.

"Doing what?"

"Looking at me."

"Sorry. I can't help it."

"Try."

A few moments later, she pulled into the parking garage for the ballpark and whipped into her designated spot.

"We're here," she said. "Get out."

He ignored her. "What are we going to do, Nicki?"

"I don't know what you're going to do, but I'm going home."

"That's not what I mean."

She sighed and let her head fall back against the seat. "I know. I'm just trying to avoid this conversation."

"Why?"

"Because I'm tired. I just want to do my job, Eric. I just want to go home, watch some game film, and *do my job*."

The weariness in her voice made him feel like a fucking heel, especially since he knew he was the cause of it. "I haven't made this easy on you, have I?"

She rolled her head to look at him, surprise lifting her features. "No, you haven't."

He scrubbed his hands over his face. Apologies had never tasted very well on his tongue, but he would at least give it a try. "I'm sorry. You were right yesterday. I've made this entire thing about what I need. I didn't stop to think about how my actions were affecting you."

"I'm sort of used to that."

Wow. Ouch. Verbal fastball.

"Do you still want me to quit, Eric?"

"No." He shook his head and stared out the windshield. "That was a fucking shitty thing to ask of you."

"Apology accepted. Does that mean you're willing to work with me?"

"I don't know," he admitted, because why not? They were apparently trying a thing called honesty for a change, and it's not like he hadn't already revealed himself to be a selfish bastard.

"Well, I need you to figure it out. Soon. Because my job depends on yours."

He blinked. "What? What do you mean?"

"I'm a temporary hire, Eric."

"I know, but what does that have to do with me?"

She looked at him like he'd just parachuted in from another planet. "What do you think? I'm as much of a try-out as the college kids. If I can't bring you and everyone else back to championship level, I'm gone by opening day."

His hands clenched. There was a rush of air through his ears. No. Dammit, no! He barely recognized his voice. "How could you agree to that, Nicki?"

"Do you see any other Major League teams knocking on my door? This was my chance."

He scrubbed his face again and held back the scream of

frustration clogging up his chest. He grabbed the door handle.

"Eric, look at me."

He leveled her with his gaze.

"We have to find a way to work together."

"But I don't even know what's wrong, Nicki!" His voice boomed against the confining walls of the car. "Don't you understand that? I'm broken, and I don't know how to fucking fix it!"

She met his outburst with one of her own. "Then stop fighting me and let me help you! Because whether you like it or not, we need each other."

We need each other. The words hurt again, this time in places inside him that were already bruised.

Eric threw open the door and got out.

She leaned over the console. "Eric, listen—"

He cut her off, his voice rougher than he intended. "You're a fool, Nicki. This merchandise is damaged goods."

He slammed the door and walked away.

16

ERIC KNEW the instant Nicki walked into the clubhouse the next afternoon. Not because he heard her or saw her. Not even because someone said her name. He just knew. His body had tracked hers like radar.

He braced his hands on either side of his stall and dipped his head between his shoulders. He heard her ask Zach Nelson to come outside for a moment, and then he knew the instant she was gone. The air was colder without her.

"You all right over there, man?"

Eric straightened without looking at Cal. "Tired," he lied. "Your couch sucks."

Cal snorted. "You ever going home again?"

Eric scrubbed his hands over his face. "As soon as my old man leaves."

"How long is that going to be?"

"Look, if you don't want me to stay at your house, just say so."

"Damn, man. Who shit in your Wheaties?"

Fate. Fate had shit in his Wheaties. Jeezus, he was tired.

"Your bad mood have anything to do with Nicki?"

Eric's snapped his gaze to Cal's. "Why would think that?"

"Seriously? How stupid do you think I am?"

Eric started to fire back but stopped. Cal didn't deserve his wrath.

He lowered his voice and looked at his feet. "Is it that obvious?"

"You mean besides that fact that you ran out of the party last night and never came back? Or the fact that you bark like a dog at anyone who looks at her? Yeah, it's obvious." Cal pulled his practice sweatshirt over his head. "What's the story?"

Eric sat down on the bench to untie his cleats. He shouldn't tell Cal anything because Nicki would fucking kill him, but fatigue proved a powerful truth serum.

"It was a long time ago." He pinned Cal with a glare. "And if she knows I told you even that much, she'll castrate us both."

"So you guys dated, or what?"

Dated. What a stupid word. No, they hadn't dated. They'd been in love. The real kind of love that makes the rest of the world fade away into a distant soundtrack.

Until he fucked it up.

"Yeah," he finally answered. "We dated."

"And?"

And I loved her more than air. "And then I got called up. End of story."

Eric kicked off his cleats.

"Hits before tits, huh?" Cal said, disgust dripping from his tone at the locker room phrase ballplayers used for putting the game before the women in their lives.

"Something like that." Eric could've set the record straight, but he wasn't tired enough to humiliate himself *that* much.

"Huh," Cal said.

Eric looked over. "What?"

Cal shrugged. "Nothing." He rose and bounced his fist on Eric's back. "Come on, man. I'll buy you a beer at Mac's."

They showered and changed quickly and then drove in separate cars to the bar. Eric's cellphone rang on the passenger seat, but he ignored it when he saw the call was from his father.

Mac's was nearly full already with players and team staff by the time Eric and Cal arrived. A table in the corner was unofficially reserved for upper management. Eric nodded a greeting to Hunter, Devin, and Todd Marshall. None of them nodded back.

Eric and Cal took their normal seats at the bar. "What's up with them?" Eric asked, motioning to the corner table.

"No idea."

Mac sauntered over, hacking into his elbow. "Budweiser?"

"Jameson," Eric said. "Straight."

Cal snorted. "Whiskey? You're going to feel like shit tomorrow."

"I already feel like shit. I might as well make it official."

Mac set an empty glass in front of him, tossed in a couple of ice cubes, and poured a healthy dose of the amber liquid. Then he opened a Budweiser for Cal.

Cal clinked his bottle against Eric's glass. "Cheers."

Eric sipped the whiskey and felt the burn all the way down his throat. He had never been much of a drinker. At least not the hard stuff. Being the son of an alcoholic tended to have that effect on a guy, but beer wasn't going to cut it tonight. He was out to get drunk. Blessedly, obliviously drunk.

His cellphone rang again. His father. Jeezus. What the hell did he want?

Eric ignored it and held up his empty glass to signal to Mac for another round. The drink had just appeared in front of him when his phone rang for a third time.

"Maybe you should get that," Cal said.

"It's my father."

"Then you should definitely answer it."

Eric fought the twinge of annoyance at Cal's tone. He didn't need a lecture from a man who grew up in a Norman

Rockwell painting. Cal's father was everything Chet wasn't.

The phone rang again. Fuck. Eric grabbed it and swiped the screen. "What?" he growled.

"Joe Wheeler called again. I tried to talk him out of it."

The whiskey turned sour. "Talk him out of what?"

"He said he had a journalistic responsibility to report it."

Eric didn't bother to ask what his father was talking about. He already knew the answer. His humiliating secret was about to be revealed.

"I'm sorry," Chet said. "I told him never to call me again, if that helps."

"It doesn't."

Eric ended the call and hit the icon for his web browser.

"What's going on," Cal asked.

Eric called up the USA Today website and clenched his jaw. There it was. Leading the sports section for all the world to see: *Aces eyeing Eric Weaver for bullpen.*

He didn't bother to read the column. He handed the phone to Cal, picked up the whiskey, and downed it in one shot.

"Fuck, man," Cal said. "Is this true?"

Eric signaled to Mac for another. "Yep."

"It's not a done deal, according to this."

"You really believe that?"

"How long have you known?"

"Long enough."

Another whiskey landed in front of him. Eric threw it back and grimaced against the burn. It hit his gut with a fiery punch, but at least his senses were softening.

"I guess we know what's up with them," he said, once again pointing to the crew in the corner. Those fuckers obviously knew the column was coming, and not one of them had the courtesy to warn him?

He raised his hand again for another drink. No matter what he did now, the specter of the bullpen would shadow his every move. Every homer he gave up in exhibition play, every fucking base hit, would be analyzed by the media as proof that the Aces would be better off taking him out of the starting rotation.

"Maybe you should slow down, dude," Cal said.

"Why? So I can throw tomorrow? Won't matter."

"It will matter. This isn't over."

Eric slammed his fist on the counter. "It is over. It's been over. You saw me in that last game. You saw me all of last year. I'm done."

Cal shifted in his seat to lean further on the bar. "With that attitude, you're right."

"You don't get it. I've given up everything for this game. *Everything*."

"Well, maybe that's your real fucking problem. You ever think about that?"

"Don't lecture me, man. You have everything. I have nothing outside this game."

Cal's face froze. Eric realized too late what he'd just said. He dragged a hand down his face. "I'm sorry, man. I didn't mean—"

But it was too late. Cal stood up from his stool. "I'm calling you a cab. I'll see you tomorrow."

"Cal, I'm sorry."

His friend took two steps away, but then spun at the last minute and stalked back.

"Look around you, Eric. You think any of this matters? You think it lasts forever?" Cal swallowed hard. "Whether you get moved to the bullpen or not, someday this will all be gone. And then what will you have? You might think you've got time later on to deal with the people in your life, but you don't. You think I wouldn't give up every single minute on the mound to spend more time with Sara?"

Eric swayed toward his friend. "Cal, I'm sorry."

Cal grabbed his shoulder and saved him from falling. "Talk to Nicki. Tell her how you really feel. Tonight. And fix this fucking thing with your father. Nothing else matters except the people we love. Nothing."

Then Cal was gone. Eric let go of the breath he'd been holding in his chest and planted his elbows on the bar. He stared into the ancient mirror that lined the wall behind the liquor bottles. He could barely make out his own reflection through the decades of grime and the haze of alcohol. But what he did see, he didn't like. He drained the rest of his drink, shame washing over him.

He needed air. He stood and dropped money next to his empty glass before walking on unsteady legs to the door. Just as he reached for the handle, the door swung open from the other side.

Kas walked in.

Great. The last person Eric wanted to see.

Eric stepped back to let him pass, but Kas simply moved in front of him. "Weaver, my man. Heading out so soon?"

"Move."

"Come on, dude. We got stuff to discuss. I hear you're going to be joining us in the bullpen."

Eric gritted his teeth.

"Probably for the best, don't you think?" Kas sneered.

Eric tried again to walk around him, but Kas kept sliding with him to block his way.

"Gotta say I'm surprised, though. What with Coach Bates and all being your personal pitching tutor."

Eric made a sound low in his chest. His brain told him to ignore it but every other part of him was willing his hands into tight fists.

"She bossy in bed? Women who take charge are such a fucking turn-on."

It all happened in an instant.

Eric raised his arm.

Threw the punch.

Kas fell to his knees, bellowing and holding his nose.

Mac shouted. Chairs toppled. Bodies ran toward them. Someone grabbed Eric's arm. He wrenched free.

This bastard was done, *done*, talking shit about Nicki.

Eric grabbed Kas by the front of his shirt and hauled him up. Kas let out a noise that was half shout, half shriek.

The door flew open again and someone ran inside.

Eric whipped Kas around and threw him against the wall. It was a strategic mistake because it gave someone else time to grab him and hold him back.

Eric broke free and surged.

Something hit him. Maybe a fist. He barely felt it. He was a single-cell being with one purpose. Everything else was white noise.

Kas sagged against the wall. Eric grabbed him by the shirt again. "If you ever, ever, say another fucking word about her, I will kill you."

"Eric, stop!" He barely heard the voice over the rage pounding in his ears. But it sounded like Nicki, and that made him stumble.

He was suddenly yanked backwards. Harper Brody had him by one arm and Riley Quinn by the other.

Kas laughed. *Laughed.* Blood ran like a river from his nose and dripped off his chin. "Shit, man. I've just been messing with you, but you really are banging her, aren't you?"

"Shut up, Kas!" That was from Brody, but Eric barely heard it, because he was suddenly staring down at Nicki.

"Outside," she said. "Now."

He held up his hands. Tried to slow his breathing. For the first time, he felt the throbbing in his cheekbone. And something hurt under his arm.

Fuck. What the hell had he done?

17

Nicki all but shoved Eric into the passenger seat of her car before she rounded the hood and slid behind the wheel. Eric flopped left, and she had to grab his shirt to haul him upright.

"Don't you dare pass out in here."

"Sorry." It came out shorry.

"What the hell is wrong with you? Why do you keep doing this?"

Eric swiped at a trickle of blood under his nose. "He was talking about you."

"Do not make this about me. This is your issue."

All day, she had ached for him and ached because of him. She couldn't close her eyes without seeing his agonized expression talking about his father or hear his gruff voice call himself damaged goods.

When Cal called saying Eric needed a ride, she almost

refused. But then she heard herself say, "I can be there in five minutes."

The last thing she expected was to walk straight into a fight.

A *fight*.

Damn him!

She cranked the ignition and peeled out, praying no one had a cellphone pointed in their direction.

"You're driving me home?"

"I'm tempted to drive you straight into the ocean."

"I'm sorry."

"Stop. Talking."

Eric was apparently obedient when drunk, because he didn't say another word during the entire twenty-minute drive to his house. He looked at her a lot, though, and that was just as unnerving.

She whipped into his driveway and rolled her eyes as he fumbled to undo his seatbelt.

She shook her head. "Just hang on. I'll do it."

She got out and went around to his side. He had managed to throw open the door but was still stuck in the seatbelt. She leaned over his body to search for the latch buried beneath his hip, but as she did, the hem of her shirt rid up and she felt his fingers lift the fabric farther.

She squeaked and jumped back.

"Sorry," he mumbled. "You have a tattoo."

He pointed to the black Chinese symbols along her side.

She pulled her shirt back down to cover the ink and her embarrassment.

"What does it mean?"

She ignored the question. "I'm going to get your dad."

The front door swung open before Nicki could even knock. Chet walked out, his eyes staring over her shoulder. He swore under his breath and leapt off the porch.

Nicki looked back in time to see Eric pitch sideways from the passenger seat and crash to the ground. He sprawled on his back, arms splayed wide. One leg was still caught in the car door.

Cussing, he kicked himself free and then stood with a glare at his father. "What are you still doing here?"

His entire body was rigid, like granite. He reminded Nicki of an animal in the wild, but whether he was predator or prey, she couldn't tell. She only knew that the sudden urge to take his hand was as surprising as the flood of protectiveness that made her chest hurt.

"What happened," Chet asked her.

"He had a little too much to drink."

Chet swore again. "Let's get him inside."

"I got it," Eric grumbled, stumbling as he tried to pull away from Chet's attempts to help.

"Upstairs," Chet ordered.

They followed him to his bedroom, and Eric unceremoniously fell onto the bed. Then he winced and clutched his side.

"Let's sit him up," Nicki said.

Eric's gaze was heavy on her face, but she refused to give in and look at him. Standing this closely to him in his intimate space, she wasn't sure if she could maintain the distance she needed if she looked too deeply into his eyes. Especially not with the skin of her side still tingling from the brush of his fingers there.

"I need to look at your side," she said. "Can you take your shirt off?"

He waggled his eyebrows. "Thought you'd never ask."

Her cheeks flamed at the comment, not just from embarrassment but from the heat of unwelcome memories.

Eric grabbed the hem of his t-shirt and tugged it up and over his head. He grimaced as he let it fall to his side. Nicki barely noticed his discomfort, though, because her eyes suddenly had a mind of their own.

They started at his shoulders and traveled down to perfectly sculpted pecs. A tattoo she'd never seen before, a black tribal design, crisscrossed his left shoulder and bicep. Her eyes drifted farther still, down to the ridges of his abs and a tantalizing line of dark hair that pointed toward—

Eric grinned. "Been a long time since you looked at me like that."

"Knock it off, Eric," Chet said. "You're embarrassing Nicki."

Chet's comment only made it worse.

"What doesh your tattoo mean?" Eric slurred.

She ignored the question. "Show us where you think you hurt something."

Eric lifted his left arm and pointed to a spot along his ribcage. She put her hands there and ignored the hot zing through her fingers. "Right here?"

Eric nodded. She pushed gently on a pinkish area, and he winced in response. She lightened her touch but continued to palpate the area, relief blossoming in her chest as she moved up and down.

"I don't think there's anything broken, but we should ice it tonight and have the trainers look at it in the morning."

He grunted and lowered his arm. She backed up, needing distance like air, as he fell back onto the mattress again. His legs hung over the edge of the bed.

Chet grabbed one and tugged at Eric's shoe. Eric jerked his foot away. "Leave me alone."

Nicki rolled her eyes and moved in. "Let me."

Eric's face broke into another drunken grin. "You're undreshsing me."

"Eric," his father warned with a low voice.

Eric pointed an unsteady finger at Chet. "You get out. This is between me and my girl."

"I'm not your girl, Eric."

He planted his hand over his heart. "You are in here."

Chet snorted, and Nicki's face flamed hotter.

Eric carried on blissfully oblivious. "I mean, there have been other women."

"Christ, Eric, shut up," Chet swore with an apologetic look at Nicki.

She kept her gaze downward, mostly because she didn't want Chet to see the truth on her face about how much Eric's words hurt.

"But I didn't care about any of 'em. They were just a dishtraction. Cuz they weren't you, Nicki."

Chet headed for the door. "OK. I think you can handle it from here."

No, she couldn't. "Chet, wait—"

Eric grabbed Nicki's arm, and his eyes were suddenly stone-cold sober. "Cal's sister is dying."

She blinked at the sudden change in conversation. "I know."

"He said I should tell you how I feel before it's too late."

Something akin to an electric jolt shot through her body. "You told Cal about us?"

He either didn't hear her question or was just ignoring it. "Can't move me to the bullpen," he mumbled. "Can't."

"Eric—"

"Can't let my father down. Can't let you down."

His drunken words, so unguarded and full of truth, erased all the edges of her anger. She gave up pretending she didn't care. She sank down next to him on the bed and cupped the side of his face with her hand. The sharp whiskers along his jaw scratched her skin and brought back the glow of long-forgotten mornings. He looked so much like the young man he once had been—the young man she'd fallen in love with—that regret became a physical ache.

"Why are you doing this to yourself, Eric?"

He turned into her touch.

"Why do you think you're damaged goods?"

"He was there," he mumbled.

They were having two different conversations. "Who was there? Where? What are you talking about?"

"The game. Looked up in the first inning, and he was there. In the stands."

"Who?"

"I let him down. I let everyone down."

"Who are you talking about, Eric? Who was at the game?"

"My father."

Chet. He'd been at the last game of the World Series. Of course. The broadcast crew had made a big deal out of it. Showed him in the family section. Even interviewed him early in the game.

The biggest game of his career, and Eric had been over-shadowed once again by the all-consuming presence that was Chet Weaver—the man whom Eric could never please.

That's when it hit her. A sad truth.

Eric was alone.

He'd had no one to turn to when his mother died. Chet would have been useless. Eric had no siblings to grieve with, no aunts or uncles or cousins he was close enough with to matter at a time like that. No deep friendships to sustain him, except for maybe Cal. He'd had nothing but the game to get him through, and there was no way that had been enough.

No wonder he was struggling on the mound. Why hadn't she figured that out sooner?

It was as if a blindfold had suddenly been removed from her eyes and she saw him, really saw him, for the first time. Gone was the haze that colored everything through a filter of anger, history and betrayal. She saw him not as the man who left her, but the man he had become since then. A man who had suffered, who had grown, who had matured. A man who had known soul-crushing loss.

Nicki didn't want to feel anything, but she couldn't help it. She leaned down and put her head on his shoulder. He stiffened for an instant, but then he turned toward her and wrapped her in his arms. In a single roll, he pulled her onto the bed with him and buried his face in her neck.

Every sense came alive in his embrace. Touch. Taste. Smell. Sound. The world sharpened into pinpricks of clarity, just like it always had when he was near. It was as if her imagination were a cloud and he alone provided the lens that made life vibrant and colorful.

He hung on to her, clung to her, like he'd been drowning in open water and she was a lifeboat. The crack in her heart became a chasm. Had anyone held him like this after his mother died?

She couldn't afford to feel like this. She couldn't afford to feel *anything*, but *no emotion* was broken. Her heart was running wild in her body, flipping off any and all attempts to get it to sit down and shut up.

Eric's voice was weak as he mumbled into her neck. "I need you, Nicki."

It was a miracle she could talk at all. "Then why did you leave me?"

She got no answer.

He had passed out.

Nicki sucked in a shaky breath. She disentangled herself from the weight of his arms and his confession, and then scooted off the bed.

She stood and ran her hands over her hair, glancing around the room as she did. A pile of dirty clothes spilled over a canvas hamper in one corner. The top two drawers of his dresser hung open. A line of empty, plastic water bottles crowded his nightstand.

Eric used to be meticulous. She had convinced herself after a psychology class during her junior year that it was his way of maintaining some kind of control in his otherwise chaotic home life, of containing the things he didn't want to see.

Now it was as if it had all spilled out. The past had exploded into his present until all that was left was a messy, tangled melee.

She turned around and watched the steady rise and fall

of his chest. More memories assailed her, unwelcome and wanted at the same time. Memories of kisses and laughter, of promises and vows.

Of tears and confusion.

She had to get out of there.

Nicki jogged down the stairs and found Chet in the kitchen preparing an ice pack. He looked up as she walked in.

"Thanks for bringing him home."

She was in no mood for pleasantries. "What are you doing here? Can't you see what you're doing to him?"

He puffed out a laugh. "That's what I like about you, Nicki. You've always stood by him."

She blinked in surprise.

"Congratulations, by the way," he said. "About the job. Well-deserved and overdue."

Who the hell was this man? The Chet Weaver she knew was slow to praise and quick to mock.

Nicki smoothed her hand over her head. "Look, you're going to need to sober him up so he can throw tomorrow. I assume you're pretty good at that."

"I will. And I am."

She started to leave, but then stopped and squeezed her eyes shut, suddenly ashamed of her own nastiness. She turned around. "I'm sorry. I shouldn't have said that."

"Why not? It's true, and I deserve it."

"It's none of my business."

He finished with the ice pack and set it aside. "Of course, it is. Eric is your business."

Simple words, but they were heavy with complex history. They also brought back something Eric had said during their argument in the trainer's office when he asked about her scar.

"You are my business."

She yanked away from him. "Since when?"

"Since the day I met you."

Yes, Eric was her business. And she was his.

Only now, they were simply colleagues. Her heart flipped her off again.

"You remind me of Melody, you know."

Eric's mother. What the hell was she supposed to say to that?

"Eric ever tell you that his mother was here for spring training when we first realized something was wrong?"

Nicki inched back to the island where Chet stood. "No."

Chet looked at the fridge. "She was getting out a jar of pickles. It fell from her hand, and she couldn't pick it back up. Her fingers wouldn't work."

Pickles. Eric could eat an entire jar in a single setting.

Chet was quiet for a moment as he stared at the floor in front of the fridge before finally looking at Nicki again. "They can't test for Lou Gehrig's disease. Did you know that?"

She shook her head, mesmerized by the information Chet was giving.

"They have to rule out a thousand other things with the same symptoms before settling on that," he said.

"How long did it take to get a diagnosis?"

"Months."

"Is that why you finally got sober?"

His lips twitched at the impertinent question. "No. That happened a year before she got sick." He puffed out a laugh, but there was no joy in it. "She got one good year out of me before she found out she was going to die."

He looked at his hands. "They gave her three years. She made it one."

"I'm sorry."

"I'm here now because of her. She asked me before she died that I fix my relationship with Eric."

"How's that working?"

"Not too good so far, but at least he hasn't thrown me out. He told me at the funeral he never wanted to see me again, so this is progress."

Oh, Eric. Nicki's hand covered her mouth to hold back the silent grief. She closed her eyes and shook her head. "Why are you telling me all of this?"

"Because Eric needs you."

No. It was too late. She opened her eyes. "I'm just his coach, Chet."

"You sure about that?"

"We broke up seven years ago. It's over."

Chet cocked his head, a question spanning his features. "He never told you."

"Told me what?"

"About the reason he broke up with you."

Her stomach lurched. "What are you talking about?"

Chet let out a sad bark of a laugh and turned around. He gripped the counter. "That's what all that was up there. You never knew."

"Never knew *what?*"

He faced her again. "You're telling me that this whole time, all these years, you thought he dumped you just because he got called up?"

She nodded, alarm bells blaring in her head.

"No, Nicki," Chet said. "It was my fault."

"Your fault? How...?"

"He broke up with you because I told him to."

18

Nicki had once watched a controlled explosion of a building on the campus of her college. There was a deafening roar as the bombs exploded one by one, followed by a shocking silence and rush of hot air.

Chet's words had the same impact.

"Wh-what do you mean?"

"He was going to propose. He wanted to give you the ring I gave his mom. But when he told me, I went apeshit. Told him he was throwing his career away. Told him he would end up resenting you as much as I resented his mother."

There was a weird sound in her ears, and Nicki realized it was her own rapid breathing. *He was going to propose.*

"No. That doesn't, I mean. Why? Why are you telling me this?"

"You deserve to know the truth."

She shook her head frantically. "No. I don't want to know that. How could you tell me this?"

She spun on her heel and raced out of the kitchen.

"Nicki." He chased her all the way to the door. His arm shot out and held it shut. When she looked up, his face bordered on anguish. "I told you because he needs you."

"I'm just his coach. Just his coach." The lie came out breathless, weak.

"He's on a bad path, the same path I was on once. He thinks the game is all that matters, that he's nothing but the game, because that's what I made him believe. I was wrong. Sooner or later he's going to crash. He's going to need someone to catch him when he does. I think you're the only one who can."

Oh, God. How could words actually physically hurt? Nicki pushed his arm away and threw open the door.

By the time she got to her car, she was shaking.

By the end of his street, her entire body was a trembling mess.

By the time she got home, she was numb.

Robby was sitting on the coffee table doing arm curls and watching TV when she walked in. He looked up and immediately dropped the weights. "What's wrong?"

She swallowed and walked to the kitchen.

"Is this about Eric?"

She grabbed a bottle of water from the fridge and opened it with shaky fingers.

"What did he do?"

Nicki set the water down but refused to look at him.

"Do I need to go over there and—"

"No. Just leave it alone."

Robby sighed and leaned on the island in the kitchen. "Something is obviously going on."

"Did you ever talk to Eric after he and I broke up?"

He shifted, eyebrows drawn. "Why?"

"I just want to know."

Robby scrubbed his hand over his jaw. "Briefly."

"What did you say?"

"I told him that if he ever came near you again, I would kick his ass. And that our friendship was over."

She winced. "I'm sorry."

"Why? He made his choices."

Except maybe he didn't. Her mind tried to recall all the details of that day—details she had fought so hard to forget. Were there signs she should have seen that he didn't really want to leave her?

No. She hadn't missed anything. They had been so strong together. When they found out Eric was getting called up, they talked about how they were going to make it work. They even studied the game schedule to figure out when they could see each other. They made love and promises.

The night before he was supposed to leave, they decided to go out to celebrate. Nicki had even bought a new dress.

Nicki slid into his car in front of her apartment building and leaned across the console like always to kiss him, but he turned his head. "We need to talk."

Nicki pulled back into her seat. "What's wrong?"

Eric pulled out into traffic and made a U-turn.

"Where are you going? The restaurant is the other way."

"I thought we could sit and talk for a while."

She felt the first twinge of uncertainty. He wouldn't even look at her, which was so unlike him. She usually had to tell him to stop looking at her and drive. Her eyes dropped to his hands clenched around the steering wheel. "What's going on?"

The muscles of his throat tightened as he swallowed. "Just wait, OK?"

"No. Tell me now. What is wrong?"

He swore under his breath and whipped into the parking lot of a strip mall and parked in front of a pizza place. He scrubbed his hands over his face.

"Eric, you're scaring me."

"I need—" He stopped and swallowed again. Then he gripped the wheel again and pressed his forehead to his knuckles.

Nicki unbuckled her belt and leaned over. She wrapped her hand around his arm. "Eric, please."

He rolled his head and stared at her hand. He swore again and sat up. He transformed in front of her. Gone was the man she loved. Gone was the crinkle of tenderness from his eyes that always made her heart skip a beat. Gone was the gentle smile he saved only for her. Even his voice was different when he finally spoke again.

"We have to break up, Nicki."

Nicki pulled away. Surely she had heard him wrong. Or this was a prank. Yes. A joke. A very mean one, but a joke. It had to be. She tried to come up with a laugh. "God, Eric, you scared me to death."

Except when he looked at her, there was no sign this was a joke. The oxygen left her lungs. She slumped in her seat. "Wh-why?"

"I can't do this with you anymore. I need to be focused on the game."

"The game."

He kept talking. Something about not having time and too much travel and he needed his full attention on the game.

He was breaking up with her because he was getting called up. She was THAT girl. The one that got left behind when the Majors came calling. Hits before tits.

It was an old story, but one she never dreamed she would star in, because they were never THAT couple. They were in love.

Or so she thought.

Nicki faced forward in her seat. "Take me home."

"Dammit, Nicki. I know you understand. The game has to come first."

"Take me home."

"*That's it? That's all you have to say?*"

What else could she say? There was no competing with the game.

"*Drive, or I'm getting out and walking.*"

Eric swore several times and backed up. He drove with an angry foot on the pedal all the way back to her apartment. He pulled into the same spot in front where he'd pulled up just earlier.

Was it really just a few minutes ago that she'd been watching out the window for him, her body humming in anticipation of seeing his reaction to her in the dress? He loved her in red. He always said so.

Nicki reached for her door handle. He grabbed her arm. "Wait."

She stared straight ahead. "What?"

"*I'm sorry. Maybe when things get settled—*"

"*Don't.*" *She pulled away from him and opened the door. She slammed it over his voice asking her to stop. Heavy feet dragged her back to the front door of her building.*

She never looked back.

"Nicki, what is going on?"

She blinked out of the memory and looked up at her brother. "He didn't break up with me because of the game. His father made him."

Robby's face hardened. "He told you that?"

"Chet did." She relayed the slim details Chet had given her.

"That's bullshit," Robby growled. "He was twenty-three. A grown fucking man. That's nothing but a cop out."

"You know what Chet was like. You know how complicated their relationship was."

"I don't care if Chet put a gun to his head. You don't dump the woman you claim to love."

Nicki retrieved her water and gulped down half the bottle. She didn't drink alcohol anymore and briefly regretted it. Because how nice would it be to be able to roll over and pass out like Eric had done earlier?

"Even if it's true," Robby said, "what does it matter now? How does that change anything?"

She threw the water bottle in the recycling bin. "Nothing," she said for his benefit alone. "It changes nothing."

But that was a lie.

The entire world had changed.

The very foundation on which she had built her life had shifted, like tectonic plates grinding beneath her feet. The tremors sent her stumbling to her bedroom on shaky legs, her stomach seizing.

It was almost easier to believe that Eric had just done what so many other players did when they got called up. If he had dumped her to focus on the game and all its spoils, she could almost justify everything that came after it.

She could justify the sacrifices she'd made, the complete isolation as she drove toward a singular goal.

She could justify the mantra that had defined her entire life. *The game is all that matters.*

She could justify who she had become.

Nicki made it to the bathroom just in time. Her dinner came up in a painful heave that brought her to her knees. Betrayal and confusion were a toxic cocktail in her veins, and she didn't know if she'd ever be able to fully purge them.

She undressed and climbed into the shower, cranking the water to the hottest setting. She let it wash over her, let the scalding drops sting her skin until she couldn't feel anything else.

Out of habit, she scratched absently at the spot on her upper arm where her birth control implant sat just beneath her skin. She'd been on the pill with Eric but stopped taking it after he left. So for three weeks following the assault, when she waited in agony to get her period—even though her doctor assured her that her blood tests showed no sign of the pregnancy hormone—she vowed she would never let herself be so helpless, so *unprotected*, again. She'd had an implant ever since.

She sank to the floor of the shower as questions swirled through her brain. What if she'd known the truth? Would it have hurt less when he left? And if so, would her roommate have insisted on dragging her to that party?

And the hardest question of all... If she had known the truth, would she have ever been alone in that alley?

19

"THAT'S IT. Let it all out." Chet patted Eric's back as he bent and heaved over the toilet the next morning.

Eric swiped his arm backwards but didn't connect. "Get the fuck out of here."

"Sorry. I made a solemn promise to your coach that I would have you in tip-top shape for the day."

Eric heard the shower turn on and felt a light spray of water. He recoiled with a yelp.

"Yep. It's cold, and it's going to suck. But you gotta get in."

Eric moaned and sank to the floor. "Please tell me it was a nightmare."

"Which part?"

"The part when I told Nicki that I'd slept with other women."

"Sorry, son. You were singing a goddamned sonnet to all your other girlfriends."

Eric moaned again.

Chet laughed. "In vino veritas."

"Fuck off."

"Get in the shower. I'll have breakfast when you get done. If you're not out in ten minutes, I'm coming back in."

Eric managed to peel himself from the floor but didn't bother to strip off his boxers before crawling into the shower. The shock of cold water brought a jolt of agony to his battered body. How the hell was he supposed to throw today? Shit, how was he going to do *anything* today? He braced his hands against the tile and let the cold sink into his bones. Everything hurt. His head. His fists. His muscles. His stomach.

His heart.

She had held him. Cradled him. Wrapped her entire body around him as if she were trying to protect him.

Jeezus. He was a fucking Hallmark card.

He peeled the wet boxers from his body and scrubbed away the remnants of the night before. He toweled off and dressed gingerly, every movement like a hammer in his head. He had to stop several times and bend at the knees to breathe.

By the time he got out, he felt only slightly better. His phone buzzed as he dressed. He read the screen with blurry eyes.

You alive?

It was Cal.

Eric typed out a response. **Barely**.

Good. I'll pick you up in 20.

Twenty minutes. Was that enough time to come up with an adequate apology for what he'd said to Cal last night? His fingers hovered over the keyboard but could only come up with a single word.

Thanks.

The smell of breakfast lured Eric to the kitchen, but the sight of the massive pile of scrambled eggs, potatoes, and ham in his father's hands made him long for death again. Chet set it down on the island, along with a tall glass of thick green liquid that roiled his stomach.

"What the hell is that?"

"Green smoothie."

"Looks like something you threw up."

"It's a mixture of kale, spinach, and fruit."

"*Kale?* Who the fuck are you?"

"Try it. You'll like it."

"I'll pass."

"Come on, Eric. You have to eat."

He sank onto the stool in front of the plate and gingerly tried a bite. Then another. And another. Then his stomach took over and he practically inhaled it. He could almost feel the potatoes soaking up the alcohol. God, what the fuck had he been thinking last night?

"Done?" Chet reached for the plate.

Eric nodded, relieved when his head didn't fight back. Chet carried the plate to the sink, rinsed it off, and put it in the dishwasher.

Eric opened and closed his mouth twice before finally blurting out the word that seemed so hard to say.

"Thanks." He coughed. "For breakfast."

Chet looked over his shoulder. "You're welcome. Feel better?"

"I'll survive."

"How're your ribs?"

"Fine."

Chet turned around, wiping his hands on a towel. "There's something I should probably tell you."

Great. Had he done something else last night he couldn't remember? Streaked down the street? Proposed to the neighbor's dog?

Chet scratched his jaw. "I told Nicki the truth about why you broke up with her."

Eric had to grip the counter to keep from falling off the stool. "What did you just say?"

"I told her I made you break up with her."

"No." A cold sweat slicked his skin. "You had no right."

"Why would you let her believe otherwise?"

Because the truth was too humiliating.

"She deserved to know the truth, Eric."

Nausea sent him running for the downstairs bathroom, and he heaved unsuccessfully. Clutching the rim of the toilet, he heard the scuff of his father's shoes in the doorway.

Eric didn't look up. Couldn't.

In his mind, he lashed out, charged his father, and threw him against the wall. In his mind, he screamed like a mountain gorilla until Chet withered and cowered.

In reality, Eric hung his head and closed his eyes.

"Are you all right, son?"

"What did she say?"

"Not much. She ran out."

Eric turned around to the sink, cranked the faucet to cold, and then rinsed out his mouth. He splashed water on his face and on the back of his neck, but it didn't stop the burn of humiliation.

"Eric, I don't understand why you lied to her."

Eric turned around. "Really? What exactly should I have said, Dad? *Sure, babe. I know we've made big plans, but I'm too much of a fucking pussy to stand up to my father, so we have to break up.* Is that what I should have said?"

"Is that true? You were afraid to stand up to me?"

Eric's back stiffened. "You knew I was. That's why you did it. That's why you did everything. I was an easy fucking target for your own goddamned insecurities."

Eric stormed past Chet as he left the bathroom. He heard the hum of Cal's car pulling into the driveway. He grabbed his duffel bag from the kitchen and then walked out, slamming the front door as he went. It was childish, but it felt really fucking good.

"You look like shit," Cal said when Eric slid into the passenger seat.

"It was a rough night."

"I heard."

"You should see the other guy."

Cal snorted.

Eric swallowed back a fresh wave of nausea. "I'm sorry about what I said, Cal."

"I know you are. It's OK."

"It's not. I was an insensitive, selfish asshole."

"So, what else is new?"

Eric dropped his head against the back of the seat with a quiet, relieved laugh as Cal backed onto the road. Relief was short-lived, though, because he still had to face Nicki. What the hell was he going to say to her? He thought the most humiliating thing he'd ever experience was seeing the demise of his career spelled out in bold Arial font on USA Today. How quickly things changed.

Eric's phone began to buzz.

Once. Twice. For fuck's sake, it was coming alive in his pocket.

Eric lifted his hip and dug it out. His screen couldn't keep up with the sudden burst of Twitter mentions. It took a second of disbelief to realize what he was seeing, and when it finally became clear, his stomach lurched again.

Ray Fox had pictures of them.

20

THERE SHOULD HAVE BEEN some kind of universal rule that when your entire world was upended, time paused to let you adjust.

Nicki didn't get it.

After a night of barely sleeping, she had to meet Abby and David in the conference room of the ballpark at eight o'clock to discuss the management of Nicki's social media accounts.

If Nicki had her way, she wouldn't have any social media accounts. It was like being watched by the entire world, twenty-four hours a day. But Abby insisted.

"The price of success, babe," she'd said.

So here Nicki was, barely awake, emotionally shredded, while David droned on about hashtags and Twitter chats.

Abby's ever-present phone suddenly rang. Nicki used it as an opportunity to stand and stretch, but barely ten seconds later, Abby hung up and leveled her gaze at Nicki.

"Did you drive Eric home from the bar last night?"

Nicki's stomach sank. "Yes. Why?"

"Ray Fox has photos."

David called up Ray Fox's website as she spoke.

Nicki rounded the table to look over her shoulder. She and Abby swore at the same time. The images were dark but clear. It was as if someone had been following them and snapped the pictures at the perfect time to give entirely the wrong impression.

The first one showed Nicki leaning towards him in the car. The second showed him drunkenly smiling at her. The third was of them driving away.

Harmless, but combined with Ray Fox's incessant innuendos, they were a nightmare.

"Oh my God." The words came out on a rush of air. Nicki had to grab the back of Abby's chair. She didn't think she could take one more shock to her system after the bomb Chet dropped in her lap last night.

"He tweeted out a link two minutes ago," David said, clicking over to Twitter.

Nicki watched as David did a quick search for her name.

Bile rose in her throat as the results popped up.

Ray Fox's snarky tweet had been retweeted five hundred times already. *Just friends? Yeah, right.*

The door to the conference room burst open and cut her off. Eric stalked inside. He looked awful. Dark circles. Dark jaw. Dark expression.

Nicki's heart did a flip in her chest, which made her want to scream.

His eyes did a quick sweep of the room before returning to her. "Nicki, I need to talk to you. Alone."

"You two being *alone* have done enough damage already," Abby retorted.

Nicki looked away. "We're in the middle of a crisis, Eric. Whatever you need to talk to me about will have to wait."

"It can't wait."

Nicki looked at Abby. "I'm sorry—"

Eric snapped. "You don't need to apologize for this, Nicki, most of all to *her*. Anyone who has a problem with you driving me home from the bar can go fuck themselves."

"Excellent," Abby snorted. "I'll let you write the statement. That should clear things up in no time."

Her phone rang again. She looked at the screen. "Fox Sports."

Control. No emotion. Nicki had to keep her head in the game. She let out a slow breath and faced Abby. "What should we do?"

"Nicki, please," Eric said.

Abby talked over him. "If you're intent on not doing any interviews, then we have three options. The first is that we ignore it, which I don't recommend. The second is you respond with a simple message on Twitter that attempts to make a joke of it. The third is that we just tell the truth. The *whole* truth."

"No." Absolutely not.

Abby let out a sound and fisted her hands in her hair. "You are going to be the death of me!"

"Goddammit!" Eric suddenly yelled.

Everyone froze.

Eric looked like he could barely speak through his clenched teeth. "I need. To Talk. To Nicki. *Alone.*"

"I can't talk to you right now, Eric. I can't." She hated how small her voice sounded. How weak.

"We have to. We can't let this go."

Abby suddenly cleared her throat. "Why do I get the feeling there is something deeper going on than these photos?"

Nicki's cheeks flamed.

Abby softened her voice. "Nicki, I understand your reluctance. I do know what it's like to be a woman in this industry. But I can't do my job if you're going to keep lying to me. So, here's what I'm going to do. David and I are going to leave you two alone for five minutes. When I come back in, I either get the truth, or I'm gone for good. Is that clear?"

She didn't wait for an answer. She crossed the room and left, David close behind.

Eric wasted no time. He closed the distance between them. "Nicki, what my father told you ..."

She held up her hands and backed up. "It doesn't matter, Eric."

She had planned to avoid him today, and this was why. Because she knew the instant they had a chance to talk, she would turn into *this*.

She couldn't do it. She could *be this*. There were pictures out there that needed to be explained, and a baseball team relying on her, and fans lining up for autographs, and enemies chasing her into alleys.

So she did the same thing to him that he'd done to her years ago.

She lied. Because lies were the only truth she had left to rely on.

"It doesn't matter why you left me," she said. "I wouldn't be where I am today if you hadn't."

He stumbled back as if she'd slugged him.

She hit him again. "Your leaving made me strong, Eric. It made me focus. You made me realize that if I wanted to go all the way, I would need to sacrifice everything."

His voice turned dark and hard. "And how's that working out for you?"

"I suppose as good as it has worked out for you."

He winced. Swallowed. Shook. Hardened again. "Bullshit. I might have been drunk last night, but I remember the way you touched me. The way you held me."

No emotion. No emotion. No emotion.

"Look me in the eye, Nicki, and tell me you don't have feelings for me anymore."

"It doesn't matter how I feel about you."

"It matters to me."

The only thing separating them now was an inch of air, but it was a gaping valley of potent regret. She stepped back, afraid of falling into it. And when she opened her mouth to speak, she wasn't sure she could trust her voice.

"I need you to report to the trainer's office to have him look at your ribs."

"So that's it? You're just *Coach* again?"

"That's all I can be, Eric."

He backed up and turned around. His movements were sluggish, pained. She imagined her heart looked the same.

"Never again," she blurted.

He looked back, face twisted. "What?"

"My tattoo. It means *never again.*"

Another lie. But one that seemed to do its job.

His face turned to stone. "I'll try to keep that in mind."

He opened the door with deceptive control and walked through it, leaving it open behind him. As if he no longer even cared enough to put forth the effort it would take to close it.

Abby walked back in, took one look at Nicki, and shut the door. "Oh, girl. You need a friend."

21

A FRIEND. What would that be like? To have someone she could trust, someone other than her brother, who she definitely couldn't talk to about this. Nicki had plenty of acquaintances. Former classmates. Former roommates. But the number of people she trusted? She could count them on one hand.

The game, she realized sadly, was her best friend.

Abby crossed the room and reclaimed her seat at the table. "You holding up OK?"

"I thought you were going to quit."

"I don't like to kick a girl when she's down."

"Why not? Everyone else does."

Abby got a disappointed look on her face at Nicki's silence. "Look, I meant what I said. I need the truth—"

"It was a long time ago."

"Thank you, God." Abby melted in relief, letting her head fall to the conference table with a thud.

Nicki might have laughed if she weren't fighting to keep her breakfast down.

Abby sat back up. "Details, please."

"I met him when I was seventeen. He and Robby played together at Vanderbilt. We lived only a couple of hours from there, but Eric was from Texas, so Robby started bringing him home. We called him our stray dog."

Nicki would never forget the first time she saw him. It was Thanksgiving of the boys' freshman year. Eric barely acknowledged her when Robby made the introductions to the family, but she felt the searing heat of his brief gaze. She knew it the way a girl just simply knows that a look was different.

There was a controlled stillness to him, as if all his muscles were engaged just trying to contain a current of energy coursing through him. By the end of that first long holiday weekend, Nicki knew two things as certainly as a young woman could.

She wanted Eric Weaver.

And he wanted her back.

It would take four years before she had the guts to finally act on the attraction. She was 21, a junior in college by then.

Stupid Cherry Bombs.

"Robby didn't care that you guys were dating?"

"He never knew, not until it was over. We didn't tell anyone." Even then, she'd wanted to protect her reputation, and Eric had wanted to protect his friendship with Robby.

Abby leaned her arms on the conference table. "So what happened?"

"It was awesome for about ten months, and then he got called up to the Majors and dumped me. End of story."

Except it wasn't, but there was no need to go into all that.

"How many people know now?"

"Just my brothers."

"Are you still in love with him?"

Nicki sputtered. "What? No."

Abby's answer was a sigh. "I was afraid of that."

"Afraid of what?"

"I've been doing this a long time. You know that, right?"

"Yeah. So?"

"I know how this world works. I know how hard you've worked to get where you are and to have the reputation you have." Abby softened her gaze. "Are you prepared for what all of this means? I mean, *really* prepared?"

"What does that have to do with Eric?"

"Everything. Because there is no room for error here. You don't get to make mistakes. Everything you do and everything you say will belong to the public. As much as I wish things were different, and as unfair as this is, the first female Major League coach cannot have a relationship with a player, Nicki. There is no amount of spin on my part that would save your reputation. You know that, right?"

"I'm *not* in love with him."

Abby's look screamed, LIAR LIAR PANTS ON FIRE. "It's Eric or your career, Nicki. You can't have both."

She met Abby's gaze through eyes that throbbed with unshed tears. "Tell me something I don't know."

22

ABBY PULLED into a parking space in the underground hotel garage and squinted her blurry eyes at the clock on the dashboard. Was that right? It was after ten o'clock? For God's sake, what a day. No wonder she was having sexual fantasies about a hot bath and a bottle of Riesling. She had barely eaten all day and was running on nothing but caffeine, adrenaline, and sympathy on Nicki's behalf.

When she found out who had leaked those photos of Nicki driving Eric home from the bar, she was going to cut his balls off.

Abby got out of the car, hoisted her massive bag onto her shoulder, and locked the door with her other hand. Then she fished around her for her phone.

She dialed David, and he answered almost immediately.

"The pictures are still trending," he said without a greeting.

"Anything new from Fox?" She shuddered with indignation at the mere thought of his name.

"Same crap. His original tweet with the photos is up to more than four-thousand retweets."

Which meant there were at least four-thousand people who agreed with his brand of cruelty. Social media had its good points, but it was times like this when she wished it had never been invented. Total strangers hid behind anonymous handles to taunt, tease, lie, and ruin lives—just because they could. Abby had almost felt sorry enough for Nicki that morning to shut down her entire social media profile. But that would have backfired in the end, because Ray Fox would have just floated the idea that only people with something to hide go into hiding.

Abby thanked David and ended the call. She took the elevator in the parking ramp up to the ground level of the hotel and was half-way through the otherwise empty lobby when the woman at the desk called her name.

"Ms. Taylor?"

Abby stopped and turned. "Yes?"

"I'm sorry to bother you, but there's a gentleman waiting for you in the bar. He asked me to give you this message when you got here."

A gentleman? Her Spidey sense sprang to life, and she instantly searched for the closest security guard. The woman was holding out a folded note. Abby accepted it and opened it.

Back booth. Dev

Abby smiled a thanks and tried not to let her shaky legs give her away as she rounded the registration desk to the entrance to the hotel bar. It was dimly lit inside, but she saw him immediately. He was bent over a stack of papers, a pen poised in one hand. Thick black nerd glasses were perched on his nose and his tie was loose at the neck. Next to him on the table sat a six-pack of Pabst Blue Ribbon. She stifled a laugh.

She must not have stifled it well enough, though, because he looked up. Her breath caught in her throat. God, but he was sexy. Hair slightly mussed. The shadow of late-day stubble darkening his jaw. And those glasses. Heaven above, he could get a woman pregnant just by looking at her in those glasses.

He smiled and lifted his hand in a wave. She shifted the bag on her shoulder and walked through the darkened bar. He stood as she approached, and she shivered. He was all lean muscle and long limbs wrapped in a perfect Armani package.

"Fancy meeting you here," he said.

She pointed to the beer. "I'm surprised they let you bring that in."

"I gave the guy a hundred-dollar tip to look the other way."

"That's some expensive beer."

"It's for you. It was worth it."

She shifted her bag again, wincing as the strap dug into her shoulder. "What are you doing here, Devin?"

"Hoping I can convince you to sit and get drunk with me. It's been a rough day."

"What happened to *make an appointment*?"

"I'm sorry about that."

He actually kind of looked it. "How long have you been here?"

"An hour."

"Why didn't you call or text me?"

"I wanted to surprise you."

"Are the glasses your disguise?"

"My contacts were killing me today."

Devin wore contacts. And they'd been hurting. The everyman quality of those two facts about someone as larger than life as Devin made something shift in her chest. She ignored the sensation.

"Look, I've had a really long day, and I'm exhausted, so—"

"I know. You did a great job handling those pictures today. Better than my staff."

"You're really on a mission to get laid, aren't you?"

He fake-stumbled. "You wound me."

She laughed despite her best efforts not to.

He cocked his eyebrow. "I just want to share a beer with you after a crappy day. Is that OK?"

"I'm sure there are lots of women who would love to take you up on that offer."

"Maybe, but you're the only one I'm hoping will accept."

She looked at her feet, his teasing smile and devilish eyes chipping away at the edges of her resistance.

"Come on, Abby. One beer."

One beer. That wasn't going to kill her. She set her bag on the seat and slid into the booth as Devin did the same on the other side. She watched as his long fingers pulled two cans free from the plastic ties. He opened one and handed it to her.

After opening his, he held his can up. "To Milwaukee."

Her smile was genuine as she tapped her can against his and then took a sip.

"This is my dad's favorite beer," she said.

"I know. You told me once."

"That was a long time ago. How could you possibly remember that?"

"I remember almost everything about you."

"I find that hard to believe."

"Why?"

"I read People magazine."

"The stories about me are greatly exaggerated."

Abby sipped her beer again, mostly to camouflage her reaction. It didn't do either of them any good for her to reveal how much she hoped the tales about his many super-model girlfriends were overblown.

He relaxed against the back of the booth. "What about you?" he asked.

"What about me?"

"Anyone special?"

"I'm pretty much married to my job."

"There's more to life than work, Abby."

"Says the man who's reviewing financials at ten o'clock at night."

"Touché."

They each took a drink again, and the silence inched toward awkward. She looked everywhere but at him.

"I was twenty-two when my father died."

She snapped her gaze to his at the sudden change in conversation. Shame heated her cheeks. No matter what he'd done to her in college, he had suffered a horrendous loss and she should have been mature enough to reach out to him.

"I'm sorry. When I heard he was in the South Tower, I should have called you or ... something."

"I didn't exactly give you a reason to." His eyes pinched at the corners. "He'd slept in his office the night before. He did that sometimes. My mom used to lecture him that he was going to work himself to death one day. He sort of did, I guess."

He stared into space for a moment, and she wondered where he was, what he was remembering.

"You know what the worst part was?"

She shook her head, squeezing her beer to keep her hands from reaching over and taking his.

"The wondering. Was he killed on impact when the plane hit? Did he succumb to smoke inhalation? Or did he live long enough for the Towers to fall? For years, there was this constant loop of images in my mind about all the various ways he might have died."

She gave up on not touching him. She reached over and covered his hand with hers. "I'm so sorry, Devin. I can't imagine what you and your family have gone through."

He studied their hands as if her touch surprised him. She was just about to pull back when he suddenly turned his palm up and laced their fingers together like he craved the connection. Her heart danced around her chest.

"He used to tell me that business was just a game. He said it all the time, and I never understood what it meant. I decided to take it literally."

"That's why you went to work for your uncle at the Aces instead of joining Dane Enterprises."

"I guess so."

She leaned closer, drawn by an unidentifiable force. He held her in his gaze, drinking her in.

"Why are you really here, Devin?"

"I came on too strong the other night, and I'm sorry."

"You could have told me that over the phone," she said, gently throwing his own words from the other night back at him.

"You're right. I could have. But I wanted to see you."

"What do you *want*, Devin?"

"To start over."

"It's too late for that."

"To start fresh, then."

Impossible. She pulled her hand away and reached for her bag. "Thanks for the beer," she said, sliding out of the booth.

"Abby, wait." He stood with her. "Can't we at least be friends?"

"I remember all too well what that means to you."

She hauled her bag back onto her shoulder and turned to leave, but he gently grabbed her arm to stop her.

"Abby, that was twelve years ago. We were in college. I was a stupid kid."

"You stole my idea, Devin. I almost got kicked out for cheating."

"I was desperate. I was failing."

"You *used* me." Could she sound any more pathetic?

"It wasn't like that. My feelings for you were sincere. I made a really bad choice, and I hurt you. I'm sorry."

She didn't want to hear this. She didn't want to shed the chip on her shoulder that had protected her for so many years. "It's late, Devin."

He grasped her elbows and forced her to face him. "Please, Abby."

"Please, what?"

"Give me a chance to make this right."

They held each other's gaze, and she recognized the instant he realized he had won her over. A smile broke out on his lips. His thumbs traced gentle circles on her arms.

The blare of his cellphone made them both jump. Devin clenched his jaw and bit out a curse. He let go of Abby's arms and dug into his inside jacket pocket, but his eyes never let go of hers.

"Devin Dane," he answered.

His face went lax, ashen.

"What's wrong?" she asked, stepping closer.

"I'm sorry, Cal," he said into the phone.

Oh, no. She'd never met Cal Mahoney, but she knew this could only mean one thing. His sister.

"I'll meet you at the airport," Devin said.

Abby rested her hand on Devin's hip. He ended the call and swiped his hand down his face.

"His sister?"

"They don't think she's going to make it through the night."

"Do you need to go?"

He nodded, solemn. "I'm letting him use my plane. It'll get him home faster."

His eyes bore into hers for another moment, then his hand cupped the back of her head and pulled her in.

His lips brushed her forehead. "I've missed you," he murmured.

And that was that.

One look into his remorseful eyes, and she knew Nicki Bates wasn't the only one fighting old feelings.

23

Eric promised himself he would never do this again. He would never show up on her doorstep, never seek her out, never give her another chance to reach inside the scabbed-over hole where his heart had once resided and let her rip it back open.

But then Cal's phone rang. And then he looked up to see Cal fall to his knees. And then he drove Cal to the airport where Devin kept his private plane, and then Cal got out of the car with one request.

"Will you tell Nicki?"

So, here he was, staring at Nicki's spiky green lawn and Robby's truck in the driveway. He'd been pummeled by the one-two punch of Nicki's coldness that morning and the soul-sucking agony on Cal's face that night. How much more could he take before he was too bruised to function?

Guess it was time to find out.

Eric walked with his hands deep in his pockets to the front door. He knocked once and stared at his feet while he waited.

Seconds later, the door opened. He looked up.

Ah, shit. "Robby—"

He was flat on his back, hand to his bleeding lip, when Nicki peered over him. She wore a fleece pullover and a look of pity.

"Does it ever occur to you to duck?"

She offered her hand, and he let her help him up. Robby glowered in the doorway.

Nicki crossed her arms over her chest. "What are you doing here?"

"Cal's sister isn't going to make it through the night. He asked me to tell you."

Her arms fell to her sides, the pity on her face no longer directed at him. "Is he OK?"

"No."

She swallowed, spared a glance at Robby, and then sighed. "Let me get you some ice."

Eric ignored Robby as he followed Nicki inside.

She pointed to the couch. "Wait here."

Yeah. No. He'd rather stand.

As soon as Nicki was out of sight, Robby advanced like a batter charging the mound. "I don't know what lame-assed story you concocted about why you broke up with her, but I don't believe it."

Eric held up his hands but stood his ground. "Robby, I'm not doing this with you. Whatever happens between Nicki and me is between Nicki and me. We're adults, and we deserve some fucking privacy. So back up."

Robby clenched his jaw. Then, surprisingly, obeyed. "Who leaked those photos?"

"Kas, probably. Can't prove it, but he's the only one who makes sense."

"I'm going to kill that motherfucker."

"Get in line." Eric glanced around. "Where are your parents?"

"They drove down the coast for dinner."

"Meathead?"

"Huh?"

Eric shook his head. "Never mind."

Robby studied him quietly again. Then he suddenly walked to the door and grabbed his coat from a hook on the wall. "I have shit to do. You have one hour."

Uh. OK. That was an unexpected turn of events.

Nicki walked back in a moment later. "Where'd Robby go?"

"Out."

"Does he know we're alone?"

"I guess he decided we're old enough to no longer need a chaperone."

"He's overprotective."

Eric snorted. "No shit."

"He has his reasons, Eric."

"Am I one of them?"

She didn't answer, other than to hand over a baggie of ice wrapped in a paper towel. Her arms resumed their protective crisscross over her heart. She gnawed on her bottom lip, a nervous tick he knew so well.

The girl I knew is long gone.

That's what he had said to her in the video room when he found her watching the last game of the Series. But he was wrong. She wasn't gone. She was just hiding behind a thick disguise of hard tenacity. She wore the job like a suit of armor. What it protected her from, he didn't know.

But he wanted to find out, and that was why he shouldn't have come here. She was gravity, and he was a wayward satellite, tumbling and searching for a tether to pull him back into orbit. If she cut the line again, he would freefall back into whatever far reaches of dark space he'd been floating in for too long.

She grew uncomfortable under his gaze. Her arms tightened around herself, and her toes curled in her socks.

His brain told himself to leave. To walk out the door, throw himself headlong into the game, and forget all about her. But when he opened his mouth, his heart did the talking.

"Are you happy, Nicki?"

"Happy?"

"Yeah. Happy. With life. Job. All that stuff. *Happy.*"

"What kind of question is that?"

"It should be an easy one."

"Look, I appreciate you coming here to tell me about Cal. But I've had a pretty terrible day, and I really need to get to bed."

"I had a pretty shitty day, too."

Her eyes sparked. "Are people accusing you of being a slut who slept her way to the bigs?"

"No."

She scoffed. "Of course not. You just get high-fives in the clubhouse."

"You can blame me for the photos all you want, but you know that's not what I'm talking about right now."

Her shoulders dropped, along with her voice. "I don't want to talk about that anymore."

"I do."

Her hands fluttered to the scar above her eyebrow, and it broke something inside him. Her voice made it bleed.

"Please, Eric. I just really want to go to bed."

An idea came to him. Most likely a colossally bad one. He stood and pulled off his sweatshirt.

Her eyes went round. "What are you doing?"

"You said we have to get in bed to talk, so I'm getting ready for bed." The t-shirt came off next.

"Stop it, Eric."

He toed off his shoes and raised his eyebrows.

Her voice was suddenly sharp and brittle. "You want to talk about it? Fine. But I get to start."

"Fair enough."

Her lip quivered. "Is it true?"

Now came the hard part. "Yes."

24

NICKI HAD HEARD the term "knees buckled" before, but she'd never experienced it. Not until then. Her joints went lax, and if she hadn't been standing so close to the wall, she would have collapsed into a pathetic heap.

The only thing weaker than her muscles was the sound of her voice. "*Why?*"

"Because he said I would end up resenting you the way he always resented my mother, and I believed him."

She covered her trembling lips with shaky fingers.

"I didn't want to hurt you, Nicki, and I was afraid I would have. I would have hurt you the same way he hurt my mom. I loved you too much to risk that."

Nicki choked on incredulity. "Are you actually telling me you left me *because* you loved me?"

"Yes."

Her head gave several little shakes. She stormed toward him, grabbed his t-shirt from the floor and threw it at him.

It fell at his feet.

"How stupid do you think I am, Eric? You left because you got what you wanted out of me and then threw me away."

"That's not true."

"You loved the game, not me."

"No."

"You made a choice, and I wasn't it. That's all there is!"

He gripped her biceps. "That's *not* all there is. Why didn't you fight for me?"

"What?" He couldn't possibly mean ...

"You just sat there. You didn't cry, didn't call me names. You just let me go."

That was exactly what he meant. It left her stuttering. "A-are you saying it was *my* fault?"

"No, but – "

"But what? You dumped me as some kind of test of loyalty? To see if I would fall to my knees and beg you to stay?"

"No, but you could have tried. Why didn't you?"

"Because it was pointless! I took one look at your face and knew."

They were both yelling now. "Knew what?"

"I couldn't compete with the game. And you let me believe that, Eric. *Why?*"

"Because I was ashamed of the truth!" He let go of her and jerked his fingers through his hair. "What kind of man breaks up with the woman he loves because he's too fucking afraid of his father?"

Nicki felt a jolt, like a rubber band snapping inside her.

Just like that, it broke – the thin canopy that had kept a tenuous shade on the scorching, confused rage that had been scalding her body since last night. It was sudden. It was fierce. And it sent her stalking to the center of the room where he stood.

"You left me!" She slugged him in the center of his bare chest. He stumbled back with a grunt.

"You abandoned me!"

She struck him again, and her fist left an angry mark on his right pec.

She raised her hands to hit him again, but he grabbed her wrists.

"You bastard," she choked. "You don't get to rewrite history now just because you want to blame your father for your own mistakes."

She tried to pull free of his hold, but he crushed her against his chest and wrapped his arms around her.

"Stop, Nicki. Listen to me."

She struggled against him, but the more she fought him, the stronger he held her until her body gave up the fight and reacted to just being near to him. Her breasts against his naked chest. Heart pounding against heart.

His voice met her ear. "It was hell for me to leave you. *Hell.*"

"But you left anyway."

"And I regretted it the minute you got out of my car."

She started to push him away but couldn't.

Instead, she tangled her fingers into the wiry, dark hair blanketing his pecs. He sucked in a breath at her touch and tightened his hold on her hand.

It would be so easy. She could turn her face and press her lips to his hot skin. Let her hands explore every ridge and valley of his body the way they'd been aching for him to do since last night. He would welcome it. He'd respond and touch her the same way.

It would be so easy to let the old traces of herself take over.

And that's what scared her.

"Just—just out of curiosity," she whispered. "How long did it take you to stop loving me?"

He bent his lips to her ear. "Who says I did?"

If Chet's words last night had been an exploding building, Eric's now were an asteroid breaking the earth. Everything shook. It was violent and hard and painful and she did the only thing she knew to do, the only thing that felt natural.

She turned her face to his skin and pressed her lips there.

He responded like she knew he would, like she wanted

him to. His hands slid up her sides, skimming with the lightest touch across the side swell of her breasts.

She didn't stop him. She should, but she didn't, because, dammit, she wanted it. She wanted his hands on her. She wanted his touch, his words. She wanted to feel heat and fire and healing and *him*. Only him. The only man she'd ever trusted and ever would.

His hands cupped her face and tilted it up until their lips nearly touched. His breath mingled with hers as their chests rose and fell, as they struggled to decide. Cross this line, or not? Give in, or not?

He swayed achingly closer for one breath of a second, and then he made the decision for them. His face shifted, and the warm pressure of his lips covered her scar. She gasped, tightening her fingers against his chest. With one hand, he cupped the back of her neck, never breaking contact with the spot that reminded her every single day of violence.

His lips migrated to the corner of her eye, to her temple, and then back to her scar. His attention asked nothing of her but offered a comfort she'd long forgotten she needed.

It was his tenderness that was her undoing. "Eric..." she breathed.

With a sound low in his throat, his mouth covered hers and started a war inside her. A war of heart and mind, logic and longing, past and present. A war between Nicki and Coach Bates, of who she used to be and who she'd become.

And she knew before his hands found a home against her back, before his fingers awakened a riot of sensation with a tender brush across her nipples, before he pulled her tight against his body, she knew before all of that which side would win.

So she surrendered.

She surrendered to the want, to the hot press of his lips against the frantic pulse in her neck, to the roaming, urgent hands kneading her heavy, achy breasts. She surrendered to the throb of desire between her legs, to the pounding of her heart, to the force that had always and would always pull them together.

She surrendered to the fire.

And let it burn.

25

Eric had never believed in love growing up. He never knew what it could be like—that two souls could merge until one doesn't exist without the other. In his world, love had always been a weapon. A prison.

And when you didn't believe in something, it was easy to give it up. You could justify throwing it away, because how could it last? How could something so hot, so passionate, be anything other than a flash-in-the-pan flame that would eventually sizzle into smoke?

And when he did—when he threw it away—he learned too late what he'd really had with her. He learned too late he'd been too scared to trust it, trust her, trust himself. He learned too late that tearing their souls apart would create a physical wound, a black hole in his chest that would never heal, never stop bleeding.

The pain had been a constant presence, a dull ache, ever

since the moment he watched her slam the door on his car and never look back.

Until now.

Because now, she was here. Back in his arms and back in his life. And the pain in his chest was different.

Eric wrapped an arm around her waist and pulled her flush against his body. She moaned, opened her mouth wider and deepened the kiss.

Skin. He needed to taste her skin. Tearing his mouth from hers, he kissed a trail along her jaw and down to her neck. She let out a sound—half moan, half gasp—and clung to his shoulders as if she were afraid of falling.

He knew the feeling.

They tumbled against the wall. He tried to cushion her with his arms, but his hands wouldn't stop moving. They grazed taut skin, ridges of defined muscle that hadn't been there before. Her body was both familiar and new, and he wanted to roar over the changes. Over their lost time when she'd had a life without him and, fuck, probably other men, and it was his own fucking fault.

Her breasts grazed his chest. He had to see them. Taste them. He reached down to grab the hem of her shirt, and she lifted her arms to let him pull it from her body. With greedy fingers, he shoved aside the lace of her bra, and then he bent to cover the hard, exposed nipple with his mouth.

She let out a sob and quivered. He nipped and tugged and sucked until her legs nearly gave out. He caught her around the waist and kissed his way back up her neck until their mouths merged again. He could kiss her forever and never be satisfied.

She was panting and shaking. So was he.

God, he could do this better but there was no time because her hand was, oh holy fastballs, her hand was inside his pants.

He groaned into the heat of her mouth. Then he shoved his hand down the front of her yoga pants and found the center of her.

She cried out.

He wrenched his mouth from hers and opened his eyes. He wanted to see her, watch her features transform as he coaxed and teased the pleasure from her body.

Her lips were swollen, her eyes were closed, her cheeks were flushed, and she was the most beautiful woman he'd ever seen. This woman who was back in his life and back in his arms.

Her head fell back and she rocked against him. His name on her lips at the peak of her climax was the most erotic sound he'd ever heard and nearly sent him over the edge in his own damn jeans.

He swept her up in his arms and lowered her to the floor. She was still weak and trembling when he came down next to her and picked up where he'd left off. His hands shook as he pulled her pants from her body. Then he unzipped his jeans and shoved them down.

She wrapped her hand around his hard length. A deep, guttural sound erupted from his mouth and he pressed his face into her neck, as she stroked him and guided him.

And then he was inside her.

He was home.

She was his home.

He groaned against her mouth as he slid in and out. Slowly. Tenderly. Until they found the rhythm they'd perfected years ago. Until they were both shaking again. Until he felt that first tremor that told him she was going to come a second time. Then she cried out and arched her back.

It was more than he could take. The world blew up. He shuddered again and again as hot, wet waves exploded into Nicki's body.

It had never happened like that before. Never.

He went lax against her and panted into her neck. "I've missed you so much, Nicki. So much."

She wrapped her arms around his back and held him there. Still inside her, still part of her, still home.

And he never wanted to leave.

SHE WAS SHAKING.

It took him a second to realize it, but when he did, Eric rose up on his elbows to gaze down at her. "Babe?"

The muscles of her throat convulsed as she rolled her face away from him. In slow motion agony, he watched as a tear rolled down her cheek.

Holy shit. "Nicki, what's wrong?"

"I need... I need to get up."

Eric rolled off her, and she shot up. He reached for her, but she scrambled away from him. His pulse picked up. "Nicki, what is going on? Why are you crying?"

He watched as she covered her breasts with her arm and grabbed her discarded t-shirt from the floor.

"Babe, talk to me."

She darted down the hallway toward her bedroom and shut the door.

Dread pooled in his gut. What the hell was going on? He jumped off the floor, yanked his pants back up, and followed the path of her panicked retreat.

He tried the door handle, but it was locked.

Fuck. "Nicki, what's happening here?"

He heard the faucet turn on in her attached bathroom, followed by several splashes as if she were throwing water around. Was she... was she *washing* herself?

Eric jiggled the handle again, more insistent this time. "Nicki, open the door."

"Leave me alone, Eric. Please."

"Babe, you have to talk to me." He swallowed back a threatening gag as a thought hit him. "Did I-did I hurt you?"

"No. I just need a minute, Eric. *Please.*"

Her voice broke on the last word. Holy shit.

He braced his hands on the doorframe. "Ok, listen. I get that you're sort of freaking out right now. I mean, I kind of am, too. This is a big deal. Please, just open the door and talk to me about it."

The water shut off. A moment later, the handle moved as she unlocked the door and pulled it open. She was wearing her t-shirt and nothing else.

He reached for her.

"Don't." She held her hands up to ward him off. "Please. Don't touch me."

His arms fell to his sides and he stared blankly for a moment. Then he let out a breath and gripped the back of his neck. "OK. I'm a little confused here, Nicki. Did we or did we not just make love?"

Nicki covered her face with her hands. "Please don't call it that."

"What the hell should I call it?"

"Nothing. Don't call it anything. Please, God, never speak of it again."

"*What?!* Are you kidding me?"

She let her hands fall away. "I-you have to leave."

"No freaking way. I'm not going anywhere until you start making sense."

"This never should have happened."

He heard the words, but it took a moment for the meaning to follow. *Never should have happened.* "You regret this?"

Her eyes flashed. "Of course, I regret this! We didn't even use a condom!"

"Y-you're not on the pill?"

"I have an implant, but that's not the point!"

Oh, thank god. Relief hit him hot and hard. Followed immediately by a surge of disbelief. "Jeezus, Nicki. I'm clean. Is that what you're worried about?"

She groaned and turned away from him. "That's not the point, either."

"Then what is the freaking point?"

She whipped back around. "I lost control!"

Her words exploded from her and bounced off the walls.

"Babe..." he breathed, reaching for her again. "You're supposed to lose control. That's what makes it good. That's what has always made it good between us."

She shook her head and backed away from him. "No. I'm not allowed to lose control. Not anymore."

"Not anymore? What the hell does that mean?"

Her lip trembled. "You don't understand."

"You're goddamned right I don't understand! Five minutes ago, I was picturing happy ever after, and you're telling me this was just some kind of mistake to you?"

"Eric, please," she begged, voice cracking. "I need to think. I need to process this."

He gripped her shoulders and bent to press his forehead

to hers. Not for her benefit, but for his. He was on the verge of losing it.

She tried to pull away, but he held tight. "Please don't ask me to leave you right now. It was hell walking away from you before. Don't ask me to do it again."

She twisted away from him. Her fingers fluttered to her scar. Her eyes darted around the room.

But suddenly, as if someone had flipped a switch inside her, she went still. She drew herself tall, transforming like she'd done before. He might have had Nicki in his arms a few minutes ago, but this was Coach Bates.

"You don't know what hell is," she said, pinning him with a flat, empty stare. "Please, Eric. I need you to leave."

Then she walked quietly to her bathroom again and shut him out.

The click of the lock echoed throughout the room. A lonely sound in a lonely space.

Eric dry washed his face with his hands and swallowed against a growing lump in his throat. What had just happened? *You don't know what hell is.* What did that mean?

He zipped up his jeans and looked down at his shoes, still on his feet. He'd never even taken them off. He'd lost control, too.

Nicki was just panicking. So was he. The reality of *after* was a scary thing because there was no going back to the *before*. This was the line of demarcation—tonight. The world was a different place than it had been an hour ago. Hell, yeah, he was panicking. But he was going to panic a lot more if he couldn't get through to her.

He walked to the closed bathroom door and leaned his head against it. He opened and shut his mouth several times as he tried to figure out what to say before settling on the one thing he *needed* to say.

"Nicki, I'll go if that's what you want, but—"

His voice shook. Fuck! He cleared his throat. "I'm not walking away from you again."

Her silence on the other side gutted him.

26

Nicki listened to Eric's footsteps as he walked away. Her legs gave way, and she sank with a whimper to the cold tiled floor. How could she want to celebrate and cry at the same time?

Her stomach churned, but not from regret. Her body still hummed with pleasure she never thought she'd feel again. Her skin burned with the imprint of his touch, his lips. Her mind replayed his words over and over again, words she'd longed to hear seven years ago but were too late now.

He thought he knew what hell was, but he didn't. He had no idea.

Hell was spending weeks staring into space feeling like you'd lost a piece of yourself.

Hell was walking home alone and hearing the voices behind you. Hell was cowering half-naked on dirty asphalt and praying for the ground to swallow you whole. Hell was knowing they were going to get away with it.

Hell was discovering the foundation on which you'd built your life was a crumbling lie.

Hell was knowing there was nothing you could do about it.

He said he wasn't going to leave her again. Didn't he understand? It wasn't his decision, not this time.

She was so close to getting everything she'd worked for, fought for, bled for. She was so close to victory.

She couldn't risk it all now, no matter how much her heart suddenly wanted to.

Nicki fell onto her side.

Who says I did? His voice was as loud in her mind as if he were standing before her.

Nicki covered her ears to drown it out. It was too late. Too late.

She curled into a ball.

And let her tears drip onto the floor.

27

THE PHONE RANG at five-thirty in the morning. Eric shot up in bed. He grabbed his phone from the bedside table and squinted at the screen, heart pounding, hoping.

Nicki.

He answered so fast, he almost dropped the phone. "Babe?"

He heard her sniff. He broke inside. "It's going to be OK, honey. We can do this."

"Cal's sister died."

He sank against the headboard.

She sniffed again. "He asked me to tell you."

And then she hung up.

Eric gripped the phone in a white-knuckled fist.

And whipped it against the wall.

28

The haunting melody of a harp rose and fell with the muted hum of conversation as Eric and Nicki ducked around small huddles of people in the funeral home outside Ann Arbor, Michigan.

It was two days later. Two hell-filled days later in which Nicki had refused to treat him as anything but a colleague. He knew he was officially over the edge when he realized he looked forward to the fucking funeral because it meant getting her almost alone. Devin used his private jet to fly them up for the funeral, and the rest of the team had stayed behind. The game didn't even stop long enough for a teammate to bury his twin sister.

Now, all around them families in their church clothes nibbled on cookies, sipped punch, and did their best to corral children who didn't understand. Beneath the forced air of civility, grief filled the spaces between the people with a choking presence. It was in the balled-up tissues in the women's hands, the nervous handshaking of the men. Some turned and smiled. Eric nodded in acknowledgement even though he didn't know any them.

Eric remembered very little of his mother's funeral. Most of it was a blur of grief and rage. But he did remember that look. The sad, I-don't-know-what-to-say smile was as much a part of funeral attire as a dark suit.

Eric settled his hand on Nicki's back as they walked through the room. Touching her was torture, but at least she didn't pull away. They'd had no time to talk, and every time he tried to get her alone, she shook her head and walked away.

Cal's father suddenly stepped in front of them. Eric shook his hand and introduced Nicki.

"It means a lot that you're here," the man said. "I know Cal will appreciate it. He's out back, if you're looking for him."

Eric thanked him and then walked with Nicki through a kitchen area toward a back door. It led to a large porch overlooking a massive, rolling lawn. The grass was pockmarked with patches of snow that were fighting the approach of spring.

Sara's daughters—Emily, Kelly, and Annie—played listlessly on a swing set off to the side of the deck.

From a hidden corner, Cal watched over them, leaning against the railing as if it were the only thing holding him up. He had the cleaned-up but haggard appearance of someone who had gone too long without sleep and was hanging on by sheer will alone.

Eric could relate. He'd been seeing the same sucker-punched expression on his own face in the mirror for the past two days.

Nicki rushed to Cal's side and pulled him into a tight embrace. Eric felt a misplaced twinge of jealousy, which he quickly shook off. Cal pulled away from Nicki and nodded at Eric, hand outstretched.

Eric ignored it and pulled his friend in for a back-pounding hug. "You all right, man?"

Cal withdrew and shoved his hands in his pockets. "I don't know half the people in there, and it's about ninety degrees in every room."

"We passed a bar on the way here. Wanna take a break?"

Cal looked back the girls. "I shouldn't leave them."

"I'll stay," Nicki offered.

Cal shook his head. "You don't have to do that."

"I'd be happy to, Cal. Introduce me. I'll play with them until you get back."

They followed Cal down the stairs of the deck and over to the play structure. The girls looked up as one. The youngest, Emily, held up her arms. Cal scooped her up.

"Girls, this is my friend, Nicki. She's going to play with you for a while, OK?"

Emily ducked her chin toward Cal's chest but studied Nicki through upturned eyes. Then she held out her arms. Nicki took her and hugged her close.

Warmth spread through Eric's body. Nicki was a natural with children, always had been, and he wondered if she still wanted to have any. She always used to.

Then another thought came to him—the thought of Nicki having children with someone else. Someone other than him.

He felt sick.

The little girl looked at Eric. "Who are you?"

"I'm Eric. I'm Uncle Cal's friend. You probably don't remember me because the last time I saw you, you were just a baby."

"Do you play baseball?" It came out *batheball* with her lisp.

"I do."

Emily leaned her head on Nicki's shoulder for a moment. And then with typical childlike innocence, she said, "My mommy died."

Cal coughed. Eric looked over, and there was a wetness to his friend's eyes that hadn't been there before.

Cal ruffled Kelly and Annie's hair. "You guys help Nicki with Emily, OK? I'll be back in a little while."

Kelly, the oldest, nodded. Eric watched as Nicki set

Emily down and took the little girl's hand to lead her to the slide. The pain in his chest made him wince.

The bar was a block away, so they walked. It was dark inside and practically deserted. A handful of people sat at booths, but the bar itself was empty. They each grabbed a seat and ordered a beer.

"How are the girls doing?" Eric asked.

"Emily is too young to really understand what it means. I think she expects Sara to come back. Kelly and Annie are putting on a good face, but I know ..." He stopped and swallowed hard. "I know they're struggling."

They drank in silence for several minutes, staring blankly at highlights of the Red Wings game on the TV behind the bar. At a break, the screen flashed back to the studio at Fox Sports Detroit. Suddenly, they were staring at Cal's face.

As we reported earlier, our condolences go out to Michigan native and Vegas Aces pitcher Cal Mahoney. His twin sister, Sara Shane, lost her battle with cancer earlier this week. Sources tell us Mahoney flew home from the team's spring training facility in St. Augustine, Florida, to be with his sister when she died.

Eric barely recognized Cal's voice when he growled at the bartender. "Turn it off."

The bartender glanced quickly between Cal and the TV, only then apparently realizing who Cal was. He mumbled an apology and changed the channel. The entire bar seemed suspended in tense silence.

"You OK?"

"I should have been here," Cal said quietly.

"You had no way of knowing when—"

"We knew it was close. We knew she wouldn't hang on much longer, but I went to Florida anyway." He clenched his jaw. "For the game. The fucking game."

Eric was silent for a moment, took a pull on his beer and then leaned forward on his arms. "At least you made it in time to say good-bye."

With a strangled cry, Cal bolted to his feet and whipped his bottle at the TV with all the speed and velocity of fastball. The bartender ducked with a surprised curse and a woman in the back exclaimed.

Eric jumped up and grabbed Cal's outstretched arm, his fingers wrapping around Cal's clenched fist.

"Cal—"

"I didn't make it." His voice ricocheted off the wall.

"What?"

Cal wrenched his arm free and pounded his fists on the bar,

"She died while I was on the plane. And they said—" He pounded the bar again. "They said she woke up. Right before she died, she opened her eyes, and I wasn't fucking here."

His voice broke. "She opened her eyes and looked

around. And I can't-I can't sleep because I wonder if she was looking for me."

Tears flowed freely down Cal's face. He raised his fist to his mouth, and the grunt of a hard sob tore from his chest. The bartender stared, customers whispered, and Eric wanted to flip them all off.

Instead, he pulled his wallet out and dropped a large wad of bills on the counter. "Buy a new TV."

Eric grabbed Cal's elbow and pulled him away from the bar.

Cal stumbled out into the blinding sun and turned away from him.

Eric pressed his hand between his shoulder blades. "It's OK, man."

Cal whipped around. "It's not OK. None of this is OK. It's bullshit. They treat us like heroes just because we can throw a ball, but I wasn't here when my own twin sister ..."

He cleared his throat and pressed his thumbs to the corners of his closed eyes. "My family needs me. The girls need me."

"Of course, man. I'm sure management will give you time. You don't need to come back right away."

Cal blinked several times, some undefinable expression crossing his face. He faced Eric square on. "I'm not coming back."

"*What?!*"

"I quit. I'm done with baseball."

NICKI KNEW the instant they returned that something had happened while they were gone. Cal's eyes were swollen and red, which was to be expected. But it was Eric's face that made her forget she was supposed to be pushing Kelly on the swing. His ashen skin covered a stunned expression.

The girls took off running when they saw Cal. He dropped to his knee and pulled them close for a hug.

Eric hung back. Nicki went to him, wary. "What happened?"

Eric opened and closed his mouth, as if he couldn't form words. "He's quitting."

"Quitting baseball?" That wasn't possible. Major League pitchers didn't just up and quit. No matter what was going on in their lives. "He's in the middle of a contract."

"He said he doesn't care. He'll give the money back, if he has to."

"He's just upset. He doesn't mean it."

"I think he does."

Cal rose, and he and the girls walked toward them. Cal patted Kelly's head. "You girls run inside, OK? I'll be right there."

Nicki hugged each of them and waited until they were out of earshot before rounding on him. "Cal—"

"It's my decision, Nicki. I can't do this anymore."

"How can you just walk away from the game?"

"Because the game isn't everything, you know."

"I know," Nicki said automatically, but the words were sour in her mouth.

"Do you?" Cal asked, his tone angry. "Sometimes we tell ourselves that the sacrifices we make are worth it, but they're not. I hope you and Eric figure that out before it's too late."

Nicki began to sweat. "What are you talking about?"

"You love each other. Don't fuck that up for the game. The game is never going to love you back."

He brushed past them and jogged up the stairs of the porch. Nicki watched, stunned and shaken, until he disappeared inside the funeral home.

A breeze blew in off the lawn, lifting her hair and sending a shiver down her spine. She was frozen, but not from the air. The entire world was crazy and inside out, a tornado twisting and turning until nothing seemed right and she had no sense of direction.

"Do you think he's going to be OK?" she whispered.

Eric's long sigh drew her gaze. "I don't know. He's punishing himself pretty bad right now."

"Is that why he's leaving the team? To punish himself?"

"I think this has forced him to get his priorities straight."

Unlike me. The thought came out of nowhere and left her empty inside. She hated all these emotions, all these feelings. She had never doubted her life or her choices before. The confusion left her bitter and angry.

Eric moved into her space, enveloping her in his scent and his presence. She shivered again.

"Cold?" he asked.

"I'm fine."

His hand reached out, hovered, and then dropped. "I want to touch you so bad right now."

Her eyes slid shut. "Don't."

"What Cal said—"

Her eyes flew open. "Stop."

She stormed past him. Cal was grieving. And his grief was making him do and say stupid, crazy things. That's all there was to it. You didn't just give it all up. Not after everything you had to do to get there. Cal would come to his senses. He would return to the game and he would realize that the sacrifices were worth it and that she and Eric—

"What if we hadn't broken up?"

She tried to block out the question as she stomped up the stairs of the deck. Eric's long stride and his voice followed her to the door that would take them back inside the funeral home.

"I've been torturing myself with that question, Nicki. Would we be married? Would we have kids? Which one of us would they look like? Hopefully you."

She whipped around as a fist gripped her heart. "Marriage? Kids? What the hell are you talking about?"

"I asked you once if you're happy, but you didn't ask me."

Her throat struggled against the clutches of panic. *Please, Eric. Please don't do this now.*

"I'm not happy, Nicki. I'm not happy without you."

He advanced on her and gripped her shoulders. His expression left her breathless.

"You've ignored me for two days, Nicki. Two fucking days. But right here, right now, it's just us. Say something. *Anything.* Just, please, fucking *talk to me.*"

It was what he didn't say—what he communicated with his eyes alone—that made her heart race and her breath catch in her lungs. The weight of their entire history hung heavy in his hooded gaze. All the pain. All the passion. All the regrets and lies and *love.*

Who says I did?

Oh, God. She fell back against the brick exterior of the funeral home.

Cal was right. She loved him, too. And there was nothing she could do about it.

His forehead came to rest on hers, his hands pressed to the wall on opposite sides of her body. "Please, Nicki. You can tell me anything. *Anything.*"

She wanted to. She wanted to so badly that her lungs burned with the need to explain everything to him. But she couldn't. Ever. It was her dirty little secret, and she would carry it to her own grave. Because the minute she told him, he would know the truth about her, and he would never look at her the same again. He would see her for the weak person she'd once been.

"I'm sorry," she whispered.

He cut her off with an angry curse. His hands became fists, and they crashed against the wall on either side of her. She choked on a cry. Not because she was fearful—never of him—but because she knew she was hurting him.

But then, suddenly, they were kissing. She didn't know who made the first move, and it didn't matter. Their lips brushed lightly. Once. Twice. Like the hesitant joining of a first kiss. But this wasn't their first kiss, and in an instant, their bodies remembered. The fire. The heat. The need. The kiss was raw emotion, a tempest of unspoken want, fueled by desire and pain and hunger.

He quickly took charge. He blocked her in again against the wall and plundered her mouth.

His kiss made no demands. Only promises. Of laughter and friendship and understanding. Of days long gone and days yet to come. They tugged with gentle persuasion, edging her mouth open wider. The tip of his tongue grazed hers. He felt so good and she needed this so much.

He slid his hand to the back of her neck and held her to him. Deeper and deeper, his mouth probed hers, searching for the thing they both wanted but couldn't have. The need between them ignited and burned. So hot. Too hot. The kind of fire that would leave a scorched Earth in its path.

And then, just as suddenly as it had begun, it was over.

Eric wrenched his mouth from hers. When he looked down at her this time, it was through a tangled expression of anguish and need.

"We can't go on like this, Nicki. It's going to kill us both."

Without another word, he turned away and left her.

She was alone in the cold.

29

THE PLANE RIDE home was an experiment in pain. Eric looked across the aisle to where Nicki sat alone, staring out the window. Her hands were fisted in her lap, her shoulders rigid. She didn't say a word to him during the drive to the airport, but the fact that she chose a seat away from him spoke volumes.

He felt Devin's gaze on him and looked up at his boss. He was as fine-pressed and groomed as when they'd left that morning. Eric, on the other hand, felt like he'd been dragged through a shit pile at a Texas rodeo.

Devin sipped the glass of Scotch in his hands. He'd offered one to Eric, but Eric declined. He didn't want to lose the taste of her on his tongue. How fucking pathetic was that?

"Did he tell you?" Devin asked.

Eric answered with a single nod.

"I could refuse to let him go. He still has forty million left on his contract."

"Don't be a dick, Devin."

"You could probably change his mind."

"Why would I want to?"

"We can't win without him."

"Maybe winning isn't everything."

Nicki's head suddenly jerked in his direction.

It took every ounce of willpower he possessed to stare straight ahead and not meet her gaze.

"Never thought I'd hear those words from you, Weaver," Devin mused.

The tone of his voice sent Eric's nerves into full fuck-you mode. "Maybe you don't really know me."

"Or maybe you're giving up."

"You throwing the bullpen in my face again? Now?"

"No. Just gauging your dedication."

"Stop it, Devin."

Nicki's voice was subdued, weary. Eric would have laughed at the surprised expression on Devin's face if he could get past the sudden tightness in his chest.

"Something to add, Nicki?"

"Eric has given everything to this game. You can criticize him for a lot of things, but don't you dare criticize his level of commitment."

Devin's eyebrows shot high on his forehead. "Thank you for your input, Coach."

Nicki's gaze strayed from Devin to him, and he couldn't breathe. Even though she had kissed him as *Nicki*, the look she gave him now told him *Coach Bates* was all she could give him.

She was choosing the game over him.

The cruel irony burned a hole in his gut.

The lights were still on in the house two hours later when Eric got home. Chet was still awake. Probably waiting for him. Chet always waited up for him.

Eric had hated it as a teen and often had reason to fear it. If he stayed out too late, he got a lecture about not taking his pitching seriously. And that was on a good day. On the bad days? He still had a scar on his left hand from an infected blister caused by the rub of his glove after three hours of throwing in the dark.

He had no reason to fear his father's wrath anymore. And wonder of wonders, he was now glad for—if nothing else—the fact that his house wasn't empty.

Eric hit the garage door button and eased his Escalade into the space. The smell of food hit him as soon as he opened the door to the house. His father hadn't lied about the cooking thing. He actually knew what he was doing in the kitchen.

Eric's stomach growled in response to the aroma, and he quickly calculated how long it had been since he'd last eaten. Hours. Eric dropped his keys on the island and headed for the fridge.

"You hungry?"

Eric peered over his shoulder at his father and realized he no longer had the energy or the desire to argue. He let the door to the fridge swing shut again and turned around. "Starving."

His father's smile hit him like a guilt stick.

"I'll fix you a plate," Chet said. "I made a pot roast. Your mother's recipe."

Eric sank onto one of the bar stools at the island and rested his elbows on the smooth granite. He dug the heels of his hands into his eyes.

Chet pulled a pot out of the fridge and set it near the sink. "How's Cal?"

"He, uh..." Eric was still finding it hard to believe, much less say it out loud. "He's leaving the team."

Chet dished up a heaping helping of meat, potatoes and carrots onto a plate before shoving it all in the microwave. He busied himself putting the pot away and hauling out the milk.

"You OK with that?"

"Fine," Eric said, the one-word answer emerging automatically, only this time it came with a side helping of bullshit.

He sighed. "Actually, I'm not fine."

Chet's voice was too casual. "Because of Cal, or because of Nicki?"

"I don't know," Eric answered honestly. Again, would the wonders never cease? "Both, I guess."

The microwave chirped. Chet pulled out the plate and set it, along with a full glass of milk and some silverware, in front of Eric. Jeezus, but it smelled good. Eric dug in and shoveled a huge bite into his mouth.

"Your mom used to make that every Christmas Eve, remember?"

Eric glanced up. His father stood on the other side of the island, watching him and waiting for a response.

Yeah, he remembered those Christmas Eve dinners. He remembered his mom in an apron—the one she only wore on holidays—and his father messing with the tree or the lights or some shit. He remembered how his mom insisted on eating with the fancy plates and starting with a prayer. He remembered looking forward to it every year, because it was the only time he could count on his father being half-way decent and his mother wholly happy.

Eric knew what Chet wanted him to say, but Eric couldn't give it to him. He was already so chest-deep in mindfucking feelings that he feared he would completely lose his shit if he attempted a stroll down memory lane with his father.

Chet seemed to accept Eric's silence. He lightly bounced a fist on the granite. "Well, I think I'll go back to my book."

Eric watched his father's stiff-backed retreat and felt something akin to panic.

He dropped his fork, the clatter of silver like an alarm bell. He dry washed his face and tried to breathe.

He thought of his father sitting in the living room with nothing but a book to keep him company.

He thought of Nicki, vulnerable and scared.

He thought of Cal, sleepless with guilt.

He thought of another goddamned night alone in his room.

"You want to come to Tampa for the game against the Yankees?"

The words were out of his mouth before his brain had time to catch up. Chet stopped and turned around. The expression on his face was like a kid whose parents had just surprised him with a trip to Disneyland.

Eric stared at his plate, choking on the fastball-to-the-chest feeling that came out of nowhere. *It's just a fucking exhibition game*, he wanted to yell.

"Sure," Chet finally answered. "Sounds good."

He left then, and Eric let out the breath he'd been holding.

He picked up his fork again and finished off his food.

Every bite was a memory he suddenly wanted to savor.

30

Abby punched up the volume on the TV in the conference room, which had become her unofficial-but-don't-anyone-else-dare-use-it office inside the ballpark.

ESPN had been teasing for more than an hour a panel discussion about Nicki and the Aces pitching staff. It was finally here.

Avery Giordano of the New York Times was one of the panelists. Unfortunately, so was Ray Fox.

"I think it's safe to say the Vegas Aces experiment has worked," Avery said. "We're now two weeks into spring training, and Aces management has to be happy with what they're seeing."

Ray Fox scoffed. "Are you kidding me? Are we watching the same team? They've lost a third of their exhibition games."

Somehow, Avery maintained her cool. "Ray, I've been

here the entire two weeks, and I can tell you the staff is improving. Harper Brody is averaging ninety-six miles per hour during bullpen sessions. That's a full two miles per hour faster than last season. Zach Nelson is showing amazing strength and control. And Eric Weaver has gotten back the spin to his curve ball—"

Ray snorted like the pig he was. "Yeah, well, who knows what kind of individual attention he's getting."

Ugh. Abby shut off the TV and reminded herself it would be bad form to throw the remote. Thank God for Avery Giordano. If Abby had been forced to debate Ray one-on-one, she'd end up in prison.

He had no idea what he was talking about. Abby had never seen a person work harder than Nicki the past two weeks. She was obsessed. Even more so now than at the beginning of spring training. It was as if she had returned from the funeral with an even narrower focus on the game. Abby couldn't put her finger on it. Nicki was just *different*.

Abby had no doubt the change had everything to do with Eric.

Abby gathered her things and shoved them in her bag. She shut off the lights to the conference room and headed to the elevator at the end of the tunnel. Devin's office was on the top floor of the office wing.

She fought the goofy smile that teased her lips as she walked into the elevator. She didn't know if she could say she and Devin were dating, necessarily. They'd gone out to dinner twice, and after the second one, he'd kissed her in his car like she was his sole source of oxygen. There had been phone calls and texts, too. Some of them heated.

Who was she trying to fool? Yes, they were dating.

The hallway leading to his office was deserted. His door was open, and she heard his voice.

Or, wait. It wasn't his voice. It was someone who sounded a lot like him, though. On speaker phone maybe?

"This has gone too far, Devin."

"I'm sure you'll survive." Devin's voice was tired, scratchy.

"Do you have any idea what this is doing to Mom? You should have heard the questions that damn reporter asked her today! As if Mom has anything to do with the running of that damn team."

Abby hugged the wall so she couldn't be seen. She should probably feel guilty for eavesdropping on what was clearly a private discussion, but she couldn't have pulled herself away even if the fire alarm sounded above her head.

"I can't control the media, Bennett."

"Yeah, but you can damn well control your team. Are they sleeping together or not?"

Abby's skin prickled with indignation as she waited for Devin to respond. He didn't get a chance, though. A child's voice called out in the background.

"I want to talk to Uncle Devin!"

Uncle Devin? Abby smiled despite her annoyance.

"Put her on the phone," Devin ordered.

"Fine. But I'm not done with you yet."

There was a rustling sound, and then a little girl's voice filled the room. "Hi Uncle Devin!"

"Hey, squirt. How's my girl?" Abby could hear his smile, which made hers grow.

"My birthday is next week!"

"I know. What do you want from Uncle Devin?"

"Can I meet Nicki Bates?"

"Of course you can."

There was more rustling and then Devin's brother ordered his daughter out of the room.

"I'm not messing around this time, Devin. This is one embarrassment too many."

Devin's voice took on a hard edge. "Meaning what, Bennett?"

"If those two are sleeping together, you need to cut her loose. Or I'll cut you loose."

There was a click and a silence. What the hell?

"You can come in now, Abby."

Her cheeks blazed as she pushed open the door.

Devin pointed to the windows flanking the door. Amusement tinged his voice. "I could see your reflection in the glass."

He was sitting behind his desk, looking better than any man had a right to. His hair was slightly mussed at the front, as if he'd been running his hands through it. His jawline was dark beneath a layer of growth. He'd lost his tie at some point, and now the collar to his shirt hung open, revealing a hint of dark chest hair.

Abby cleared her throat. "I'm sorry. I didn't want to interrupt."

"Why not? It's always fun to be part of another round of," his voice dropped to a mocking tone, *"You disappoint us, Devin.* It's my brother's favorite game."

"What was he talking about? He wants you to fire Nicki?"

"He's all bluster, Abby. It's nothing to worry about."

"But you would stand by her, right?"

That brought him up short. He blinked. "Do you really think I wouldn't?"

She shook her head. "I'm sorry. I'm just sensitive about her."

He winked. "Don't I know it."

He stood then and yawned behind his fist. His other hand scratched low on his stomach, his fingers lifting the hem of his untucked shirt just enough to reveal tight skin and more dark hair. She started to sweat.

He rounded his desk and propped one hip on the corner. Their eyes locked. His glowed like amber gems in the light from his desk lamp. The effect on her was swift and complete. A wave of heat rushed up her spine.

"Have dinner with me tonight."

There could be no denying the hidden meaning in

his tone of voice. *Have dinner with me* was just code for, *Let's stop dancing around this thing and get it on already.*

And, oh boy, was she ready, but disappointment was a cold shower. She cleared her throat. "I can't. I'm leaving."

His expression sobered. "Leaving where?"

"I have to go back to New York."

"*Today?*"

"Tomorrow morning. Early. I need to pack tonight."

"Why?"

"I have other clients who are starting to feel neglected, and I have several meetings lined up this week. I can handle Nicki from there."

His eyes sparked with an expression that robbed her of all coherent thought. It wasn't just that his gaze was laden with blatant desire—which it was. It was the *way* he looked at her, as if he could see straight through to the part of her heart that wanted him, too.

He looked at her as if he dared her to deny it.

She couldn't. Her entire body screamed for him, ached for him in places that had been dormant for so long. Making love to Devin again would either be the most exhilarating experience of her life, or another mind-numbing mistake that would leave her even more broken than she already was.

He rose from the corner of his desk and sauntered over to where she stood. "Tell me what you're thinking right now," he whispered, reaching over her shoulder to push the door shut.

"I'm thinking that for some people the attraction is too strong, no matter how much they want to fight it."

His arms snaked around her waist and tugged her gently against him. "Do you want to fight it?"

"No."

His nostrils flared. "How long do you have to be in New York?"

"I don't know."

"But you're coming back."

"When I'm needed."

His head dipped until his mouth hovered over hers. "You're needed."

Then his lips lowered fully to hers. Their mouths joined in an explosion of sensation and wonderment that stole her breath. His hand cupped the back of her head, holding her in tender possessiveness. And she liked it. Liked being possessed by him and devoured by him.

His mouth kissed a trail down her jaw to the hot pulse of her neck. "Tell me what you're thinking now," he said, his mouth dancing over her collarbone.

Her breathing hitched. "I'm thinking that I can't stand to get hurt again."

He met her gaze. She cradled his cheek. "Please don't hurt me, Devin."

"I won't."

She searched his eyes, looking for signs of deceit or any other reason to stop this now. She couldn't find one. Where she once saw arrogance, she now saw sincerity. Where there was once selfishness, there was now compassion.

"I believe you," she whispered, unable to keep the surprised wonder from her voice.

He suddenly hefted her up in his arms. She laughed and wrapped her legs around his waist to hold on. "I have to pack," she breathed against his mouth.

"I've waited for this for twelve years. You're going to leave me now for luggage?"

She laughed again. He crossed the room with her balanced in his arms until they reached the couch along the wall opposite his desk. He set her down gently, reverently, and then stripped them both of their clothing.

When he covered her body with his, she knew.

This time it would be different.

31

A WEEK WENT BY, and then another. The Aces continued to struggle in exhibition play without Cal.

But not Eric. He was a machine again, and fuck if he knew what magic fairy dust his father was sprinkling on his food, but it was working. Every time Eric started, the Aces won.

His father attended every game now, and a tradition had been created. Game, then dinner out. Tonight, they chose a swanky steakhouse with a view of the ocean and slabs of meat so huge that it was no wonder the place was popular among the ballplayers.

He and his dad opted to wait at the bar until their table was ready. His father ordered ice water; Eric, a Budweiser. A row of TVs above the center of the circular bar were all tuned to different channels. ESPN was one of them, and they sat down in time to see highlights of the day's various exhibitions.

Eric watched his own slow-motion delivery from the mound as he struck out his fifth batter of the day. Damn, that had felt good. He struck out eight total, and the Aces beat the Washington Nationals 4-1.

"You looked really good out there today," Chet said.

"Thanks." He had *felt* good out there.

"Nicki knows what she's doing as a coach, doesn't she?"

"Better than anyone I've ever worked with."

She was a machine, too. The damn Energizer Bunny of baseball. She and Hunter had decided to move Zach Nelson into the starting rotation to replace Cal, but the kid wasn't ready, which meant Nicki was throwing herself into the job even more. Eric wondered if she was sleeping at the ballpark, because it seemed like she never left.

As if on cue, ESPN showed a clip of Nicki coming out to the mound midway through the seventh inning that day to consult with him and Riley Quinn. Eric clenched his jaw. The catcalls from the Nationals crowd were lewd and loud, but Nicki had kept her cool the entire time. Not once did she let on that she even heard what they were saying. But Eric heard. Every fucking word. And he shut them up by striking out the next batter.

The best way to beat guys like that is to win. Maybe she was right.

A loud, booming laugh from the front of the restaurant

made his ears prick up. It was followed immediately by the lyrical lilt of an Italian accent.

Eric turned to look just as the entire Bates clan spilled into the bar area in one loud group.

Of course. Of course he and his father would choose the same restaurant as Nicki and her family. The Aces were playing the Red Sox tomorrow, and it looked like the entire gang was in town for the show.

"Is that Nicki's family?" Chet asked.

Eric didn't have time to answer, because Isabella suddenly spotted them and let out a boisterous gasp. "Look who's here!"

She raced to the bar. Chet stood up and was instantly dragged into an Isabella bear hug.

"Oh, Chet. How wonderful to see you."

"It's been too long, Isabella."

"Too long. I'm so sorry about your Melody. Dear woman. So terrible."

"She is missed," Chet said.

Eric waited for resentment to surge but, strangely, it didn't.

Isabella tugged Eric in next. "My boy." She pulled back and pinched his cheek.

"Oh my gosh," Isabella whipped around to look at her family. "They should eat with us!"

"Absolutely," Andrew Bates said. He stuck out his hand to Chet, and the two men greeted each other with one-armed hugs.

Isabella didn't wait for Eric or Chet to agree. She walked
to the hostess stand, and Eric heard her tell the woman they
needed to add two people to their reservation.

The woman added more menus to the stack in her arms
and then asked the group to follow her. Eric paid for their
drinks at the bar. He looked up to find Nicki watching him,
but she glanced away as soon as their eyes collided.

The restaurant had given them a large private room in
the back. One entire wall was made of windows overlooking
the ocean. As they all filed in, he and his father were greeted
by more hearty hugs and pounds on the backs and how-the-
hell-are-ya's and one I'll-still-kick-your-ass glare from Meathead until Eric ended up in front of Robby and Nicki.

The room got eerily and obviously quiet. Eric tried to
keep his expression neutral but was afraid his face screamed,
YES, I HAD SEX WITH YOUR SISTER AGAIN.

"Nice job today," Robby said.

One giant exhale filled the room. "Thanks. It felt good."

There was a clinking noise, like someone hitting a bottle
with a spoon at a wedding. Nicki and Robby shared an eye-
roll. It could only mean one thing. Andrew Bates was about
to give a toast.

Eric's lips cracked with a smile. Andrew's dinner toasts
were legendary. He could find any reason on any occasion to
stand in front of his family and impart wisdom, gratitude, or
a bad joke that inevitably led to ribbing from his kids.

God, he had missed this.

"Robby, Nicki, please come here," Andrew said.

Nicki groaned. "Dad, no."

"Hush, Clutch. If there was ever a time for a toast, it is today."

Nicki and Robby eye-rolled again, this time dramatically for effect, and joined their father at the head of the table.

Once again, Nicki met Eric's eyes but quickly looked away.

Andrew cleared his throat. "I will never forget the first time my baby girl told me she wanted to play baseball like her brothers. There was nothing that could keep her away from the field. At first we thought she just wanted to tag along—"

Eric smiled behind his hand. He'd heard that speech so many times, he could practically recite it.

"And when we began to realize how special her talent was, that she was every bit as good as Robby, well... frankly, I was terrified."

Eric wrenched his gaze back to Andrew. This part was new.

"You see, there is nothing harder for a parent than to realize you cannot protect your children from everything. And your mother and I both knew, Nicki, that the path you were seeking was going to be very, very hard, and there would be people who didn't want to see you succeed. The obstacles you have faced would have stopped the strongest of men. You literally bear the scar of it."

Andrew's voice wavered slightly, but Eric barely noticed. His eyes were locked on Nicki, whose face had paled. The scar. What the hell had happened to her?

"But you have overcome every one of them," Andrew continued. "You have worked harder than anyone I have ever known, and now here you are. The first woman ever to coach in the Major Leagues."

His voice became thick, growing deeper with his emotion. He raised his glass.

"Tomorrow we will watch my daughter, my Clutch, coach against my son, Robby. I have never been prouder as a father than I am at this moment. Cheers."

They all raised their glasses and repeated the word.

Robby waved his hands. "OK, OK, enough of this crap. Where's the steak?"

It was like musical chairs. The entire family scattered and battled for a seat. And when the music stopped, the only two left open were right next to each other. Nicki looked pointedly at him before claiming one of them.

Eric lowered himself into the other. He waited a full ten minutes—until everyone had ordered and lost themselves in their own conversations—before looking at her.

She let out a long-suffering sigh. "Stop, Eric."

He dropped his voice. "What happened to you?"

"You're never going to let it go, are you?"

"No. Especially not after what your father just said."

Her mouth closed. He watched the muscles of her throat work as she swallowed, and his mind remembered the feel of his lips there. Finally, she gave up with a shake of her head.

"I got mugged in college. OK? That's it."

He was quiet for a beat, his chest tight. "You have to give me more than that. Who mugged you?"

"Just some guys. I was a senior. It was October. I went to a party with a friend. She got drunk, so I got annoyed and decided to walk home alone. It was stupid, but I took a shortcut through an alley. A group of guys followed me, started harassing me. When I told them to shove it, they beat me up."

Bile stung the back of his throat. He tightened his hold on her arms. "How bad?"

"I had a lot of bruises and some cuts—"

Eric let out a growl-like noise, which earned him a warning glare from Nicki. She was lucky he wasn't screaming out loud.

Her senior year. October. That was just a couple of months after he'd been called up. After he'd left her. "You should have told me."

"Why would I? You were gone by then."

And she believed he didn't care. Didn't love her. It's exactly what he'd wanted her to believe then.

Dinner dragged on for what seemed like hours. He put

on a good show, at least he thought he did. He answered when spoken to, laughed when expected to. But his mind was stuck on her.

By the time it was over, he was ready to claw at his own skin. Chet surprised everyone by secretly picking up the entire bill, which earned him another Isabella hug, this one with tears.

Eric saw and heard little of it. After saying their good-byes, Eric told his father to go on home without him.

Fifteen minutes later, he claimed his stool at Mac's. Ten minutes after that, he regretted it. Someone had dumped about fifty dollars into the juke box and programmed it to play nothing but Garth Brooks. Eric was one guitar solo from whipping his beer at the machine.

Mac set a Budweiser in front of him. "Bitch—"

Eric held up his hand. "Don't say it."

Mac shrugged and then looked over Eric's shoulder. "A Red Sox player in an Aces bar. That's something you don't see every day."

Eric followed Mac's gaze.

Ah, shit. Robby.

32

Robby stood just inside the doorway. Catching Eric's eye, he tipped his head toward the door behind him and then walked out.

Eric could only think of a few reasons why Robby would be there, and one of them meant Eric was about to die. He drained what was left of his beer, stood, and dropped a ten on the bar.

"Call the cops if you hear anything strange."

Mac snorted.

Eric spotted Robby standing next to his black Yukon in the parking lot, arms crossed and stance wide. Like he was waiting for a fight. Shit.

Eric took his time. "What do you want?"

"Get in. We're going for a drive."

And end up the next Jimmy Hoffa? No way. "I'm not going anywhere with you."

"I need to talk to you, and I can't do it here."

"What about?"

"Will you just get in the car?"

Eric rounded the front of the SUV and hauled himself into the passenger seat as Robby climbed in and started the car. They were silent as they pulled out of the parking lot and onto the quiet road that led away from downtown.

Eric looked in the backseat for duct tape and a shovel. "I'm kind of a big deal, Robby. If I go missing, people will notice."

Robby managed a snort-like laugh. Neither spoke again for another fifteen minutes until Robby turned into the entrance to a roadside beach and picnic area. It was weedy and dark with a crooked, rusty grill that looked like a tetanus shot waiting to happen.

"Wow. You really know how to show a guy a good time."

"Just get out."

Eric pushed open the door and climbed down onto the sandy soil. A moment later, he joined Robby in front of the car. Robby handed him a beer, peeled one for himself from a six-pack, and then set the rest on the hood.

"You're going to get me drunk before you kill me?"

"I'm not going to kill you."

"Then what are we doing here?"

Robby cracked open his beer and leaned back on the grill of the car. He swallowed and dug the toe of his shoes into the sand.

"Just say it, Robby."

"I need a favor."

"*You* need a favor from *me*?"

"Don't make this any harder than it needs to be."

"What do you need?"

"I'm worried about Nicki."

Eric spoke carefully. "So am I."

"I know. I saw how you looked at her tonight when my father mentioned her scar."

"She told me she got mugged."

Robby took a long drink. Then he cursed under his breath and peeled away from the car. He headed toward the water. Eric's mind called up a long-forgotten memory. Sophomore year. Spontaneous road-trip to the beach with some of the guys from the team. Getting wasted on the beach and laughing their asses off at the stupidest crap. Drunkenly telling Robby his sister was hot. Getting knocked on his ass in the sand for it.

Eric watched as Robby set his beer down and then grabbed a rock. He whipped into the water. Whatever the hell was on Robby's mind, it was serious. Eric set his beer on the car and then joined him at the water's edge.

"Talk."

Robby planted his hands on his hips and stared at the water. "I need to tell you something. And if you care at all about my sister, you will listen and swear on your mother's grave that you won't breathe a word of it to anyone. Especially Nicki."

"OK." He dragged the word out.

Robby hit him with a serious glare. "I mean it. Nicki would kill me if she knew I told you."

"Then maybe you shouldn't."

"I can't do this alone anymore. And neither can she, whether she'll ever admit it or not."

He heard the ring of an alarm in his mind. "What the hell are you talking about?"

Robby stared again at the water. "She didn't get mugged. That's what she tells people, but it's not true. She didn't want anyone to know the truth. My family and I are the only ones who do."

The alarm became a siren. "What's the real story?"

Robby swore again and looked at the ground. Eric fisted Robby's shirtsleeve. "You'd better spit it out, because I'm about to lose my shit."

"It wasn't a mugging. They knew who she was. Recognized her from the Sports Illustrated cover. They beat the shit out of her. Told her she didn't belong, told her to quit."

They told her to quit. Just like Eric had.

Bile rose in his throat as the siren became a deafening roar.

"That's not the worst part, though," Robby said.

"What do you mean? What could be worse?"

Wait.

No.

The world tilted beneath his feet. He bent and put his hands on his knees. "Don't say it, Robby. Please."

"She was raped."

Robby's voice had dropped so low, Eric wasn't sure he'd heard him. Or maybe it was the rush of blood in his own ears that had drowned out the words. The beach, the water, it all disappeared in a red haze as rage clouded his vision.

No. Not just rage. *Agony.* A sound emerged from his chest but was cut off by the feel of Robby grabbing his shirt. "Listen to me."

Eric blinked and looked up, trying to focus on Robby's face.

"I know how you feel right now. I know you want to scream bloody fucking murder and then go kill something. But you need to listen to me. OK? She can't know that you know."

Robby let go, and Eric felt his knees give way. He sank onto the sand. Everything he ate and drank that day staged a grief-stricken revolution in his stomach. He rolled onto his knees and threw up on the sand.

"I know, man," Robby said. "I did the same thing."

Eric dry-heaved a few times and then sank back on his ass. He used his sneakered foot to bury the mess in the sand and then fell onto his back. The sand was cold and wet, and he could feel it seeping through his jeans and his t-shirt. Robby dropped down next to him.

"How did I not know about this? The trial would have been all over the news."

Robby scoffed. "There was no trial."

"They were never caught?!"

"She couldn't identify them. The rape kit didn't match anyone."

Eric's stomach roiled again at *rape kit*. He threw his arm over his eyes to block out the images his brain was determined to force on him. Nicki, alone in an emergency room. Bloody and beaten. Forced to endure another violation so investigators could collect evidence.

"They got away with it," Eric said.

"Not according to Nicki. She says the best way to beat them—"

"Is to win," Eric whispered.

Robby rolled his head and looked at him in surprise.

"She gave me the same speech when I went after Kas in the clubhouse."

It hadn't made sense to him then. In fact, her attitude had seemed infuriatingly naïve. Now he understood everything—the mask she wore, the empty determination, her reluctance with him.

He finally understood *her*.

Robby hooked an arm under his head. "She changed after it happened. I know any woman would. But Nicki suddenly cut everything out of her life except baseball. I've never seen anyone so focused. So driven. I've never seen anyone work so fucking hard. And not just at baseball. She got her master's degree and then her Ph.D. It was like she had something to prove."

His voice trailed off for a moment.

"She doesn't see it, though," he continued. "I've tried talking to her about it, and she just tells me to shove it. My parents are afraid she's never going to date again, never get married. You were the last guy she was with. How's that for some cruel irony?"

Eric thought he couldn't be any more destroyed than he already was, but then the weight of Robby's latest bomb settled on his chest.

He'd taken her on the goddamned floor. Was that the first time she'd had sex since—Oh, God. That's why she had flipped out afterward.

He was going to be sick again. Eric sat up and shot to his feet. "You have to take me back."

Robby jumped up and grabbed his arm. "Hey. Whatever you're thinking right now, forget it. You can't let on that you know anything about this."

"You can't ask that of me. I can't pretend."

"I can, and you will. Because if she knows I told you, she will never speak to me again."

Eric felt like his air was being cut off, like somone had wrapped their hands around his throat and squeezed. He was trapped. Screwed no matter what he did. There was no way he could keep Robby's secret. Not after making love to her. He had to know she was OK. He had to apologize for the way they'd done it, gather her close, and promise to cherish her if she'd just give him the chance to make it right.

But he sure as shit couldn't tell Robby *that*. Because it would kill Nicki if he told Robby about *them*.

Eric clenched his fists and let out a shout of frustration, punching the air.

"You need to keep it together, Weaver. I told you this for a reason."

"What?" Eric growled. "What possible reason could you have if I can't do anything about it? Just to torture me? Do you hate me that much?"

"I used to, but here's the thing." Robby stepped closer. "I also think you still love her."

Eric froze. Every muscle tensed. He didn't deny it because there was no point. "What do you need me to do?"

"Watch out for her. Be there for her. Because once she gets this job, once she achieves *this*, I don't know what comes next. No one can go this hard for this long without crashing. And when she does, you might be the only one who can catch her."

Eric studied his former friend—the defeated hang of his shoulders, the forlorn darkness in his eyes. He had never taken the time to mourn the loss of their friendship, but he felt it now. Robby had been like a brother. Eric lost a lot when he walked away from Nicki. He didn't know if they could ever get past that, but they shared at least one thing.

They both loved the same woman and would do anything to protect her.

The fact that Robby, despite all the history between them, trusted him to be the one to take care of her meant more than Eric could have articulated. So, he went with the only language ballplayers understood. "Fuck, Robby."

Robby's mouth twisted into a grimace. "Yeah." He sighed then and turned toward the car. "I gotta get going. I'll take you back."

They rode in silence again, enveloped in darkness, lost in their own regrets. Eric stared out the window until the bar came into view again. Only then did he look over at Robby.

He had a thousand things he needed to say but couldn't find the right words to say them. "You remember that time I got pulled in the seventh, and then that stupid fucking reliever lost my lead?"

Robby snorted a laugh as he turned into the parking lot. "Yeah, I remember."

"You got me drunk and forced me to play Halo all night until I stopped bitching about it."

"Which you never did."

"Do you remember what you said to me that night?"

Robby's hands tightened on the wheel. "I'm not letting my best friend quit just because the bases are loaded."

"I still play Halo when I need to settle down over a loss. I think about what you said every time. Thank you for that."

"You didn't need to thank me. That's what friends do for each other."

"I'm sorry I fucked that up, Robby."

Robby nodded and slowed to a stop in front of the bar. Eric hesitated, but then grabbed the door handle.

"Eric."

He looked back. Robby held out his right hand. Eric stared at it, surprised and overwhelmed. Then he reached across his body to accept the handshake. It wasn't exactly a truce. It was barely a peace offering. But it was a far cry from a punch in the face, and that mattered. It mattered a helluva lot.

They squeezed hands one more time, and then Eric hauled himself out of the car. Robby drove away with a small wave. As he watched his old friend's taillights disappear, Eric exhaled for what seemed like the first time in hours.

The drive back to his house was a long exercise in torture—like watching another team's home run make that painful, slow-motion flight over the wall.

But for the first time in Eric's life, the comparison didn't seem an equal metaphor. Baseball didn't even come close.

He weighed a thousand pounds as he walked into his house. The glow of the backyard lights drew him through the kitchen and across the living room. He looked out the sliding-glass patio doors and saw his father sitting alone on a deck chair, a glass of water in one hand while the other toyed with edges of a book on the table next to him. The old man went through a book a day, it seemed.

Eric studied Chet for a moment, really studied him. The man who once twitched with impatience now exuded a calm sturdiness. Sobriety had eased the lines around his eyes and the clench in his jaw.

His entire life, Eric had wondered why his mother stayed with his father. What makes a woman as amazing as his mom stay with a man who couldn't keep his dick in his pants around other women? Who loved the game more than his own family and just expected them to accept it? Why would she stand by a man who made her cry far more often than he made her laugh?

Maybe this man, the one sitting before Eric now, was the man she'd fallen in love with, the man whose return she'd been waiting for.

Eric opened the door and walked out. His father looked up. "Wondered when you'd get home."

"I, ah, I met up with Robby for a drink." Which was sort of true.

Chet adopted the sad smile Eric had come to recognize. His father felt guilty about something.

"I'm glad you two seem to be friends again."

Eric shrugged. "Not sure if I'd call us friends yet."

"I hope you can someday."

"Me, too."

Chet stood with a war-weary sigh. "It's amazing," he said, pensive. "The ripple effect your actions can have."

He scuffed along the concrete patio toward the edge of the pool that Eric almost never used.

"They warned me about that in rehab," Chet said. "The hardest part sometimes is coming to terms with all the ways you've changed the world around you. It's easy to not see it when you're a drunk. Addiction is self-serving. It allows you to ignore everything except your own needs. And then you get sober and you look around, and you see the path of destruction you created in every direction."

Chet turned around. "It was nice being with the Bates family tonight, but I saw the destruction again. Where would you be, where would Nicki be, if I hadn't made you break up with her?"

The air seeped from Eric's lungs. A hundred responses flitted through his mind, but when he finally spoke, the words surprised them both.

"It's not your fault."

He could blame his father for a lot of things—for hurting his mother, for being a demanding asshole, for countless things. But Eric couldn't blame his father for what happened with Nicki.

It wasn't his father's fault that Eric had been too immature back then to trust Nicki enough to stand by him if he failed. It wasn't his father's fault that Eric had been too selfish to consider anything but his own needs, his own fears.

No, it wasn't his father's fault that Eric chose to put the game first.

Chet had simply given him a convenient excuse.

Eric stood taller and repeated the words that no longer seemed so shocking. "It's not your fault, Dad. The decision to leave Nicki was mine and mine alone."

He walked back inside before he did something stupid. Like hug his father.

Eric had allowed himself to believe all these years that there was no one else in the world who understood his what-ever-it-takes need to sacrifice everything for the game. But Nicki did. They were the same person fighting the same battle. He knew that now.

He had been driven by the need to win his father's approval the only way he knew how—the game.

She was driven to defeat a group of nameless, faceless phantoms the only way she knew how—the game.

How could he fault her for that?

He couldn't, because they were the same.

And that changed everything.

33

Every night, the dream got worse. More vivid. More real. It gripped Nicki in choking terror until she woke up sweaty and out of breath.

Even when she managed to fall back to sleep, morning yawned like a black hole that sucked her into a soundless routine.

Every day, Ray Fox continued his unrelenting crusade against her.

Every day, Kas taunted her.

Every day she ignored him.

Until today.

Today, more than a week after the Red Sox game, Kas went too far.

Nicki shoved open the door to the clubhouse with both hands. She didn't bother to announce herself first, which she normally did to give guys time to get dressed, if necessary. A couple of them let out surprised yelps and scrambled to cover their nakedness.

"Kas, I need a minute," Nicki said, storming through the clubhouse to his stall.

His back was to her, a towel wrapped around his waist.

"Yeah, well, I don't have a minute," he drawled, reaching for a stick of deodorant on the shelf in his stall.

"I need you to stop what you're doing and look at me."

He took his time turning around. As he did, the towel somehow managed to fall from his waist.

"Oops," he deadpanned.

Nicki didn't look down, didn't even blink. "You dropped something."

"You told me to stop what I was doing. I was trying to get dressed. Can't have it both ways, sweetheart."

Harper Brody swore from two stalls away. "For Christ's sake, Kas."

Kas responded without letting his glare stray from Nicki's face. "I don't recall inviting you into this conversation, Brody."

The clubhouse had gone silent, and Nicki felt the weight of every set of eyes boring into her back. "You missed the afternoon workout."

"I'm not doing yoga."

"I'm sure you're aware the team's policy for missing required workouts during spring training."

He scratched his dick.

"Hunter will expect your check for five thousand dollars on his desk tomorrow," Nicki said.

She turned on her heel.

"I'm not paying any fucking fine," Kas said.

"Yes, you are," she yelled over her shoulder.

She sensed what would happen next before it actually happened, but it still didn't make her reflexes work fast enough to stop it. Kasinski's arm shot out, and his fingers wrapped around Nicki's upper arm.

He jerked her around. "Listen, bitch."

The room erupted and everything seemed to happen at once. Harper Brody hurdled over his bench. Zach Nelson ran from the other side of the room with an angry shout.

Riley Quinn yelled into the shower area. "Weaver! Get in here."

Nicki barely heard or saw any of it. Every one of her senses was focused on one thing—the squeeze of Kas's fingers on her arm.

"Remove your hand," she said, amazed at how calm her voice sounded.

"Or what?"

"Or you will face disciplinary action."

The entire clubhouse held its breath. Kas snorted. "Right."

Brody took a menacing step forward. "Let her go. Now."

Eric ran into the room, hair wet, chest bare, a half-buttoned pair of jeans covering his lower half. The noise he made wasn't human.

Kas surveyed the room. What he saw apparently convinced him to let her go.

"Thank you," Nicki said crisply.

She felt the staff's eyes following her retreat through the door.

The adrenaline crash didn't hit until she made it safely through the tunnel to the dugout outside. But when it hit, it hit hard. Her hands shook as she rubbed them across her face. Then she fisted them against her stomach and tried to slow her quick pants of breath.

She'd wanted to hit him. The instant Kas grabbed her, she wanted to whip around and slug him and throw him to the ground like she had learned in self-defense classes. She wanted to kick him and pummel him and scream. The urge for violence was so strong that it burned her from the inside.

Her arm throbbed where he had manhandled her. She absently rubbed it.

"Are you all right?"

She gasped and looked to her right. She hadn't even heard Eric behind her. His hair was still wet, but he'd thrown on a t-shirt and shoes.

"I'm fine."

"Let me see your arm."

"I said I'm fine."

He stared pointedly. With a sigh, she held it out for his

inspection. He pushed up the sleeve of her sweatshirt and ran his fingers over the spot that bore the red outline of Kas's fingers.

His jaw clenched. "Does it hurt?"

"No," she lied. She pulled her arm back. "I'm OK, Eric."

"I am going to end him, Nicki."

"He's not worth it."

"But you are."

Her heart did a backflip.

This was the closest she had stood to him in days. She could smell his skin and the soap he used in the shower. She spied a miniscule speck of blood dotting his jaw. He must have cut himself shaving, and she had to put some distance between them or else she was going to reach out and touch the tiny wound.

She had felt his heavy gaze all week everywhere she went. Sometimes, he looked like a puppy she'd just kicked. Other times, he burned her with an intense stare, his green eyes laced with a restrained urgency she'd never seen before.

"I have to go." She brushed past him but he blocked her path.

"Wait," he said. "I want to show you something."

Her response was automatic. "I can't. I still have a lot of work to do."

"Ten minutes, Nicki. That's all I'm asking."

She felt hot and conflicted. "What is it?"

"It's a surprise."

"Maybe we shouldn't."

"Think of it as an adventure."

She followed him with an outward *ugh*. Inside, it was a different story.

He led her through the tunnel and into an alcove where the maintenance elevator was located.

She side-eyed him. "Where, exactly, are you taking me?"

Eric pushed the button to the top floor, and they rode up in silence. When the doors opened, she darted out ahead of him.

"Turn left," he said behind her.

She glanced briefly behind him but then did as he said. "Where am I going?"

"You'll know it when you see it."

The service hallway was long and dark, with doors lining the right side that accessed the various press boxes and VIP suites of the ballpark. At the far end was an exit.

"See it yet?"

"All I see is an exit sign."

He caught up with her. "Look out the window."

She stopped at the door and stood high on her tip-toes to look out the window. And sucked in a gasp. From this little corner fire escape, she could see not only the entire ballfield below, but also the ocean in the distance.

"Best view in all of St. Augustine," he said.

He reached around her and tried the handle, his arm brushing hers as he did.

She stepped sideways. "Won't that set off an alarm or something?"

The door opened. "Or something."

He winked. "Come on," he said, holding the door open for her.

The platform groaned under their weight as they walked out onto the fire escape. He sat first, letting his legs hang over the side of the floor. She followed slowly, warily.

"Still afraid of heights?" he asked.

"No. You still afraid of snakes?"

"Yes. Terrified."

She laughed quietly, gradually relaxing enough to lean her arms on the lower rung of the railing in front of them. She actually was still afraid of heights, but not so much with Eric next to her. He was the only person who had ever gotten her onto a roller coaster. She'd never felt safe enough with anyone else.

"Impressive, huh?" he said, leaning back on his hands.

"How'd you discover this spot?"

"Rookie prank my first year. The older guys sent me on a wild goose chase that ended here, and then they locked me out. I had to walk down the fire escape and all the way around the yard to get back in."

"Doesn't sound like much of a prank."

"I was wearing women's underwear."

She barked out a laugh that took her completely by surprise.

"Jeezus, Nicki. That sounds as rusty as that old 4Runner you used to drive."

This time she snorted.

"Do I need to pat you on the back or something?"

"Stop," she joked, but she didn't mean it. Eric could always make her laugh. She might have missed that more than anything else after they broke up.

"This is where I came after I got the call that my mom died."

"Alone?"

"I didn't want to lose it in front of the guys."

"Did you lose it when you got out here?"

His eyes stared into a distant space for a moment. "Yeah," he finally answered.

Eric had cried alone on a fire escape when his mother died. There was so much wrong in that statement that Nicki felt tears spring to her eyes. Her heart wanted to wrap her arms around him, but her stubborn fears wouldn't let her.

All she had to give him were empty platitudes. "I'm so sorry about your mom, Eric."

"So am I."

The world got wavy behind a layer of wetness. The ocean in the distance was choppy with the coming tide. White caps soared and crashed, a natural turbulence that matched her emotions. Coming up here was a mistake.

She pulled away from the railing and stood. "I should go."

"Why?"

"I still have a ton of work to do tonight." And because she was suffocating.

"Gonna lock yourself in the video room? Bury yourself in game film?"

The sharpness in his voice, so different from his tenderness before, made her skin jump. "So what if I do?" she snapped back. "Why do you care?"

"Do you really want me to answer that?"

Nicki grabbed the door handle.

Eric jumped up. "Wait."

He covered her hand with his. She didn't pull away. Couldn't.

They were inches apart. He reached up with his other hand and let his thumb caress her bottom lip.

"Don't," she pleaded. Yet she didn't put any distance between them.

"I've missed talking to you," he said.

Without even trying, he managed to draw her closer. Just the heat of his touch had her leaning, slowly, inch by aching inch, toward the grounding he alone had ever offered.

"You were my best friend, Nicki."

She leaned until their breaths mingled, until their noses touched.

"I would give anything to go back in time," he said.

He dipped his head to hover above her lips, barely touching. He nudged her mouth and she nudged back.

Her eyes slid closed as she lost herself in the what-if. What if she leaned all the way and let his lips cover hers? What if she sank into his strength the way she wanted to? What if they *could* go back in time?

At least to that question, she had an answer.

"I shouldn't have gotten out of your car," she whispered, the truth a tiny bomb inside her. "I should have fought for you."

He let out a groan, letting his forehead drop to hers as his hand fully cupped her cheek. "Fight for me now," he whispered, voice rough and painful.

She turned her face away. "I can't."

"You can. We can fight together."

"It would ruin me."

"Or save us both."

Nicki tilted her face to the sky. Everything hurt. She couldn't have come out here. She turned the door handle, his hand falling away as she did. The door swung open, and she walked through.

Her voice acted on its own as she spoke over her shoulder. "I lied to you about my tattoo. It doesn't mean never again."

"What does it mean?"

"Never stop fighting." Oh, God. She couldn't breathe. "I have to go home."

Her feet carried her back inside, down the hallway, all the way to the elevator. But with every stop, the word echoed in her mind.

Home.

Eric was her home.

But she was too lost to find her way back.

One week later, Nicki stopped taking Robby's calls.

Busy, she texted him.

Make time, he texted back.

She turned off her phone.

ERIC HUNG up the phone and swung his legs off his bed. The ice pack taped to his shoulder and bicep dripped onto his leg.

I'm worried about her, Robby had said. *This is what I was afraid of.*

Eric stood and tore at the tape holding the ice to his skin.

This had gone on long enough.

He had given her enough space.

It was officially time to play ball.

36

Someone was beating on her front door. Nicki stumbled on her thirty-fifth push-up. Her elbows weakened, and she fell to the floor of the living room. Who the hell would be at her door at ten o'clock?

A gruff won't-take-no voice yelled through the door. "Let me in, Nicki."

She grabbed the towel next to her, mopped the sweat from her brow, and padded to the door. She pulled it open and nearly fell down as he barreled inside. He spun, took one look at her, and swore.

"Are you *training* right now?"

"So what if I am?"

"It's ten o'clock at night, Nicki."

"So?"

"It's a little obsessive, don't you think?"

She folded her arms across her chest. Sweat slicked her

arms, her abdomen. So what if she'd been working out? She was an athlete. That's what athletes did. "What are you doing here?"

"Checking to make sure you're not dead. Did you turn your phone off?"

"I-yes."

"Why the hell have you stopped talking to Robby?"

"H-he called you?"

"He's worried about you."

"I'm fine."

"Dammit!"

She jumped at his sudden exclamation.

"I'm sick of that word, Nicki."

"But I am fine."

"You're not fine. You haven't been fine for weeks."

"Go home, Eric."

He grabbed her shoulders. "Not until you talk to me."

No. I can't. I can't talk to you. I can't see you. I can't be around you. I can't.

He lightened his grip. "Babe, please. Talk to me."

She pulled free of his hands and his penetrating stare. "I have to take a shower. I have to go to bed. You have to go home."

She turned.

He gripped her elbow.

She spun around.

He dropped his voice. "I know you didn't get mugged, Nicki."

It took a moment for the words and the meaning behind them to register, and when they did ... No. No no no no no. That wasn't possible.

"Robby.... Robby told you?"

Why couldn't she breathe?

Eric tried to draw her close, an unbearable sadness on his face. "He was worried about you."

Nicki yanked away from him and raced to the bathroom. She shut the door. Cranked the shower on hot. Why couldn't she breathe? Why was her heart racing? Why would Robby do that? Why...?

Shit. She was lightheaded.

She stepped into the shower and leaned on the wall.

Why were her legs so weak?

Her knees gave way, and she sank to the floor of the tub. What the hell was happening? The water was hot and punishing against her skin. Her work-out clothes clung to her.

She curled into a ball.

She heard a sound.

Realized it was from her own chest.

37

ERIC STOOD OUTSIDE THE BATHROOM, arms braced on either side of the doorframe. He heard the shower turn on. He could wait her out. Did she think he would just leave because she was in there?

But then he heard something else.

A thump.

A keening.

Fuck.

He threw open the door and stalked inside. He jerked the shower curtain so hard that half the rings broke. What he saw gutted him like a baseball bat to the stomach.

He reached over and turned off the water. Nicki jumped and tried to sit up. "Get out of here, Eric."

He bent and slid his arms under her. She beat against his shoulders. "Get out!"

He lifted her out of the tub, water soaking his shirt and

his pants. She continued to beat on his arms, his chest. And holy crap, was she strong, but he turned and whisked her out of the bathroom and into her bedroom.

"Eric, please...." Gone was the anger, the shouting. Her voice was a desperate plea now. "Let me go."

He lowered them both to the bed and held her on his lap. He wrapped an arm around her waist to anchor her to him and palmed the back of her head to hold her face to his neck.

"Please..." she whimpered.

He tightened his hold on her. "Talk to me, baby. Just talk to me." Dammit, he'd waited too long. He had given her too much space, too much room. He should have been taking care of her.

"You don't understand," she sputtered. "I can't... I can't...."

"You can't what, Clutch?"

She suddenly burrowed her face into his neck and grabbed his shirt and shook. She was crying. Fuck. Fuck. She was crying.

He grabbed the blanket that was balled up next to them and pulled it over her body. Then he slipped his hands underneath and stroked her wet skin. Her back. Her hips. Her stomach. Her arms. He caressed and held her and pressed kisses to her temples and her wet hair, and he let her sob against him, every shake of her body a knife to his heart.

It seemed to go on forever, but finally the sobs began to

slow. Her breathing hiccupped and caught. He felt her swallow. Another minute passed, and her hands loosened against his shirt. Then she cleared her throat, and she uttered words that slayed him to the bone.

"I tried to fight back."

Just four simple words that in any other context would have been small, insignificant, nothing. But here, now, they were everything.

The air escaped Eric's lungs in a single breath. "What happened?"

"I went to a party and left alone."

He pressed his lips to her temple, silently encouraging her to go on even as he dreaded hearing it from her voice.

"They started following me. One of them said he recognized me." She swallowed. "You're that bitch on the baseball team. That's what he said."

He closed his eyes and sucked in a breath.

"Then they all started in. Yelling stuff. I tried to run through the alley."

Her hand started playing with the chest hair sticking out of the top of his t-shirt. "It happened so fast. I turned around and told them to fuck off. I knew it was going to be bad as soon as I said it. They caught up to me. One of them grabbed me."

He was afraid to move, afraid to breathe, afraid to do anything that might make her stop talking, even while his entire soul was screaming for her to be quiet. Robby had given him just the most basic of facts. Nicki was painting the entire brutal picture.

"He grabbed my arm. And then another one grabbed my other arm. And then another one punched me in the face. He had a ring on his finger. I couldn't see anything for a second because blood dripped into my eye."

The scar. Eric couldn't hold back the sound that emerged from his chest.

"He got in my face. He started saying things like how I shouldn't be on the team. I started to fight back. I started kicking with my legs. I got one of my arms free and hit him."

She was talking fast now. Words spilled from her mouth as if she couldn't stop them even if she tried. "He went crazy. He started attacking me. The other guys couldn't even hold on to me. I fell to the ground and he started kicking me. And then he told his friends to hold me down."

Eric was going to throw up. Bile rose in his throat, riding a wave of rage and helplessness. He turned his face fully into her hair and closed his eyes.

"I couldn't stop them. I was strong, but they were bigger than me. And there were so many of them. The one who hit me, he got on top of me."

She burrowed into his chest. "I remember ... I remember kicking as hard as I could. And then he yelled something, and I felt ... I felt my pants being pulled down, my underwear. And then ..."

She stopped cold.

Eric squeezed his arms around her. He could barely get words out around the lump in his throat. "You don't have to say it, Nicki."

But she did. She said it.

"He raped me."

Eric let out a sound that was half-sob, half-growl and rolled with her on the bed. His lips kissed her hair, her face.

Her hands fisted his shirt again. "I just stayed there after they left. I don't even know how long. The pavement was dirty and wet, and I just sort of curled up. I just kept thinking about the game. Practicing pitches in my head. Then I snapped out of it. I fixed my clothes and went to the hospital."

He tried to block the picture from his mind, but he couldn't. And it was that image—of her laying there, beaten and scared, left naked and crying on the dirty pavement like so much garbage—that finally sent his emotions out of control. She'd been battered and beaten and violated, and then she'd cowered on the ground practicing pitches in her head. He buried his face in her neck and let the tears that had been threatening for so long finally break through.

He was crying. Fuck. He was crying big heaving cries.

He splayed his hands against her back.

She felt her hands on his face. "Eric."

He clung to her.

She forced his face up to hers.

And she kissed him.

He was robbed of breath. Robbed of thought.

"I need you," she whispered. And then she kissed him again. Longer this time. Deeper.

Eric groaned against her mouth. He needed her, too. He needed her like air.

But not like this. He rose onto all fours and buried his face into the crook of her neck. "No, Nicki. Wait."

She moaned and tried to pull him back.

"Not like this, baby. Please."

She slammed her hands into his chest and shoved him away. "What? I'm unclean now? You don't want me now?"

"What? No. Jeezus, no." He cupped her cheek. "You can't think that, Nicki."

She rolled out from under him and evaded his attempts to hold onto her.

He jumped out of bed and followed her as she fled back to her bathroom. "I just meant that I don't want to take advantage of you right now."

She tried to shut the door. He shoved his arm in the way.

He watched as she yanked a towel off the metal bar on the wall. "I don't need your fucking pity, Eric."

She turned her back on him and whipped her wet work-out tank over her head.

"You know that's not what I meant. I want you so much it hurts."

He reached out to brush the cold, wet hair from the nape of her neck and replaced it with his lips. His arms slid around her waist from behind, and his mouth kissed a path around to her shoulder.

"They were never caught," she whispered. "That's why I have to win. That's why I can't stop. I have to win. So I can beat them."

"I know, baby. I know."

He turned her around in his arms and leaned his forehead against hers. They stood like that, breathing each other in, for several long moments. He didn't know what made her move, but she finally lifted her lips and pressed them against his.

God, he wanted her, but he held himself back.

She wrenched her mouth away with a frustrated argh. "I'm not fragile, Eric."

"But I am." His forehead came down on hers again as his hands cradled her face. "I can't do this and then lose you again, Nicki. I can't. I won't survive."

"I don't understand you. I thought this is what you wanted. What do you *want*?"

"I want forever."

38

Forever. The word floated. It soared and sank, burrowed inside and warmed her within.

And then it burned. Because it wasn't possible. Not anymore.

"I want to kiss you until you make that little whimper noise you make." His voice was deep, raspy, like it hurt just to talk. "I want to lay you down in my bed and claim you every night."

No. Stop. She wanted to cover her ears to block out the words and the impossible images they created.

"I want to go to sleep with you in my arms and wake up with you next to me. I want to hold your hand on roller-coasters and share popcorn at the movies."

She tried to pull away, but he held her. "I want to binge-watch Netflix with you and get mad when you watch an episode without me. I want to wear stupid Halloween costumes together and kiss you on New Year's Eve—"

"Halloween? Netflix? Those things belong to other people, Eric. Not me. I don't get to have those things."

"Why not?"

"Because.... because I can't!"

"Then what exactly do you think you've won?"

"Nothing! That's the point! I don't even have the job yet."

"The job." His voice was flat, and for the second time that night, he looked like she'd slapped him.

He let go of her and stepped back. "Who gives a shit about the job right now? Did you not hear what Cal said to us? Do you really think he wouldn't give up every single year of his career for one more day with his sister?"

"What the hell does Cal have to do with us?"

"What happened to you was horrible, Nicki. And it kills me to know you went through it. But if you use it as an excuse to live some empty life with nothing but the game to come home to, then you haven't won anything. The game will never love you back."

Throwing Cal's grieving words at her was a low-blow. She lashed out with a fist to his chest. "You left me!" The words burst from her on a sob. A tear escaped down her cheek. "I loved you, and you left me!"

"I know," he whispered, reaching up to wipe the tear

with his knuckle. "But we have a second chance, Nicki. Right now."

"No." She pushed his hand away. "It's too late, Eric. For us."

He gripped her arms. "It's not. Don't say that."

"You're the one who sent us on this path, not me! I wouldn't even have gone to that stupid party if not—"

She stopped. She couldn't say it. She didn't blame him. Not anymore.

His features froze. "If not for what?"

She squeezed her eyes shut. "Nothing."

"If not for *me*?"

She opened her eyes. His image danced before her through tear-coated eyelashes. "The only reason I went out that night was because my roommate said I was being pathetic for crying over you."

His face twisted. He let her go with such force that she stumbled back against the doorframe. But in the very next instant, he crushed her against his body and buried his face in her neck with a gut-wrenching sound. "I'm sorry. God, Nicki. I'm so sorry."

He started to shake against her, and she wanted to scream. She wanted to lash out at the world for the injustice, for everything they'd lost. Instead, she clung to him, held him, rocked him as he cried against her shoulder.

"It's not your fault, Eric," she choked. "It's their fault. Only theirs. I don't blame you, but it happened. We can't change it. We can't undo it. All we can do is live with the consequences."

He dragged his forehead to her temple. His wet, bristled cheek was like sandpaper against hers. He held the side of her head with his hands and sucked in a shaky breath. Then he dragged her mouth to his and kissed her. Frantically. Desperately. Their tears mingled and dripped, and when she pulled back to take a breath, he held her.

"I can't live with the consequences anymore," he said.

"We don't have a choice."

"We do. All you have to do is say it. Just say the words, and we will figure it out."

"What? What do you want me to say?"

"Tell me you love me."

Her lips trembled against the words, against the truth, as she whispered into the crook of his neck. "I love you."

His mouth crushed against hers again. He slowed down only long enough to bend at the knees and hoist her up in his arms. She wrapped her legs around his waist and buried her face against his shoulder as he carried her back to her bed. He lowered her down and followed gently.

Passion became wonder. Urgency faded into content-ment. Desire became something more. His hands cradled her head, tenderly holding her in place as his thumbs rubbed lazy circles against her cheekbones. He kissed her like he would never tire of it.

The tremble in his voice matched the tremor in her heart.

"I love you so much, Nicki. I always have."

She threaded her hands in his hair. "Show me."

And so he did.

He cherished her with his lips. Nicki arched into him as he slid down her body, leaving a hot trail of kisses until he hovered above her belly button. She looked down at him to find his eyes trained on hers.

"I want to do it right this time, Nicki," he vowed.

"You've always done it right."

He shook his head. "Never. It's never been enough. Tonight is about you. What you want. Tell me what you need."

Tears burned her eyes again at the tenderness of his words, his gaze. She threaded her fingers in his hair. "I just want you."

His hands tugged gently at her pants, and she lifted her hips to help him ease them off her.

"Eric," she moaned, tugging him back up to her. She needed him. Needed his kiss and his strength. He kissed his way back up her body and met her seeking lips with his own. He kissed her until she was achy again and writhing beneath him.

The outside world disappeared. The past faded away. There was only now. Only him. Only them, and a profound sense of safety.

There was a time when she believed she would never feel safe again.

Until now.

He shed his clothes. They made love slowly, their bodies moving with the gentle rhythm of promises. Afterward, he pulled her tightly against his body. "We'll make this work," he vowed.

"How," she whispered.

"I don't know. I just know we don't have a choice anymore."

For now, she would cling to that.

And hope the morning never came.

THINGS WERE JUST GETTING good with what's-her-name when Ray Fox's cellphone rang next to the bed. He groaned and grabbed the back of her head. She had a tongue like a lizard and the imagination of a porn star.

"Right there, right there," he grunted.

She obeyed, and he felt the stirrings of his release. His phone switched to voicemail but then immediately started ringing again.

"Fuck!" Ray slammed his fist onto the bed and pushed at what's-her-name's head. "Get off me."

She rose up on her knees. "Can't you let it ring?"

He ignored her and rolled over. He grabbed the phone and answered without bothering to look at the caller ID.

"This had better be fucking good," he growled.

"Oh, it is," said the voice on the other line. "It definitely is."

SHE WAS STILL THERE. Devin knew it before even opening his eyes. He could feel the warmth of her body and smell the fruity scent of her shampoo. His body woke up ready to go, but when he rolled over and saw her there, sound asleep, her lips parted slightly and her naked skin barely covered by the sheet, he didn't have the heart to wake her. Abby rarely got enough sleep as it was, and it had been a late night.

He had picked her up at the airport last night after she returned from another quick trip to New York. She insisted she needed to work until well past midnight, but then he'd kept her awake for far different reasons.

Oh, man. He had to get up. Otherwise, Abby would definitely not be getting any more sleep.

Careful not to disturb her, he rolled out of bed and pulled on the pair of jeans that he'd tossed onto the floor the night before. He padded out of the bedroom and into the kitchen. The coffee was already brewing, thanks to the daily clock function. He poured a cup and headed for his home office.

He was only part-way through last night's emails when his phone buzzed. It was a text from Todd Marshall. **You see this? Why didn't they quote us?**

He included a link to the Wall Street Journal business briefs.

Devin had to scroll through several items to find what he was looking for.

ACES TO GO PUBLIC?

DANE ENTERPRISES MIGHT BE *ready to take the Vegas Aces public. Sources say Bennett Dane III, head of the Dane corporate empire, has held talks with several potential investors and hopes the move will keep the team alive but off the family books. But it would also mean an end to one of Major League Baseball's longest-running family-owned baseball franchises and raises questions about what will happen to current Aces president and Dane-family playboy Devin Dane...*

HE COULDN'T READ ANYMORE. Rage turned his vision red. He dialed his brother's cellphone.

"You sonuvabitch."

Bennett laughed. "Is that any way to talk to your boss?"

"What the hell is this? What are you trying to pull?"

"I'm trying to help you out, little brother. Some gratitude would be nice."

Devin shot to his feet. "Gratitude? You motherfucker—"

"Calm down. You're clearly in over your head with this Nicki Bates thing. I figured I'd give you some extra incentive for fixing this debacle."

"Devin?" He spun around. Abby stood in the doorway, stifling a yawn. She wore his button-down from the night before, and it hung loosely on her small frame like an invitation to see what was inside. Her hair was messy from sleep and sex, and her eyes were pinched with fatigue and concern. He got that wind-knocked-out-of-him feeling he always felt when he looked at her.

But it was different this time. Because the entire world had changed in the past two minutes.

"Devin!" His brother barked on the other end of the phone.

Devin ended the call and dropped the phone. "Did I wake you up?"

Abby shook her head. "I smelled coffee. But then I heard you talking in here and –"

"What did you hear?"

She blinked. "Nothing. Why?"

Oh, good. That was nice. Way to raise her suspicions.

He shook his head. "I'm not really awake yet. You should go back to bed. It's early."

She walked into the room and, yawning again, grabbed the remote from his desk. "I'm usually up by five. This is sleeping in for me."

She turned on the TV and changed the channel to ESPN. She then stole his coffee mug from the desk. Mesmerized, he watched as she brought it to her lips and took a sip. He loved her lips. He loved what she could *do* with her lips. He loved the way they looked when she smiled and laughed, when she pulled them together in concentration, when she chewed on them in nervousness, when she touched them to his and whispered.

He blinked. She had just spoken to him.

"I'm sorry. What?"

Her eyebrows drew together. "Are you sure you're OK?"

"I haven't had enough caffeine."

For a fleeting moment, he thought about telling her about Bennett. Hell, it was in the Wall Street Journal. She would find out anyway. But he couldn't stand to be face-to-face with her when she realized he was still just a puppet on his family's strings. He couldn't stand for her to find out yet he wasn't really the man she thought he had grown into.

The air escaped his lungs. He couldn't do this. He couldn't do what he needed to do to save his team and still be the man Abby mistakenly believed him to be. But he couldn't stand to think of the alternative, either. She was in his house and wearing his shirt and drinking his coffee and he never wanted her to leave because she belonged there.

Desire, hot and desperate, raced through his veins. He had to have her. Now. He needed to feel her warm tightness wrapped around him and hear her gasping in his ear. It was selfish but he didn't care. He was an immediate gratification kind of guy.

"What do you have on under that shirt?"

Her smile turned coy. "What do you think?"

"Come here." His voice was hoarse.

She took her time, sashaying toward him with a seductive sway to her hips that made the shirt open and close like a peep show.

By the time she reached him, he had lost all control. He yanked the shirt off her shoulders and threw it. He crushed his mouth against hers and plundered with his tongue. His hands cupped the round cheeks of her butt and pulled her against his leg. She moaned and ground against him.

Screw foreplay. He let go of her and undid his jeans. She helped pull them down over his hips., and then he hoisted her up in his arms. She wrapped her legs around his waist as he thrust inside her.

Abby cried out as he pushed her against a wall and pounded into her. His hips found a frantic rhythm. Her nails dug into his back. His fingers squeezed her ass. She bit his shoulder.

This wasn't love making. This was fucking. Desperate, wild fucking. And even as he felt his explosion building, he felt guilty. Because Abby deserved better than this. She deserved better than him.

He ground into her harder and harder and he could feel the intimate muscles inside her begin to contract and shudder with her pending release. Then her legs tightened around his waist as her orgasm rocked through her limbs. A primal scream erupted from her mouth and she called his name. Over and over. Devin. Oh, God. Devin. Devin.

And then he joined her with a final, shuddering thrust, her name on his lips, his seed spilling into her, his mind reeling, his heart shattering.

She went limp in his arms. Her forehead dropped to his shoulder, and she was trembling. He realized a moment later that she was laughing.

"Before I get really insecure," he panted. "What is so funny?"

She pulled back and cupped his cheeks with her hands. The look on her face was so tender and full of trust that it nearly crushed his chest.

"I'm just..." She paused to catch her breath. "Wondering what...has gotten into you this morning."

"You," he whispered.

She let out a little gasp and her eyes got wet and she kissed him.

That's when it hit him—what he felt for her. It wasn't

lust. It was another 'L' word. And it couldn't have happened at a worse time.

41

BUOYANT. That's how Nicki felt when she woke up just after dawn. Her eyes were puffy, her cheeks raw, her body sore, but her chest ... buoyant. As if an anchor that had been weighing her down had finally snapped, the chains broken and gone.

Eric had loved her for hours before they fell asleep, physically and emotionally exhausted. His arm was now heavy across her waist, his body spooned against hers from behind. His soft, rhythmic breathing sent shivers down her spine.

This was one of the things she'd missed most when they were apart. The simple intimacy of waking up next to him—of stretching and feeling him stir, of finding hands under the covers, of warm skin brushing warm skin, of snuggling deep into his muscled chest, of lazy smiles and tender teasing.

She needed to get up but didn't want to. She wanted to

hide under the covers with him all day and pretend the rest of the world didn't exist. She wanted to hear him say the words he'd vowed last night over and over again. *I love you, Nicki.* She wanted to make it dark again, because in the dark the promises they made faced no obstacles.

She reached for her phone on the bedside table and checked the time. Ugh. It was after eight. They had less than an hour until they needed to be at the ballpark. The exhibition game against the Detroit Tigers started at noon, and they had to go through warm-ups, batting practice, and all the pre-game publicity stuff.

Eric let out a deep breath in his sleep. In repose, his face was soft, relaxed. The whiskers that had already started to grow last night were now sharp and pronounced along his jaw. She wanted to feel them against her skin again.

Instead, she rolled with a sigh and rose as quietly as possible. His t-shirt was on the floor. She grabbed it and pulled it on, taking a moment to breathe in the scent of him that lingered along the collar before letting it fall loosely over her naked body.

There was no time for her normal morning workout or breakfast. In the kitchen, she gathered items for a protein smoothie—bananas, strawberries, protein powder, almond butter, and ice. The blender whirred, and she winced. She wanted to let him sleep as long as possible, but seconds later, she heard him shuffle into the kitchen.

She looked over her shoulder and tried not to openly

drool. He wore nothing but his jeans, the faded denim low-slung on his hips. She'd seen his bare chest countless times, but it was different this morning. Everything was different this morning.

"Sorry, did the blender wake you up? I was going to let you sleep a little longer. I was just making a protein shake. I made enough for both of us, in case you want some."

He smiled at her babbling and slid his arm around her waist from behind. "Hey."

She swallowed away her nervousness and looked up at him. He dropped his mouth onto hers, quick and hard. When he pulled back, his eyes glinted with amusement. "'Mornin'."

He stepped back and stretched with a yawn, and she ogled the way it made his pants dip even lower, revealing the tip of dark hair below his waist.

"This is when I remember that you don't drink coffee," he said, roughing his hand over his hair. He slouched against the counter and stifled another yawn.

"You shouldn't either," she chided. She poured the shake into two glasses and handed him one. "This is better for you."

He winked. "Ok, Coach."

He took two long drinks and set the glass down behind him. Then he held out his hand to her. "C'mere."

She took his hand and let him tug her against his body, nestling her between his splayed legs. She immediately went hot. He slid his finger beneath her chin and tipped her face up to his. He smiled softly before settling his lips against hers. It was tender, gentle, and said more than words ever could.

She pressed her cheek to his chest and closed her eyes. Why couldn't they hit the pause button on the outside world?

He rested his chin on the top of her head and ran his hands up and down her back. "Don't do that."

"Do what?"

"Start thinking about all the things that could go wrong."

She didn't bother denying it.

"I meant what I said last night." He tilted her face up to his again. "We will figure this out. All of it. Because not figuring it out is no longer an option."

His face dipped to the exposed column of her neck. He nuzzled, and she shivered again.

"My shirt looks pretty good on you."

"It smells like you," she murmured.

"That's not always a good thing."

"It is this morning."

His hands found the hem of the shirt and worked upward, his fingers brushing her backside up and down with feather light caresses. Against her abdomen, he went hard. She moaned and pressed into him. "We don't have much time."

"Join me in the shower?" he suggested, licking beneath her ear.

God, yes. She had such exquisite memories of showering with him. She followed him wordlessly and let him pull the shirt over her head. By the time they climbed into the hot water, she was shaking with need. But no memory of previous times could compare. Maturity and appreciation for everything they'd lost and gained made it a whole new experience this time.

As the bathroom steamed and the water beat down, his hands were slow and gentle, his words erotic and loving. She came first, and he held her until her quakes subsided before taking himself to peak with a throaty declaration of love.

Then he held her and caressed her with slow, languid kisses that made her wish again they could just lock themselves inside and forget the rest of the world. Forget all the reasons this was risky. Forget Ray Fox. Forget reality.

But as soon as they turned off the water, reality came crashing in.

ERIC WAS so busy admiring the sight of Nicki bent over drying her legs and wondering if they had time for another round that he almost didn't hear the ringing of their phones.

Both their phones.

Nicki let out an *ugh* and dashed from the bathroom.

Seconds later, she let out a soft curse. Eric wrapped a towel around his waist and walked into the bedroom in time to see her hold the phone to her ear.

"What's wrong?"

"There's a picture on Twitter."

"What kind of picture?"

She turned away when whomever she had called answered their phone "It's me," she said.

Eric bent to grab his jeans from the floor and pulled his phone from the pocket. He called up his Twitter app and—

"That's it?" It was a picture of his car outside her house. True, it was taken in the middle of the night, but it was still just his car.

Then he saw that Ray Fox had retweeted it with a snarky message. *Friends? Right. These two give new meaning to conference on the mound.*

Eric ran a hand down his face. They hadn't even gotten one fucking day of peace.

"No, I haven't seen it," Nicki said into the phone. She turned around again, and he reluctantly showed her his screen. Her face fell.

"We'll be there in twenty minutes," she said.

She hung up and dropped her phone onto the bed before running her fingers through her wet hair. He wrapped his arms around her from behind.

"Why can't he just leave us alone?" she asked.

He kissed the tense reeds of her throat. "No idea."

"Who took that picture? Who sent it to him?"

He nuzzled her again. "I don't know. But we're in this together. We'll deal with it together."

She turned in his arms and did what he'd been longing for her to do for weeks.

She leaned on him.

42

THEY DRESSED QUICKLY and drove in separate cars to the ballpark, where a security guard waited to usher them in unseen. Like criminals. He left them in the conference room with an order from Abby to stay put and to not check social media.

Nicki immediately ignored it. She called up Twitter on her phone. "Two thousand retweets."

Eric didn't even want to think about the comments attached to them.

When Nicki dropped into one of the chairs at the conference table, he crossed the room and knelt before her. "Babe. It's going to be OK."

She leaned forward and pressed her forehead to his shoulder. He turned to kiss her hair.

The door suddenly burst open. Abby marched in like a general charging into battle. She dropped her massive black bag on the table and swept a stern gaze from him to Nicki and back.

"You two had a very simple job. Stay away from each other. Was that so hard?"

The door opened again. Hunter walked in, took one look at Eric holding Nicki's hands, and let out a sigh. "Well, I guess that answers that question."

Nicki yanked her hands back.

"You're on the mound today, Weaver," Hunter said. "You have to be on the field in fifteen minutes for warm-ups."

He walked back out.

Abby cleared her throat. "It's time to do an interview, Nicki."

Nicki's eyes tightened at the corners. "What does that accomplish?"

"The only thing people know about you is what Ray Fox wants them to, and you're letting him. This endless drip, drip, drip of rumor and innuendo is never going to stop. He controls the narrative. Let's take it back."

"How?"

"Tell the truth," Abby said.

Nicki looked up into his eyes, and Eric watched the indecision play out on her face. He mentally kicked himself because they could have avoided all of this if he'd just been smart enough to park around the corner. But he hadn't been thinking that far ahead when he pulled up in front of her house, and he definitely hadn't been thinking about his car after he went inside.

Still, they would have had to deal with this sooner or later. They couldn't stay hidden forever.

Abby's phone rang. She pulled it from her bag and sighed. "ESPN."

Nicki reacted with a hard swallow and a deep breath. He could almost hear the two sides of herself arguing inside her head. He knew them both now. Knew what each one wanted and feared.

He loved them both.

"Hey." Eric reached out and tucked a strand of hair behind Nicki's ear. "Never stop fighting, right?"

She smiled and pressed her forehead to his chest.

Abby's phone buzzed with a text. "Avery Giordano wants a statement. Decision time, boys and girls."

Nicki's hands sought anchor on his hips, and he bent to kiss the top of her head. "We're in this together, Nicki."

She straightened with a nod. "OK."

Abby let out a whoop. "Let me get working on it."

The door once again burst open, followed by an angry voice. "You have to be kidding me."

Nicki jerked away from Eric just as he whipped around.

Devin stood in the open doorway, chest heaving beneath his crisp, white shirt like he'd just run a mile. He stormed farther into the room. "Are you two really fucking each other?!"

"Devin!" Abby's voice rose in anger and surprise.

Nicki's face drained of color.

"I can't believe this." Devin jerked his hands through his hair. "You have no idea what you've done."

"This happens to be none of your fucking business, Devin," Eric snapped.

"I own you!" Devin boomed. "Both of you! Everything you do is my business."

Abby grabbed his arm. "Devin, what is wrong with you?"

"End it, or find a way to deny it," Devin said, pointing a finger at Nicki. "Now. Or I can't promise that I can save you."

The he whipped around and stormed back out.

"Oh my God."

Nicki's panicked exhale sent Eric spinning back around. "Babe—"

"Don't." She held up her hands.

The door opened again, and Hunter stuck his head into the room. "Let's go, Weaver."

Nicki looked up at him. He understood her fear, her reluctance. He did, but the look on her face was sending waves of ice through his veins.

"Nicki, I know this isn't the timeline we planned on for going public, but—"

"We never talked about going public at all, Eric."

The world compressed, narrowed, until there was

nothing but the words she said. "How did you think this was going to work, Nicki?"

"I don't know!"

"Were you expecting me to just be your dirty little secret again?"

"You heard Devin! We might not have a choice!"

Hunter growled. "Now, Weaver."

Nicki shook her head. "Just go, Eric. We don't have time to talk about this."

Disbelief. Fury. Pain. They became his lifeblood. "Fine. I'll see you on the field, *Coach*."

43

NICKI HAD NEVER FELT SO EXPOSED. The lens of every camera in the ballpark focused on her the instant she left the safety of the tunnel and entered the dugout. The firestorm had only grown in the hours since the picture first appeared. The social media monster had been let loose from its cage, and there was no pulling it back in.

Nicki would have given anything to stay inside during pre-game but she couldn't hide forever. Not from the crowds, the media, Ray Fox. Or Eric.

Eric.

She saw him on the field, warming up with Riley Quinn. Even from a distance, she could tell he was stiff and angry. His jaw was clenched, his throw fierce.

Someone in the stands made a whistling noise. "Weaver, where's your coach?"

He whipped the ball to Riley and then glared into the

stands. His gaze strayed down to hers but quickly moved away. Her puffy eyes stung with new tears. Dammit! Why didn't he understand?

Devin couldn't have been any clearer.

She could have Eric. Or she could have her job.

"Hey baby." Nicki jumped at the voice, her creep radar on high alert. Kas sidled up next to her and dipped his head close to her ear. "How'd you sleep last night?"

Harper Brody interceded. "Knock it off, Kas."

"Fuck you, Brody."

Kas leaned down again and slid his hand to her waist. "You giving private lessons to everyone, or just Eric? Because I've been having some trouble finding the sweet spot and—"

Someone hit him.

Kas let out a noise and held his bloody mouth, stumbling back.

Then her hand started to hurt. Crap, her whole arm hurt.

Shit. *She* had hit him.

"You fucking bitch."

Kas advanced, and the world started to move in slow motion.

44

Eric heard the chaos before he saw it. Riley shot to his feet behind the plate, whipped off his mask, and pointed at the dug-out. Eric turned just in time to see Kas punch Nicki square in the face.

Nicki crumpled like a rag doll.

Eric screamed her name and began to run.

Harper Brody pulled Kas back.

Eric leaped down the dugout stairs, eyes clouded with red rage. Kas and Brody saw him at the same time. All three went down as Eric launched himself at Kas. He got in three solid punches before Riley pulled him off.

Eric struggled to pull away.

"Someone help me!" Riley yelled.

Another player latched onto Eric's other arm and held him back as Kas rolled off Brody and stood. Blood smeared across his face.

On the other side of the dugout, Hunter yelled for someone to call for doc.

Eric deflated.

The guys let him go and he raced to Nicki's side.

He fell to his knees next to her. He was only vaguely aware of Brody and Riley dragging Kas away. Eric cupped Nicki's cheek. She was out cold.

"Nicki, baby." God, there was blood. Kas had cut her cheek. "Nicki, please."

She let out a moan and rolled her head. Thank God. Her eyes fluttered open and looked up at him, unfocused and confused.

"Hey," she whispered.

He laughed. He didn't know what else to do. "Nice job, Clutch."

He leaned forward and kissed her.

And felt her gasp against his lips.

45

ABBY SLID into the passenger seat of Devin's car. He hit the accelerator before she'd barely had time to shut the door.

"How bad is it?" he asked, voice clipped.

"Her vision is blurred and she threw up in the ambulance."

"Concussion?"

"Sounds like it."

Devin pounded his hand on the steering wheel, and Abby jumped in her seat.

"What the hell is wrong with you, Devin? What was all that in the conference room?"

"Does Nicki have any fucking idea what she's done?"

Abby's mouth fell open as a creeping dread spread through her limbs. "Excuse me? *Nicki*? Kas should be in jail right now."

"I won't argue that point, and trust me, we will deal with that, but fuck!"

The uncharacteristic profanity sent the dread to Twilight Zone levels. "You're going to protect her, though, right? You didn't mean what you said in there."

He didn't answer.

"Devin—"

"Did you know about them?"

She hesitated. "I only knew that they were a couple a long time ago."

"Dammit, Abby! Do not *ever* keep anything about the team from me."

"Do not ever order me around like one of your minions. I don't work for you or the goddamned team, Devin."

His jaw tightened. "How are we going to deal with this?"

"*I* am going to work it like a professional. You are going to stop acting like a damn Neanderthal."

Devin whipped into the parking lot for the emergency room. Abby grabbed the door handle, but felt his hand on her arm. She swung around.

"I'm sorry," he said. "I shouldn't have yelled at you."

"You're right. But you have a helluva lot more to apologize for than that."

She got out and slammed the door.

～

ERIC WAS EJECTED from the game before it even started.

Like he gave a fuck. He didn't bother changing out of his uniform before racing through the building toward the parking garage. He ran into his father in the tunnel.

"Which hospital?" Chet asked, jogging to keep up.

"Memorial."

"I'll drive," Chet said.

Photographers and reporters swarmed like buzzards to a fresh kill as soon as they arrived. Drooling and snarling, they took their bites as Eric and his father tried to push through the hospital doors.

"Eric, how long have you and Nicki been sleeping together?"

"What did Nicki say to you before you kissed her?"

"Did you and Nicki have sex before today's game?"

Eric swung around on that one, but his father grabbed him and pulled him through the emergency room doors.

Bile stung the back of his throat. This couldn't be happening. How was it possible that just a few hours ago, Nicki had been in his arms?

The staff at the hospital was well-acquainted with dealing with the celebrity that the team brought to town. As soon as Chet ushered him inside, security guards blocked the doors to keep the press out. The hospital's public relations director greeted him with a firm handshake and a no-nonsense nod.

"Please follow me, Mr. Weaver. I'll take you to a private waiting area."

Whispers and points followed their every step. They reached the end of a long corridor, and the PR woman unlocked a door. Inside was a luxuriously decorated waiting room with a giant TV and leather couches.

"We reserve this room for high-profile guests," she explained. "A security guard will stand outside the door. No visitors will be allowed in without your approval."

She pointed to a small kitchenette. "The refrigerator is fully stocked with various refreshments. If you require anything special, please call my cell phone. The number is posted on the fridge."

Eric growled. "I don't give a shit about the refrigerator. Where is Nicki?"

The woman offered a warm smile. Eric felt like an ass for treating her like that, but he couldn't bring himself to care.

"I'm sorry," the woman said. "Of course I should have covered that first. Ms. Bates is being evaluated. Shall I arrange for a doctor to come and give you an update?"

"I want to see her."

"I'm afraid that's not possible right at this minute. But we will keep you posted regularly and let you know as soon as she's able to receive visitors."

Eric groaned and fisted his hands in his hair. The woman smiled again and then left. Eric made a slow circle in the center of the room and then punched the air. "Fuck!"

Chet handed him a bottle of water. "Drink."

"I'm not thirsty."

"Drink."

He accepted the bottle and swallowed several gulps. There was a knock at the door. He sloshed water on his uniform twisting around.

Abby walked in, followed closely by Todd Marshall and Abby's partner, David. Great. The whole corporate crew. What did they do? Rent a bus?

Devin barreled in next. "What do we know so far?"

"You have a lot of fucking nerve coming here," Eric said.

"That's not what I asked."

"Fuck you, Devin."

Chet set his hand on Eric's arm. "She's being evaluated," he said. "They said they would send a doctor when they have any information."

Todd's phone rang, and he ducked out again. Abby approached Eric, her expression wary, like she'd just come across a mountain lion while jogging. "How did she look?"

He shook his head, his voice blocked by something in this throat. For the rest of his life, he would never forget the moment he saw her fall. Or the moment he realized she'd been knocked out cold. Or the moment she realized he had just kissed her in full view of the entire world.

"What have you done," she whispered.

Devin spoke up. "Eric, I hate to voice the obvious, but I need to know the truth."

"Yes, you're an asshole."

Devin clenched his jaw. "Don't fuck with me right now. You are in no position to do so."

Eric got in Devin's face. "And what does that mean?"

"You beat the shit out of a teammate. You're looking at a suspension, at the very least."

"Me?! He knocked Nicki out cold!"

"And he will be dealt with. But I can't have one of my players running around like some goddamned overprotective boyfriend!"

Eric grabbed Devin by the shirt and shoved.

Chet jumped in between them. "Enough!"

Eric shouted over his father's shoulder. "Are you asking me if I'm sleeping with her? Is that what you're asking? Have I been *fucking* my coach?"

Devin's face turned red with anger. "You know damn well what I'm asking."

"I'm in love with her. Does that matter to you?"

Devin threw his hands in the air. "Well, that's just great. Beautiful. When's the wedding?"

"Everyone shut up!" Abby stood in the center of the room and shouted. The room went quiet but for the labored breathing of too much testosterone. She planted her hands on her hips. "Do you want the entire hospital to hear this?"

She pointed at Devin. "You. Go find that Stepford wife

of a PR woman and tell her to set up a barricade around the hospital. There's no reason for the press to be that close to the entrance."

Eric clicked his teeth at Devin. "That's right, Devin. Run along."

Devin growled again, but Abby blocked him with a hand to the chest that would've made a Heisman winner proud. "Go, Devin!"

Devin turned around and stormed through the door.

Abby swiveled and pointed at Chet. "You. I'm putting you in charge of contacting Nicki's family. They're probably worried sick, and I doubt she has her cellphone with her."

Chet nodded obediently.

She finally pointed her finger at Eric. "And you, Mr. I'll Beat Everyone's Ass. Can you chill the hell out for one second, please? We have major damage control to do, and I need to know that you're not going to go Hulk on us at the wrong time and break Manhattan."

"I don't give a shit about damage control."

"But you do give a shit about Nicki. Right?"

He deflated. He cupped the back of his neck and answered with a crisp nod.

She let out a breath and tugged on her suit jacket. "Good."

Todd Marshall burst through the door. "Turn on the TV."

Eric swore. Nothing good ever followed those words.

Chet grabbed the remote off the table next to the couch. The TV was already turned to CNN.

A slow motion clip showed Eric bending and kissing Nicki.

Abby sighed. "Well, I guess there really is no denying it now."

46

Nicki was numb, detached, like she was floating above her body and watching everything unfold on a movie screen. The only connection she had to reality was the pounding in her head that had begun seconds after waking up on the floor of the dugout to find Eric leaning over her.

"*Nice job, Clutch.*"

And then he kissed her.

In front of everyone.

Oh, God. What had he done?

What had *she* done?

The door to her room opened, and a man in scrubs walked in. He introduced himself as Dr. Something or Other. She listened with half an ear as he talked about running this test and that. They were pretty sure there no broken bones in her hand, but X-rays would tell them for sure. And a CT scan would let them know if she had a concussion.

She snapped to attention. "A concussion? Just from getting punched?"

He smirked. "This isn't the movies, Nicki. A blow to the head from a Major League Baseball player the size of Al Kasinski isn't much different than slamming your head on the dashboard in a car accident."

Her stomach roiled. He must have recognized the signs, because he thrust a plastic bin under her chin.

She sank against the pillows and pushed it away. "I'm fine."

I'm sick of that word, Nicki.

"Just hang tight," the doctor said, setting the bin on her lap, just in case. "We'll know soon enough. You need anything in the meantime?"

"The remote to the TV."

"You sure about that?"

"Oh yeah. I'm my own reality show."

"I'll have someone bring it in." Then he gave her a sympathetic smile and left.

For a few blissful hours, she had deluded herself that somehow they could make it work. Now she knew the truth. Last night had been too good to be true.

Were they out there somewhere—the ones who had hurt her. Were they watching the clip of Eric kissing her? Were they laughing?

They were going to win. She was going to lose her job, and she would never defeat them.

She let her head fall back and the tears flow.

If Todd Marshall didn't stop cracking his knuckles, Eric was going to break his face. Devin had mysteriously disappeared twenty minutes ago. Abby was working her phone and alternating between swearing and barking out orders.

No one would tell him anything.

He was officially in hell.

The door opened. Eric shot away from the wall he'd been holding up as a doctor in scrubs walked in. The room erupted as everyone shouted over each other.

The doctor held up his hands. "Hang on. Hang on. I don't have much to tell."

Eric pushed past his father and Abby. "How is she? Where is she?"

"First of all, she's OK. We have her scheduled for X-rays and a CT scan."

His gut pinched. "What for?"

"Possible concussion."

Eric planted his hands on his head. Kas had hit her that hard? He was going to be sick. He felt his father's hand on his shoulder.

"The cut on her face did not require stitches," the doctor

said. "We've bandaged that up. But that's all I can tell you until we get a look inside her."

"I want to see her."

The doctor winced. "I would advise giving her some time."

"I'm not exactly a stranger off the street. Where is she?"

The doctor raised his hands again. "Mr. Weaver, I understand you're upset—"

"What. Room."

The doctor let his hands drop. "Room two."

Eric practically bowled the man over as he raced out.

The doors to the emergency room were around the corner and down one long hallway. No one stopped him. He pushed through the swinging doors and nearly collided with a frazzled orderly. She jumped out of the way.

He pushed open the door to room two and felt his chest split. Nicki was propped against pillows, her knees drawn to her chest, an ice pack wrapped around her throwing hand and a butterfly bandage on her face. There was blood on her uniform.

Her eyes were locked on ESPN on the TV opposite the door. Ray Fox was smug and victorious on the screen.

"Devin Dane has no choice but to get rid of her at this point," the asshole said. "She has been lying all along. She has tarnished the reputation of a great American game."

"Babe ..." Eric let go of the door, and it swung shut behind him.

She looked over, her face hardened into a stranger. A pitcher on the mound. Coach Bates once again.

He eased toward the bed. "Nicki, we can get through this."

"Why did you do it, Eric? I could have maybe survived the fight and the picture. But you kissed me. In front of everyone. Why?"

"Because I was scared shitless! You were dead to the world when I got to you, and you were covered in blood. Do you have any idea what that did to me? And when you woke up, Jeezus. I didn't plan it. It just happened."

"Right. After our argument over doing an interview, it *just happened*. And now we have to live with the consequences."

She had said the same thing last night. Except last night it was an absolution. Today it was an accusation.

"You—" Shit. He had to stop and collect himself. "You think I did it on purpose?"

The muscles of her throat worked as she swallowed, and she turned back to the TV.

Avery Giordano was now talking.

"I never thought I would agree with Ray Fox," the woman said. "But if there is, in fact, a relationship between Nicki Bates and Eric Weaver, a relationship they've lied about, it might not be something we can tolerate. A boss can't sleep with her employee in any industry without it being a problem."

Boss.

Employee.

Eric swallowed against a suddenly dry throat. "Nicki, look at me. We can handle this together."

"I don't think there can be a *we*."

Her words erected an invisible wall, and he hit it head-on and hard. It knocked him back, stunned.

"You don't mean that, Nicki. You're just scared."

She didn't even look at him. "I have to save my career."

"Even if it means the end of us?"

"Yes."

No single word had ever hurt as much. It was a giant fist slamming into his chest and yanking out every vital organ.

But pain quickly became rage. It made him want to roar like a wild animal. It made him want to grab the nearest heavy object and throw it. It made him want to break windows and crash cars.

It made him the Hulk, and he was going to break Manhattan.

"You know what your problem is? You've never really pulled yourself off the ground."

Her face whipped to his and drained of color. "What did you say?"

"You're still cowering half-naked with your hands over your face."

"How dare you."

"You can get all the tattoos you want, but you're still just practicing pitches in your head, afraid to throw the real heat."

She yanked a pillow from behind her and threw it at him. "Get out!"

The pillow hit him with all the force of a marshmallow but the finality of a walk-off grand slam.

Game over.

He stared at it on the floor. Pictured her hair spread out on it. Her face turned toward his. Her lips swollen from his kiss. Her eyes smiling at him.

"I'm all out of pride here, Nicki. I have nothing left but honesty. And the truth is, I'm dying right now. I'm not sure how I'm even going to walk out of here. But I feel even worse for you, because one day all of this will be gone, and then what will you have?"

"Victory," she spat out.

"Well." He cleared his throat against the lump there. "I hope you're happy together."

He fisted his hands and stalked to the door. *Call me back, baby. Please.*

He gripped the handle. *Come on, Nicki. Don't let me leave.*

"You bastard."

He walked out. And left his heart behind.

47

FOR FUCK'S SAKE. Was the entire hospital staff outside the door, listening to his complete and total destruction? They jumped and scattered the instant Eric limped out of her room and her life.

Just one person remained.

His father.

"Son—"

Eric pointed. "Don't. Don't say anything."

His cleats beat an angry staccato on the tiled floor as he got the hell out of there. He pushed through the swinging doors.

And came face to face with Devin.

For Christ's sake.

Chet instantly wrapped his arms around Eric to hold him back, but then let go when he realized it wouldn't be necessary.

Eric was all out of fight. He'd been coming out swinging his whole life, and it had left him nothing but bloody and broken.

Devin was stone-faced. "Two game suspension. Brody gets home opener. You won't start until the second week."

It was amazing how little he cared. "What happened to moving me to the bullpen?"

Devin gripped the back of his neck and grimaced. "Yeah, well. I was never really going to move you to the bullpen. I just wanted to light a fire under your ass."

Fucking Devin. "You really get off on manipulating people, don't you?"

"It worked, didn't it? You finally got your shit together on the mound."

"That had nothing to do with you."

It had everything to do with Nicki. The magic fairy dust that had given him his throw back? It was her. She was what had been missing, and now she was gone again. Devin had just handed him his spot in the starting rotation. It's what he wanted, but it didn't matter anymore. Not without her.

Fatigue settled in his bones. He was so tired of this shit.

Eric turned around and looked at his father. "Was it worth it?"

Chet paused, lips parted. Then he let out a sad, quiet breath and shook his head, as if he knew exactly what Eric was asking.

326 LYSSA KAY ADAMS

"No, it wasn't. I'd give up my entire career if I could get your mom back and fix things with you."

Eric nodded and looked down. Emotions were hitting him fast and hard, and he sure as shit didn't want his father to see that. But he couldn't stop himself from asking something else.

"What if I hadn't been any good?"

"Good at what?"

"Baseball. What if I'd sucked at it?"

"If you don't know the answer to that, then I sucked at being a father even more than I thought."

The floor wavered through a watery lens.

His father reached out, his hand hesitating a second before closing over Eric's arm. "Baseball isn't who you are, Eric. It's just what you do for a living. It's a job. Nothing more. I learned that way too late in life."

Fuck. The lump in his throat threatened to block his airway.

"I didn't know how to show you that I cared. I didn't know how to be both—a player and a father. Baseball was all I knew, so I pushed you into it. I pushed you too hard, and I pushed you away. I destroyed myself and my family. For the game. The fucking game."

Fuck. FuckfuckFUCK.

"I should have made sure you understood that I didn't care if you became a garbage man. I would have loved you the same, no matter what. You're my son. That's all that matters to me."

Christ. He was fucking *crying*. In the middle of the damn hospital. With people walking by and the entire baseball press corps outside.

His father wrapped his arm around Eric's back and pulled him into his embrace. Eric choked on a sob. And for the first time since he was a child, he wrapped his arms around his father's back.

His dad cupped the back of his head. "God, son. I've missed you so much."

Eric couldn't talk. He felt like a little boy again, being comforted after falling down.

Maybe he was.

Eric took several deep breaths.

Behind him, Devin cleared his throat.

Eric pulled away and turned around. He wiped his cheeks with the back of his hand.

"Tell you what, Devin. I'm really tired of being owned by you. So, how about this? How about I don't start at all?"

Devin blinked. "What does that mean?"

"I quit. I'm done with baseball."

48

It was mid-afternoon before Nicki's doctors confirmed the diagnosis. A *concussion*, they told her. *You have anyone who can stay with you?*

"No," Nicki answered, raw and drained.

Having no one to stay with her meant she had to spend a night in the hospital for observation. She was being observed, all right. The parking lot across the street had been taken over with satellite vans and white tents where reporters gave live, official-sounding updates even when there was absolutely nothing new to report. Rumors and speculation were enough.

But this was her *life* they were talking about. They mocked and analyzed and debated and speculated, but not once did they ever stop to realize that she was a living, breathing human being.

Abby showed up around three and zapped off the TV. "I

thought I told you not to watch this junk." She dropped a duffel bag at the end of her bed. "I brought you some stuff."

Nicki dove into the bag and pawed through clothes and toiletries. "I need my cellphone."

"I couldn't find it."

"What about my iPad?"

"Couldn't find that either."

"My laptop?"

Abby handed her a novel. "Bought it downstairs."

Nicki sank back against the pillows. She knew Abby was just trying to protect her, but it was pointless. She'd already seen the worst of it on TV. The endless replay of the fight and Eric kissing her had already been turned into Facebook memes and YouTube parodies.

She was officially the laughingstock of baseball. They didn't care that beneath the uniform, she was just a woman. A woman whose entire career was flashing before her eyes. A woman whose heart was breaking.

Abby dragged the chair by the window over to the bed and sat down. "Eric has been suspended two games."

She already knew that. ESPN gleefully reported it every ten seconds or so. Still, just hearing his name gouged a new hole in her heart. "What about Kas?"

"No official word yet, but he's likely looking at an indefinite suspension. That's the good news in all of this, if there is any. People are definitely on your side in the fight."

She knew that, too. CNN had done a Twitter poll. It showed overwhelming support for her in punching Kas.

The relationship with Eric was another matter. One fan who was interviewed actually said she deserved to have Kas come on to her in the dugout if she was sleeping with Eric.

She had it coming, in other words.

"Any word on me, yet?"

Abby touched her arm. Not a good sign.

"Try to get some rest," she said. "You really do need to take care of yourself. A concussion is nothing to mess around with."

Nicki nodded and fingered the edges of the book, a murder mystery. At least it wasn't a romance. She couldn't take any happy-ever-afters when her own had been destroyed.

How naïve she'd been to think she could ever have one.

Abby's phone buzzed with a text message. She stood and read the screen. A dark expression passed over her face.

She was distracted when she looked back at Nicki. "I have to go. I'll be in touch."

Nicki turned back on the TV after Abby left. CNN blared to life just in time for the breaking news.

Sources: Aces Owner Dane to announce Nicki Bates out following dugout fight, affair rumor

"YOU SONUVABITCH."

Devin paced in his office in the ballpark. If he could crawl through the phone and choke his brother, he'd already have his hands around the bastard's throat. Not only had Bennett leaked a false story that Devin was going to fire Nicki, he wasn't even ashamed of it.

Bennett laughed. "You obviously needed a nudge. I did you a favor."

"I haven't made a decision about her yet."

"Exactly. You think you have a choice. You don't."

"This team is mine."

"That team is part of Dane Enterprises. You are my employee."

Panic crept up his spine. Bennett was bluster. Nothing more. "Spit it out, Bennett."

"You want to keep your fingers in the family bank account? Then listen up, baby brother. Fire. Nicki. Bates."

The panic spread through every limb like a virus seeking a host. "How much time do I have to decide?"

"Twenty-four hours."

The line went dead.

Devin stared at the window, squeezing his cellphone and wishing it would break. A flash of movement in the reflection caught his attention.

He spun around. Abby.

He watched as she approached. There was a deceptive calm to her steps. She was vibrating with energy and anger, but her movements were controlled. She carried a lone piece of paper in one hand.

He itched to touch her. He wanted to crush her to his chest, strip her clothes off, lay her down on the couch, and forget everything but the feel of her skin on his.

"It was a false story, Abby. I haven't made a decision about Nicki yet."

"How much time did he give you?"

"Who?"

"Your brother. That's who you were talking to, right?"

Sweat pooled under his arms. She was too calm. "Abby—"

"How much time did he give you?" she repeated.

"You don't understand."

"How. Much. Time."

He sank into his desk chair and scrubbed his face. His tie tugged at his throat, a noose that got tighter with every movement. He sighed and looked up. "Twenty-four hours."

"And if you don't fire her?"

"I lose access to family accounts."

"So, it's Nicki or your money."

Her eyes slid shut, her limps trembled. The sight incited a riot of emotions in him, but the only one that came out was defensive asshole. He tossed his phone onto the desk.

"I don't have time for this, Abby. I can see you're mad at me, but maybe you should direct some of that anger at your client. She brought this on herself."

Abby opened her eyes. "That's all you have to say?"

"What would you like me to say?"

"That you'll protect her. That you'll do the right thing."

Defensive asshole rose again as he shot to his feet. "I will do what I have to do to protect my team."

"You mean protect your money."

"Same thing, Abby."

She cleared her throat and smoothed her suit jacket. "That might be the only thing you've ever said to me that I believe."

She walked the rest of the way to his desk and slowly set down the piece of paper.

"What is that?"

"Thought you'd like to see the email I just received informing me that I've been fired from my firm."

What?! He grabbed the paper. Skimmed it. And felt the air seep from his lungs.

"They fired you because of me?"

"I believe David's exact words on the phone were that my relationship with you created a conflict of interest, which resulted in damage to our client's reputation."

"Why? I don't understand—"

"Todd Marshall is the leak. We hired a private investigator to find out who it was. David blames me. He said I was too busy fucking you to notice what was happening right in front of me. And he was right."

No. Devin rounded the desk. "That's bullshit, Abby. You have to fight—"

She backed away from him. "There was something else in that report, Devin."

He swallowed hard. Couldn't breathe.

"You lied to me." Her voice shook. "You were the leak that first day. I asked you directly, and you *lied to my face.* Which makes me wonder what else you've been lying about."

"Not us, Abby. I never lied about us."

"Everything about us is a lie, Devin."

He watched, frozen in place, as she turned and left his office and then disappeared from sight.

His mind screamed at him. *Don't let her go. You fucking idiot. Get up and go after her.*

"Abby, wait." Devin ran after her.

The elevators. He ran down the hallway. "Abby!"

He turned the corner. The doors were sliding shut.

"Abby, wait!"

The doors closed in his face. He slammed the palm of his hand against the cold metal.

He barely remembered dragging himself back down the hallway to his office, but suddenly he was back at his desk.

His cellphone rang.

It was Bennett.

Devin picked up the phone.

And whipped it against the wall.

49

NICKI FELT their hands on her. Their voices taunted her. She fell to the ground and curled into a ball and let the cold, wet pavement seep into her bones.

She woke up choking on air and darkness.

"Hey ... hey. It's OK."

She sank back against the pillows and turned her face toward the soothing reassurance.

Robby stood next to her bed. He cocked a smile. "I guess we're going to have to change your nickname to Rocky, huh?"

She burst into tears.

NICKI BLEW her nose on the tissue Robby handed her and threw it in the trash can by her bed. He sat down in the seat

Abby had pulled over earlier. He leaned, elbows on his knees.

She sniffled and winced at her own pathetic state. "How long can you stay?"

"A little while. Our game is early tomorrow." He looked at his watch. "Today."

He was going to drive all night, after driving all the way there? She cried a little more. "Thank you for coming."

"So," he breathed. "You and Eric."

"Not anymore."

"I'm sorry to hear that."

Nicki side-eyed him. "Who are you, and what have you done with my brother?"

He offered a small smile. "You OK?"

Fine. Her automatic answer left a sour taste in her mouth. She wasn't fine. She was as far from fine as a person could be. She was tired. Tired of being mad. Tired of being scared. Tired of fighting an enemy that only seemed to grow larger the harder she pushed herself.

She looked toward the window and swallowed against the thickness in her throat. "You know what I was thinking about today?"

She felt his gaze upon her. "What?"

"Those parties we used to have after your Vandy games. Remember those?"

The window wavered before her eyes, and she could see her parents' backyard. She could smell her dad's hamburgers on the grill and hear the clink of ice cubes in tall glasses of lemonade. There was her mother, shooing them outside while she finished cooking. There was Robby, teasing her. And there was Eric, looking at her with those seductive eyes and making her heart race. They were all laughing. Always.

"What happened to us, Robby?"

"The game changes everyone."

"Why?"

"Sometimes when you chase a dream for so long, you forget to enjoy the success."

"I'm not a success."

"It was an anonymous source, Nicki. You can't believe that report."

"I'm not talking about my job." The air left her lungs as the truth of her own statement hit her. She was woozy with it. *Drunk* with it.

Eric was right. She hadn't won anything.

Even if she managed to save her career at this point, she still wouldn't have the justice she'd been pursuing for so long. Not if they let her lose the joy she felt for the game. Not if she continued this way, sacrificing everything that mattered. Not if she let them scare her into running away from the fight.

But especially not if she had to give up the person she loved more than air.

She really was still cowering on the pavement with her

hands over her face.

"I love him, Robby."

"I know." He smiled in the dark. "Go back to sleep, Nicki. We can figure things out in the morning."

"How?"

"I have no idea."

At least he was honest.

ROBBY WAITED until he was sure she was asleep again before soft-shoeing out of her room.

Twenty minutes later, he knocked on Eric's front door. Eric answered red-eyed and rough.

"Ah, shit. Robby—"

Robby punched him in the face.

"GODDAMMIT!"

Eric stumbled back into the foyer of his house and held his hand to his mouth. His fingers came away bloody. "I am really fucking tired of getting hit."

Robby strolled in like nothing had happened and swung the door shut. "Nice place, Weaver."

"What the fuck, Robby."

Chet ran around the corner from the stairs in some old-man pajama pants, took one look at them both, and shook his head. He turned back around and yelled over his shoulder. "Try not to break anything."

Robby grinned. "You look like shit, Eric."

"It's after midnight. What do you want?"

"My sister looks like shit, too."

Great. Just when he'd finally staunched the bleeding in his chest.

Eric did a slow turn of the entryway and gave up. He sat on the floor, flopped onto his back, and let his arms flop to his sides.

Robby snorted. "What the hell are you doing?"

"Just do it and get it over with."

"Do what?"

"Rip my fucking heart out."

Robby laughed and towered over him. "Get up, pussy."

"I quit today."

"You can't. You're in the middle of a contract."

"So was Cal."

"Extenuating circumstances. I don't think a broken heart counts."

"What are you doing here, really?"

"I thought maybe we could play Halo until you stop bitching."

Eric let out the air from his lungs. "Why?"

Robby held out his hand. "Because I'm not letting my best friend quit in the seventh inning. Get up."

50

THEY WERE BEHIND HER. Yelling at her. Taunting her. *You're that bitch on the baseball team.* He grabbed her arm. Hit her in the face. She winced and waited for the sting of the blow.

But it didn't hurt.

He hit her again.

She felt nothing.

Nicki shot up in bed and blinked in the dark. Robby was gone. The clock on the wall said three o'clock. As in early.

She needed a phone. Now. She leaned and grabbed the edge of the wheeled bedside table and hauled it over. She hit nine for an outside line and then dialed Abby's number.

Abby answered on the second ring.

Nicki didn't give her a chance to say *hello.* "I need a favor."

51

ABBY WAS A TWITCHY, sloppy mess. Nicki had never seen her so out of place. Her hair was pulled back in a ponytail, her face free of make-up, her feet shoved into running shoes instead of the ankle-breaking heels she normally wore.

True, Nicki had dragged her out of bed in the middle of the night, but Nicki always assumed Abby just woke up coiffed and lipsticked like women on soap operas.

It took a mind-numbingly long time to get discharged in the morning and even longer for security to clear a path so she could sneak out unnoticed in Abby's car. Now that Nicki knew what she was going to do—what she wanted— every minute standing in the way of her goal was torture.

Avery Giordano agreed to meet them at Abby's hotel. Abby secured a conference room for the interview, and The New York Times would stream it live on their website.

It was the *live* part that seemed to have sent Abby into

unhinged territory. She twitched in the driver's seat. "Maybe I should sit in on the interview, too."

"And look like I need someone holding my hand?" Nicki shook her head.

"Won't you at least let me prepare some talking points to review?"

"No. I want to speak from my heart." She shivered dramatically. "God, that sounded cheesy."

"Can we be serious for a second?" Abby said. "This is a big deal, Nicki. You've had no interview prep. No practice. And don't think for a second that just because Avery is fair, she's going to be easy."

"I don't want easy. I just want to tell the truth."

Nicki had no idea what would happen after this. She might lose her career, and that would hurt like hell, but she would survive. She might not get Eric back, but she had to try. Not trying was no longer an option.

Abby pulled into the parking garage of her hotel and drove to the staff entrance, as security had instructed. She parked in a spot near the door that had been reserved for them.

Abby squeezed her hand in the elevator. "Are you sure you know what you're doing?"

The doors opened. "I do. I'm fighting back."

This wasn't the kind of story Avery Giordano wanted to do. She was an award-winning journalist, not one of those celebrity hounds hanging around outside. But she couldn't turn down the chance to land the first ever interview with Nicki Bates, even if there appeared to be an agenda.

Avery had been taking a beating from Ray Fox and his knuckle-dragging minions for her fair coverage of Nicki so far, as if reporting the facts—like the *fact* that Nicki Bates was as good as any other pitching coach in the Majors— made her some kind of politically correct hack. But fairness worked both ways. If Nicki thought Avery was going to go easy on her now, she was wrong.

Her cellphone buzzed with a text from Abby Taylor. She looked at the videographer behind her. "They're here."

The first thing Avery noticed when Nicki walked into the room was a butterfly bandage under her eye. Oozing around it was a purple and green bruise that made her wince with sympathy.

She stuck out her hand. Nicki's grip was firm, confident. Avery reviewed the interview parameters she and Abby had settled on—fifteen minutes, one camera, no still photos—and motioned for Nicki to sit in the chair opposite hers.

Avery looked at the videographer again. "Count us down."

He nodded and hovered over the button that would take them live online. "In five, four, three, two—" He pointed.

"Thank you for joining me today, Nicki."

"Thank you for meeting with me."

Avery nodded toward the bruise. "That looks like it hurts."

Nicki's fingers brushed the bandage. "Believe it or not, I've been hit worse than this. But yes, it hurts."

Hit worse than that? There was a story there, but it would have to wait. "We will go over the fight with Al Kasinski in a minute, Nicki, but let's deal with the elephant in the room."

Nicki nodded, her gaze direct.

"Are you having an affair with Eric Weaver?"

"No."

The whooshing sound Nicki heard outside the door must have been Abby fainting dead away.

Avery leaned forward. "Nicki, he kissed you in the dugout. He spent the night at your house. Are you denying—"

Nicki held up her hand. "Think about what you asked me."

"I asked—"

"You asked if I was having an affair with him. Think about the connotation of that word. Like it's something dirty. Or illicit or wrong. Just like the thousands of people calling me a slut. Just like Ray Fox and his disgusting innuendos about conferencing on the mound."

Avery's lips thinned. "Are you, or are you not, in a non-professional relationship with Eric Weaver?"

A splinter pierced her heart. It was less acute than yesterday but no less painful. "I don't know. I don't know where we stand right now, to be honest. But you still haven't asked the question that matters."

Clearly frustrated, Avery shifted in her chair. "OK. For the sake of moving forward, what should I ask you?"

"How I feel about him."

"And?"

"I love him."

52

Nicki waited for the elevator doors to close before turning around to face Abby. "Well?"

Abby's blank stare sent a prickle of unease up her spine. Nicki thought it had gone well.

But then Abby rushed her, and Nicki nearly fell over from the crush of their awkward, tangled embrace.

"That was the best client interview I've ever seen," Abby said.

Nicki pulled back, relief making her knees weak. "Really? Do you think it will—" Her mind searched for the phrase Abby always used. "Change the narrative?"

Abby laughed. "Honey, you didn't change the narrative. You just changed the game."

～

Relief was short-lived, though. The elevator opened into the basement parking garage, and they got back into the car. Nicki wasn't interested in changing the game. Right now, she was only interested in one thing.

Abby seemed to read her mind. "It's going to be OK, Nicki."

"We said the worst things to each other yesterday. *I* said the worst things."

"People tend to do that when they're scared. But I think you just made up for it."

"I don't know. I've been such a stubborn idiot. I don't think he will forgive me."

"Is that what you want?"

"Yes." God, yes. What good was the game if she didn't have him to enjoy it with? What good was winning if he wasn't there to celebrate the victory? And what kind of victory was it if he wasn't part of it?

"Then keep fighting."

"You were the one who said I couldn't have him, that I couldn't be with him."

"I was wrong."

Abby started the car, and Nicki noticed for the first time what really looked different about her friend. She'd been crying. Nicki had been so caught up in her own drama that she had failed to notice Abby was going through something, too. "Are you OK?"

Abby pulled out of the parking garage and shrugged. "I had a rough night."

"Is it Devin?"

Abby's head snapped so quickly to look at Nicki that she was certain her friend had broken her neck. "You knew about us?'"

"I suspected. Did something happen? Was it because of me?"

Abby took her time answering. When she did, her voice was flat. "No, it wasn't because of you. It was because of me." She blinked a few times and took a deep breath. "Where to, Nicki?"

"I have no idea." She couldn't go the ballpark. She didn't even know if she still had a job. And the house? If she'd lost her job, she probably lost that, too.

Nicki heard the ringtone of her cellphone and looked around, confused.

"Glove box," Abby said. "I charged it for you."

Nicki flipped open the glove box and yanked out her phone. *Please be Eric. Please be Eric.*

Disappointment thudded hard in her ribs. "It's Devin."

Abby stiffened in the driver's seat, her knuckles going white as she gripped the wheel. The ringing stopped, and Nicki's phone alerted her to a new voicemail.

"Listen to it," Abby ordered.

Nicki pressed the button and put the phone to her ear. Time slowed.

"Nicki, it's Devin. Call me immediately. The job is yours ..." His voice paused. "If you want it, that is. You'll need to work with Carol in my office to arrange the move to Vegas. She'll take care of everything."

He paused again. "And will you please tell your boyfriend that his resignation is not accepted? I can't lose my coach and one of my best pitchers at the same time."

53

ERIC MOVED his laptop to the mattress and swung his legs off the bed. His stomach roiled, his head pounded, but he felt neither.

I love him.

She didn't deny it. She went live online and told the world she loved him. Even after everything he'd said to her.

He tested his weight and then hobbled to the window in his bedroom. The press had moved from their spot outside the hospital to the street outside his house. Vultures. All of them. But Nicki had faced them head on. She'd looked straight into the camera and told the world she loved him.

He had to watch the interview twice before finally accepting it wasn't some drunken dream.

I won't apologize for falling in love. I won't apologize for being human, for wanting more out of life than just this game. If that costs me this job, so be it. But I will not allow the pettiness and the shallowness and the jealousy of other people to decide the direction of my life. Not anymore.

He'd called her a coward, but the woman he saw on that interview was the bravest, most beautiful thing he'd ever seen. His stomach churned. What the hell had he done?

"Eric?"

He twisted and regretted it immediately. The hammer in his head beat a warning. Robby had gotten him ruthlessly drunk.

His father winced. "Yikes. You look like a mean buzzard on a hot shit wagon."

Eric managed to laugh over the alarm bells in his skull. Of all his father's Texas colloquialisms, that was one of his favorites. He hadn't heard it in a long time.

He answered with another one. "Go shit in your hat, old man."

Almost immediately, though, his throat closed and his chest began to ache. He turned back to the window and hid his face as more of Nicki's words from the interview came rushing back.

I've been fighting for something for so long that I forgot why I wanted it. I've been trying so hard for so long to make people accept me. I've given up everything, but it doesn't matter what I do or say. It doesn't matter how well I perform. There will always be someone who thinks I don't belong. There will always be someone who wants to see me fail. There will always be guys who'd like nothing better than to kick the shit out of me in a dugout or a dark alley.

And then she'd handed over a folded-up piece of paper.

On the screen, Avery Giordano looked confused as she pulled it apart and skimmed it. Her eyes went wide.

"This is a copy of a police report."

"Yes."

"It lists you as the victim."

"Yes. They beat me, they raped me, and they were never caught. And I've been curled in a ball since then, shielding my face from their punches. But I'm done being their punching bag. I'm ready to stand up, because sometimes you have to come out swinging."

Eric leaned his head against the cold glass. "I managed to fuck things up but good, didn't I?"

"Why? Because you guys got in a fight?"

"Because I said some things that can't be taken back. I called her a coward. I accused her of being scared, but I was the one who was terrified."

"People say things they don't mean when they're hurting, Eric."

Eric turned around slowly. He could tell by his father's eyes that he wasn't just talking about the fight with Nicki.

Chet walked further into the room. "Do you know why I finally got clean?"

Shit. Eric didn't know if he could have this conversation right now. He swallowed and coughed.

"Because I said something truly horrible to your mother, and she forgave me. Her forgiveness convinced me to get my life under control. And when I came home from rehab, when I struggled to stay sober, I asked her why she stayed with me. Why did she put up with me? Do you know what she said?"

Eric shook his head, afraid to speak. He'd wanted to know this for so long, but he was afraid of the answer.

"She said, 'Some things are worth fighting for.' I never deserved her, but she stuck with me. And do you know who has always reminded me most of your mother?"

Eric coughed again.

"Nicki. They have the same strength, the same loyalty. She'll forgive you, Eric. You might have to work at it. You might have to grovel. But it's worth fighting for."

Eric sucked in a breath. "Then I guess it's time to come out swinging."

He crossed the room to the bathroom.

"What are you doing," his father asked.

"I need to take a shower. I have some groveling to do."

54

THE TWO ESPN anchors shook their heads, mouths agape. The one named Jim looked at his partner.

"Have you ever seen anything in baseball like the past twenty-four hours?"

The one named Brad shook his head. "Never, Jim."

He shifted and looked at the camera. "The soap opera that is the Vegas Aces baseball team may have reached its dramatic climax today with the shocking announcement this morning by owner Devin Dane that despite previous reports, he has not fired pitching coach Nicki Bates following a dugout fight between Bates and Pitcher Al Kasinski, and after Bates confirmed in an interview with the New York Times that she has, in fact, been having an affair with another pitcher on the team, Eric Weaver."

He laughed a fake newsman laugh. "It's a mouthful, folks. We have continuing coverage."

Abby closed her eyes to ward off the wave of emotion that had been a constant threat for the past two hours. Her bags were at her feet, packed and ready to go. It felt wrong, unnatural, to be a simple bystander to the news. She should be on the phone, working her sources, working period.

But it wasn't her job anymore.

The ESPN anchor continued. "The commissioner of Major League Baseball is expected to announce today sanctions against Kasinski, which will likely include a one-hundred-game suspension."

One hundred games. Nowhere near long enough. The bastard belonged in jail.

Abby heard a knock at the door and a voice say, "Bellman."

She stood up on shaky legs and turned off the TV. Her cell rang for the sixth time in twenty minutes. She probably didn't need to, but she looked at the screen.

It was Devin. Again.

She choked on a sob and turned it off.

55

DEVIN PRESSED his foot on the accelerator and growled. He would've thrown his phone out the window if he wasn't just hopeful enough that she would call back. She should still be at the hotel. Her plane didn't leave until noon. That's what Nicki had told him.

Nicki, who by some miracle didn't hate him. Who had actually called him that morning and told him that she would think about his job offer on one condition—that he take care of Abby.

Take care of her? He could do better than that. He was going to marry her.

Her hotel came into view. He jerked the wheel, narrowly missed a cab parked along the curb, and whipped into an open space. He jumped out. He threw his keys at the waiting valet and began to run.

He raced across the lobby and around a corner to the elevators. The doors on one were beginning to close.

He ran forward and shoved his body through the opening.

There was a family of four inside. The parents looked at him like he was crazy and gathered their children close.

He didn't blame them. He hadn't showered, shaved or even changed his clothes since yesterday. He probably even smelled bad. Devin pushed the button for the tenth floor and tried not to swear out loud as the elevator stopped on four other floors. The doors had barely parted on the tenth before he ran out.

The door to her room was open. There was a maid's cart in front. He knocked over a stack of toilet paper as he dodged around it and raced into the room. "Abby!"

The maid jumped and screamed.

He spun and searched the empty room. "Where is she?"

"Who?"

"The woman who was staying here?"

"She left, sir."

No. He bent forward and pressed his hands to his knees, panting. "When?"

"About five minutes ago."

He spun and ran again. Out the door and down the hallway. He didn't have time for the elevator so he used the stairs.

He took them two at a time the whole way down, and he

was sweating by the time he burst through the door on the ground floor. An old lady with a small dog in her arms screeched and jumped out of his way.

He ran to the desk where a pockmarked college kid in a hotel uniform was biting his nails.

"Abby Taylor. Did she check out yet?"

The kid looked up. "Huh?"

Devin growled and slammed his hands on the desk. A girl on the other end looked over. "Abby Taylor? I just checked her out."

She pointed toward the door.

Devin followed her point. He saw her immediately. Standing by a cab. His knees actually shook.

"Abby!" His voice echoed through the cavernous lobby and drew the shocked silence of everyone there.

He didn't care. He ran.

He slammed his hands against the door.

She turned around.

He kept running.

Her eyes widened.

He pulled her clear off the ground and kissed her.

ABBY STRUGGLED in Devin's crazed embrace. He set her down with a sound that could have been a laugh or a grunt.

But he kept his arms around her and pressed his cheek to the top of her head.

"God, Abby. Don't ever do that to me again."

"What are you doing here?"

He pulled back and looked down at her. "I came to stop you."

Everything inside her began to hurt and break apart. "It's too late, Devin."

She backed away from his arms and turned toward the cab.

"Wait a minute."

"I have to go. My plane leaves in ninety minutes."

"Abby, listen to me. I'm sorry."

She retrieved her laptop bag off the ground. "For what?"

"For everything."

She shook her head. That was original.

He forced her to face him. "Listen to me. Please."

He looked like hell. His eyes were red and tired. He needed a shave and a fresh suit. He looked every bit the desperate man in love. It had all the makings of a grand romantic gesture. One she didn't trust.

"I can't, Devin. I have to go."

"Wait. I-I'm keeping Nicki. I didn't let her go. I offered her the job."

"I know."

"I might lose the team."

"I know."

"Bennett cancelled my access to all the Dane accounts."

"I'm sorry for you."

"Abby—"

She shook her head, mostly to distract herself from the tears that threatened behind her eyelids. "I have to go."

"Wait. I can't lose you."

She opened the door to the cab and set her bag on the seat.

He grabbed her arm again. "Abby, don't. I'm sorry I lied to you."

"You were just desperate and afraid of failing, right?"

"*Please.* It's different this time."

"Why?"

"Because I love you!"

Her lungs stopped working. Her heart shattered in her chest. She turned around and slowly lifted her gaze.

He gripped her shoulders. "I love you, Abby. And I've never loved anyone before. You-you're my *conscience.*"

It was no use. She couldn't keep the tears back any longer. They spilled from her eyes and down her cheeks. His face softened into an expression of relief. He cupped her face and said it again. And again.

"I love you. Jeezus, I love you."

She pulled from his touch. Shook her head. Backed away.

"Abby?"

She tried to form the words. The hardest words she'd ever said.

"Devin, I ..." She stopped on a sob. God, she wanted to believe, but she had believed him so many times. When was she going to learn?

He reached for her. "Babe ..."

She closed her eyes, her voice a whisper. "I don't believe you."

And before she could fall apart, she climbed into the cab and pulled the door shut.

Devin grabbed the handle. "Abby, wait."

Abby slammed the lock down.

The cab driver turned in his seat. "Ma'am?"

"Just go. Go."

She heard Devin's voice. "Abby!"

"Go!"

The driver shook his head and pulled out.

Don't look back. Don't look back.

She couldn't help it. Just one more look at him. That's all she wanted. She turned in the seat and looked out the back window. He stood in the center of the street, his hands on his head, watching her leave, oblivious to the curious, silent stares of everyone around him.

Abby sank into the seat once again.

And cried all the way home.

56

NICKI CRADLED her cellphone against her ear. She had twenty minutes until she had to be in the bullpen for pre-game warm-ups.

The TV on the wall was tuned to CNN. Abby would be so pissed.

Nicki's cheeks burned as the network replayed an interview with Brody.

"Do we care if they're a couple? BLEEP no. Dude, the whole team is in love with her. Eric Weaver is the luckiest BLEEP in America."

Except Eric Weaver wasn't taking her calls.

She dialed Robby. He answered immediately.

"He hasn't called me back, Robby."

"He will."

"No. I know him. He would've done so by now if..." *Stop.* She closed her eyes and tried to breathe. She couldn't go into the game like this. It wasn't the most important thing in the world to her, but it *was* important. She still had a job to do. A job she had fought for her entire adult life.

The door to the trainer's office suddenly opened. She turned around. "Oh my God."

Robby's voice was alert. "What's the matter?"

"He's here."

Robby laughed. "I'll talk to you later."

Nicki shut her mouth.

Eric shut the door.

She had so much to say and no time to say it. She rushed forward. "Eric. I tried to call you. What are you thinking, trying to quit?"

"Nicki—"

"I'm so sorry. You were right about me. Everything you said."

"Nicki—"

"I was afraid. A coward. I almost lost everything."

He grabbed the back of her head and pulled her mouth to his. It was short and hard. He pulled back just enough to whisper against her lips. "Stop talking."

"But—"

He kissed her again. Longer this time. Deeper. Until her feet tingled and her knees quivered and she had to hold on to him to keep from falling. Or maybe it was his arm around her that held her steady. All she knew was that he tasted so good and smelled so good and his whiskers tickled her skin and she didn't know if she should laugh or cry or both.

He pulled back again, breathless. "Don't say a word until I'm done."

"OK."

"You have nothing to apologize for, Nicki."

"But you were right."

He kissed her. Wide-mouthed with his body flush against hers. Their tongues tangled in a passionate dance that made everything sing. But he ended it again. "I told you not to talk."

"OK."

He pressed his forehead to hers. "You are a braver person than I could ever dream of being. When I saw your interview this morning, I couldn't even breathe. And I'm so sorry I pushed you into that. I know you weren't ready."

"I needed to be pushed."

"Are you purposely talking so I'll kiss you?"

"No, but I like the idea."

So they kissed again. It was a whole-body kiss, with arms and legs and wide, open hearts getting in on the action. They tumbled back against the door and laughed. She cupped his face and held his eyes. There was a peace there she hadn't seen in a long time.

She ran her hand down his cheek. "You can't quit, Eric. I won't let you give it up."

"I'm not quitting. And I'm not moving to the bullpen.

That was bullshit. Devin said he just wanted to light a fire under my ass."

Even with the warm and gooey emotions softening her limbs, she went stiff at his words. "What? Are you kidding me? That sonuva—"

He kissed her and laughed against her lips. "God, I love you."

She sank into him. "I love you, too."

There was more kissing then. Lots of it. And a dam broke inside and she might have started crying.

He wiped tears away with his thumbs. "Don't cry. Please. Everything is OK."

"I can't help it. I've been so blind, so stupid."

"No, I have."

"But I'm the one who—"

More kissing. She started to tingle all over.

"None of what happened before right now matters, Nicki. I will never, ever stop fighting for you."

A knock at the door vibrated beneath her back. Hunter called out. "Show time, kids. Wrap it up."

Nicki wiped her face with her hands and the sleeve of her pull-over. "Is it obvious I've been crying?"

Eric shook his head and caressed her bruised cheek with his knuckle. "You look beautiful."

She curled her fingers into his shirt. "What happens after this, Eric?"

He braced his hands on either side of her head against

the door and leaned in, delicious and warm and sexy. "We go to Vegas, baby."

God, that sounded good. She stood up straighter. "Ok. Let's do this."

She turned and opened the door.

And let out a shriek.

Standing outside the trainer's office, the entire team started to clap. Instead of their jerseys, they wore matching t-shirts that said, "Fight like a girl."

She busted out laughing as Eric whispered in her ear. "Surprise, baby."

He gave her a small shove, and she stumbled out in the tunnel. Claps became whistles and shouts and fist-bumps of support. Harper Brody stood at the end of the line, and Nicki felt her cheeks warm.

Eric covered the awkwardness with a well-aimed glare. "Back off, Brody."

He raised his hands in mock surrender. "Was just telling the truth, Weaver."

The team followed them down the tunnel. Nicki slowed as the dugout came into view.

The world was out there with all their cameras, their judgment, their snide Twitter remarks. She looked at the man next to her and knew it didn't matter. Whatever they threw at her, at *them*, it wouldn't matter. Not anymore.

Eric slid his hand into hers. "Ready, Coach?"

She kissed his cheek. "Batter up, babe."

EPILOGUE

The Redemption of Devin Dane

DEVIN ROLLED HIS EYES. What a stupid headline.

He threw the newspaper onto the growing pile of crap on the kitchen counter. It slid off the top and onto the floor. Nothing could have better summed up the current condition of his life.

Moving was a messy process. Selling off everything you owned was even worse. It was bad enough when it was just the house in Florida, but now he was getting rid of his home in Vegas. The crew from the estate company was pouring over everything, documenting its value. Recording it in their little books and packing it away to sell.

Every little bit helped when you were suddenly broke.

Nicki bent and retrieved The New York Times from the

floor. She, Eric, and Hunter Kinsley had arrived that morning to help—which mostly meant giving him moral support as he watched his entire material existence being carted out in boxes. Once the last of it was gone, he was taking his clothes and moving in with Hunter.

Eric and Hunter had run out a half hour ago for pizza, and Nicki was keeping him company while he sorted the last odds and ends.

She leaned against the counter. She opened the paper, flipped to the article, and took a deep, dramatic breath.

"There's a moving van outside the house on Desert Rose Drive," she read aloud, "and a for-sale sign on the sweeping front lawn. It's an unremarkable site in this part of Las Vegas, where high-rollers come and go with the constantly shifting economic breezes. What makes this scene stand out is the man watching from a dark corner of the porch. His jeans are torn at the knee, and he hasn't shaved. On his face is an expression of stoic resolution mixed with good, old-fashioned humiliation. Because in the life and times of play-boy-turned baseball mogul Devin Dane, it is a moment of both embarrassing public failure and hard-fought personal triumph."

Devin groaned and grabbed the paper from her hands. "Stop. It was bad enough reading it to myself."

Nicki shook her head. "It actually isn't bad. Especially since you didn't even cooperate with Avery."

"I hate it."

"But it's mostly accurate, isn't it?"

"Yeah. I will give her that."

"It's almost like she had an inside source."

Devin shrugged again.

"Someone who knows you pretty well."

Devin looked up. Nicki raised her eyebrows.

He shook his head. "Not possible."

"Why not?"

"Because I doubt she would have anything good to say about me."

He waited for Nicki to contradict him. She didn't. He'd be a liar if he said he wasn't disappointed.

But now that the elephant in the room had finally trumpeted its presence, he could at least ask the question he'd been dying to ask all day. "How is she?"

"She'd like me to believe that she's fine and everything is perfect."

"You don't believe that?"

"No." She shrugged. "I mean, her business is going really well. Three of her clients from the old firm moved with her, and she has picked up some new ones pretty quickly. She's branching out from athletes and sports teams, which I think is probably a good thing. But personally, I think ..."

Nicki's voice trailed off.

"You think what?"

"Devin, have you thought about just *calling* her?"

"Not really. I mean, you know, only about twenty times a day." He shook his head. "I'm like a fucking drug addict."

"That's kind of romantic."

He managed a laugh.

Nicki bit her lip. "I don't know if I'm supposed to tell you this or not, but I guess you would probably find out anyway."

He raised an eyebrow.

"She's been hired by the VA hospital here in Vegas."

His stomach dropped to his knees. "For what?"

"To do PR for some new program helping veterans with PTSD. There's some new doctor coming in, I guess. That's all I know."

Devin's pulse skyrocketed. "So she's ..."

"She's going to be in Vegas a lot."

Holy shit. Holy fucking shit. Devin turned away from her and tried to slow his breathing.

There was an awkward silence. "Can I ask you something?"

"Sure." His voice practically cracked.

"Is *everything* in the article true?"

"For the most part."

"Even the part about the money?"

"Even the part about the money."

"So, your mother gave you back your trust fund, and you rejected it?"

The incredulity in her voice made him laugh despite the sick feeling in his stomach. "I did."

"Why?"

"There are too many strings attached to my family's money."

"And the team?"

"Bennett is determined to take it public. I'm going to fight him on my own merit."

Nicki was quiet. He looked over at her.

"Would you find it patronizing if I told you that I'm proud of you?" she asked.

He laughed. "No."

"Then I'm proud of you."

She gave him a hug. He didn't deserve her friendship, or Eric's. But by some miracle, he had it. Eric and Hunter walked in just then, loaded down with pizza and beer.

Eric stopped short. "Hey, hey. Hands off my woman, Dane."

Nicki laughed and pulled back. And, just to goad her future husband, she planted a kiss on Devin's lips. Eric made a growling noise.

Devin disentangled himself from Nicki and pushed back. "When's the wedding?"

"Right before Christmas," Nicki said.

Eric handed him a beer. Devin accepted it with a thanks

and then pretended not to notice the hungry look that passed between the two of them.

He exchanged an eye roll with Hunter. They were both still coming to terms with the weirdness of one of their coaches dating one of their players.

"You guys eat. I'll be right back," he said.

He needed some alone time to process what Nicki just told him. He walked down the hallway and turned left. The walls were bare, all of his artwork already packed away for sale at Sotheby's.

His heart stopped. The paintings.

He spun around.

The woman in charge of his estate turned the corner. He descended on her like a wild beast. "Where are the paintings from the Florida house?"

"They're packed already. We're having them appraised."

"I need one of them back."

"Which one?"

"The Faragamo. I'm not selling that one."

"But, sir, we estimate its worth at more than two hundred thousand dollars."

"I'm not selling it. Get it back."

She blinked and nodded before turning away.

Two hundred thousand. Christ, he needed that money.

But he knew someone who would appreciate the painting for far more than its monetary value.

He sank against the wall, his knees suddenly weak and his stomach queasy. Abby was going to be in Vegas. Often.

He had to get her back.

He had to.

TO BE CONTINUED ...

AFTERWORD

Thank you for reading *Seventh Inning Heat*! I hope you enjoyed Eric and Nicki's story! I first came up with the idea of these two characters more than ten years ago, so finally bringing their story to readers gives me all the feels.

This is the first book in a series about the Vegas Aces baseball team. Book two, *Seventh Inning Hero*, will feature Aces Manager Hunter Kinsley and will continue the story of Abby and Devin (who will get their own book in my fourth release, *Seventh Inning Redemption*). Book three, *Seventh Inning Hope*, tells the story of Cal Mahoney, one of the starting pitchers we meet in *Heat*.

Want sneak peaks at all these future Vegas Aces books? Want to be the first to know about release dates? Sign up for my newsletter by clicking HERE. You'll receive information about new releases, contests and giveaways, and other exclusive content, such as deleted scenes and excerpts.

Now that you've finished *Seventh Inning Heat*, would you consider leaving a review on the site where you purchased it? Reviews make sure that other readers can find my books! Good or bad, I would be grateful for your review!

ABOUT THE AUTHOR

Lyssa Kay Adams is the pen name of an award-winning journalist who gave up the world of telling true stories to pen emotional romances. She's also a diehard Detroit Tigers fan who will occasionally cheer for the Red Sox because her husband is from Boston.

Lyssa lives in Michigan with her family and an anxiety-ridden Maltese who steals food and buries it around the house and who will undoubtedly be a character in a future book.

Things Lyssa loves: Baseball pants, mashed potatoes, and that little clicking sound that scissors make on the cutting table at fabric stores.

Things she doesn't love: Mean people, melting ice cream cones, and finding food in her underwear drawer.

Keep up with Lyssa on Twitter at @LyssaKayAdams. Please note: She mostly tweets about baseball pants and mashed potatoes.

ACKNOWLEDGMENTS

A book is never the work of one person. An author relies on the help, guidance, and comforting shoulders of many people to bring a story to life.

Huge thanks to my family, first and foremost, for putting up with the insanity of living with a full-time author. I really DID hear someone knocking on the door that one time. It wasn't just a deadline-induced hallucination. Maybe.

And a major shout-out to the writing friends who have helped me and inspired me along the way. To my original critique group – Mary, Jennifer, Dana, Michelle, and Paula. You will always be my "girls in the basement." Further thanks to my Romance Writers of America friends: Jennifer Lyon, Marianne Donley, Alyssa Alexander, Isabelle Drake, Jenn Stark, MJ Summers, and so many more that it would take an entire book to list them all.

And finally, to Michelle Baty, cover designer rock star...
I got you hooked on romance novels. Don't try to deny it.

Made in the USA
Columbia, SC
06 July 2024

38216022R00228